Dead Ringer

An Eddie Malloy Mystery

Joe McNally

The Eddie Malloy Series in order of publication

Warned Off
Hunted
Blood Ties
Running Scared
The Third Degree
Dead Ringer

Eddie also appears in *Bet Your Life* alongside
Frankie Houlihan who makes his debut in
For Your Sins

Author's note

ACKNOWLEDGMENTS

My partner in crime-writing for more than twenty years, Richard Pitman, retired in 2013. Richard's hard work turned my first poor attempt at a manuscript, Warned Off, into something Hodder & Stoughton were willing to publish. We've been writing together since although Richard, for some time now, has been urging me to strike out on my own.

Richard, as a top jockey, was a boyhood hero of mine. You can imagine then how much our partnership has meant to me. Very few are lucky enough to work with one of their heroes. Our idols can often turn out to have feet of clay. Not Richard. I've never known him deny help or a favour to anyone. Not long after his sixty-ninth birthday, Richard became an altruistic kidney donor.

Some lucky person is now living life anew, thanks to the selflessness and kindness of a very fine man.

Thanks Richard. I shall miss you.

I'd like to thank the following, who helped with research for Dead Ringer...

Weatherbys are racing's administrators in the UK and Ireland. The company has been in business since 1770. I've had quite a few dealings with Weatherbys over the years, and have found them, not only helpful, but extremely gracious, polite, and quick to respond to enquiries, often in substantial and painstaking detail.

A perfect example of this furnished me with the key facts which drive the plot of Dead Ringer. Those facts came from Paul Palmer, head of Horse Registry at Weatherbys. Thank you, Paul.

Others in the racing industry have been helpful, although they have opted to remain anonymous in these credits, as have some of my contacts in the police force...you know who you are, and I'm grateful to you.

Finally, to my proof-reader, and lifelong friend Charlie Smith, thanks, pal!

Joe McNally
January 2014

For Margy, with love

ONE

We were turning toward the straight at Ascot for the last time. I was crouched on a veteran steeplechaser swinging my whip, talking to him, urging him on through the cold blinding rain in pursuit of three others. The ground was like pudding and the brown horse below me plodded on as he'd been doing each winter for nine years. We had no chance of winning, but he kept going. His name was Excalibur. I reckoned he had cleared more than seven hundred fences in his life.

Excalibur had long ago mastered the art of efficient jumping, spending minimum time in flight, battle-scarred belly brushing through black birch, empty scrotum ensuring painless contact, at the price of castration when still a colt, condemned by his lack of speed never to mount a mare.

On we went.

Three to jump in the gathering gloom, then a wash-down for the old gelding and a shower for me. His horsebox would carry him home to a familiar, welcoming stall. I faced an hour's drive to an empty house, though no less comforting for that.

Weary, winnerless and wondering what to do in the two-day break before Christmas, I got into the car and took my phone from the glove-box. New rules on integrity banned jockeys from using mobile phones on racecourse premises. Some of the lads carried them anyway. I preferred to leave mine locked up. My history made it vital for me to be above suspicion. I minimized risks where I could.

Three voicemails waited. The last one was from Jimmy Sherrick. He sounded anxious. I called him.

'Jimmy'

'Eddie.' He was on hands-free.

'Any luck today?' I asked. He'd been riding at Haydock, two hundred miles north of Ascot. 'Waste of time, Eddie. Two rides. Two losers. You?'

'I can beat you. Three rides, three losers. The best that can be said is that I'm going to be home a hell of a lot quicker than you are.'

'I'll be taking it easy. No point bursting my balls to get back. Traffic is shit as usual.'

'You okay? Your voicemail sounded a bit edgy.'

'Nah, things aren't right. I wanted to talk to you.'

'I'm about to head home. I can put this on hands-free.'

He didn't answer. I thought we'd lost the connection. 'Jimmy?'

'Eddie, I'm chucking it with Bayley. I wanted you to know first, since you got me the job.'

'What's up?' Jimmy had been riding for Bayley Watt for the last three seasons, and the new season wasn't that old.

'Ahh, things just aren't right. I had a call last night from the *Racing Post* asking if I'd do one of these interviews for the Sunday edition. You know the usual crap, what's your favourite horse and all this?'

'An honour.' I joked.

'They must be well short of subjects to be phoning me. Anyway, one of the questions is "How would you like to be remembered?", and that's what decided me.'

'What, you'd like to be remembered as a guy who packed in the best job he's ever had?'

'There's jobs and jobs. You know that. Every man has his price, so they say, but look, I'll tell you about it over a drink. All I'll say now is that you really need to think about things if Bayley offers you anything. Come over for a bite tomorrow.'

We arranged to meet at Jimmy's place next evening.

Jimmy was a bit like the old gelding Excalibur. He'd been around for years, plodding through his career in the lower half of the jockeys' table. In his forties now, Jimmy was a grinder; a reliable, workaday jockey whose dreams of stardom ended as mine were beginning. One of the things that had affected his career was the time he saved my life.

He got a lot of praise for that, but a few whisperers questioned his "commitment" at a crucial time for him - heartless bastards.

Jimmy threw a big race to help me.

I was just nineteen and still claiming. Young professional jockeys start their career with a weight allowance which is supposed to offset their experience. The more winners they ride, the smaller the allowance they can claim until the allowance is 'ridden out'.

I was still claiming five pounds on the day of the fall. This meant the horse I was riding didn't have to carry the ten stone eight pounds the handicapper had allotted; my claim reduced that to ten stone three. This was in a big race at Kempton. Prize money to the winner was forty grand, which was a lot fourteen years ago.

I was a bold young buck, throwing horses at fences with a belief in my timing and talent that far outstripped caution and experience. Death seemed centuries away.

My mount was a front-runner. Some horses just like to lead, he was one. But another horse, a grey, took us on from the start that day and I stupidly pitched myself into a "oh no you don't" battle right from the off.

In front of the packed grandstands, I called on my horse for a big jump, hoping to dishearten the grey. My mount did all he could but I'd asked him up way too soon and he smashed into the fence, front legs piercing the black birch two thirds of the way down, chest hitting the top of it, spine flexing as his back end tried to continue at thirty miles an hour. They told me the final somersault was spectacular; firing me out of the saddle like a missile, head first, straight into a blackout.

I was young. So were the two medics who came to help. I'd stopped breathing. They figured out I'd swallowed my tongue but my jaw had locked. They told me afterward that they'd been frantic and scared trying to get my mouth open. The man admitted to crying in fear and frustration, and the woman, his colleague, was trying to calm him as well as help me. All this while the race continued. Fourteen runners were on their way toward us and the finish. Seven tons of horseflesh travelling at thirty miles an hour.

But the fence I lay in front of, the second last in the race, had been dolled off with markers to warn the jockeys and send them round the wing. Jimmy Sherrick turned into the straight well clear on the chestnut mare whose name I can't recall. As he galloped past the dolled-off fence he looked across and saw the medics struggling, the man crying, my face going blue. And he did something unheard of. He pulled his horse up. Jimmy sacrificed the race by stopping and turning back to jump off and land beside us. He knew what had happened and he pushed the crying medic away with such force the man rolled underneath the white rails. Then Jimmy punched me hard on the side of my jaw.

Unlocked.

The female medic reached and hooked my tongue out of my airway.

I sat up to see the horse I'd been riding cropping grass on the infield. He was okay, and so was I.

An anonymous donor sent Jimmy the money he would have earned from his percentage of the prize money. Jimmy made the international news bulletins. But at the end of the season his contract with that trainer was not renewed and Jimmy found himself drifting to the edges, freelancing, scrabbling for rides.

When I recovered, I'm ashamed to say that I didn't do half enough to try and help Jimmy Sherrick. Oh, I thanked him, posed for pictures, bought him champagne, offered him a holiday abroad. Material stuff thrown his way by a cocky kid on the road to the top; to being Champion Jockey at the age of twenty-one. Too busy playing the big star to stop and think and help a man who loved race riding as much as I did. A man who'd wanted to succeed, as I did. A man who had not lost perspective, or his sense of humanity.

I'd lost mine.

I remember asking myself, if the positions had been reversed, would you have sacrificed that race to save Jimmy Sherrick?

No.

My arrogance and self-perceived "professionalism" persuaded me that I should be proud of that answer. When fate took its revenge on me by way of a frame-up in doping allegations which got me warned off, I had five years in the wilderness to reflect on what a prick I had been after Jimmy Sherrick saved my life.

When I finally regained my licence, seven years ago, Jimmy was still clinging on. He was working the fringes, riding the slow horses, the poor jumpers, the heart-breakers and soul-eaters who trailed home in the dying wake of winners, passing the post as the stands emptied, banished to a blind world where nobody watched anymore.

Older, sorrier, wiser, I had tried to do for Jimmy what I should have done all those years ago.

When I couldn't take a ride, Jimmy was always the guy I suggested as a sub. Any owners I met, I'd talk Jimmy up. 'There's nobody better, believe me. Jimmy's experience can't be bought.'

'He's an old man. Past it.'

'Don't you believe it. He's tough and as fit as he ever was.'

When Bayley Watt offered me the job of stable jockey, I'd persuaded him to give it to Jimmy Sherrick. OK, perhaps that was no great sacrifice. Bayley was just a permit trainer, restricted to training horses owned by himself and immediate family, but he'd had some good animals over the years. This had been his best start to a season. He had fewer than a dozen horses but he'd already won some good prizes, and looked set to break his own records.

That's what made Jimmy's decision so puzzling. Christmas was days away. A hell of a time to give up security and good horses.

As I passed Jimmy's dark house on the way home, I considered calling on him later that night rather than waiting twenty four hours. I slowed and stopped close by to consider the options. He had two hundred miles to travel. I knew that once I reached home I'd be reluctant to come back out. I drove on. Tomorrow night would do. Even my curiosity could hold out that long.

I suspected Jimmy had simply had enough of Bayley Watt. The trainer could be eccentric. He'd tried a few crazy schemes to improve horses. Maybe he'd just worn Jimmy out with them. Jimmy was forty four, a man of routine. He didn't like surprises. I smiled as I pulled into my driveway, already looking forward to Jimmy's story.

But I never got to hear it.

When I called on Jimmy next evening, I found him hanging from a rusty chain, looped through the rafters in his cellar. A wooden chair lay on its side and his body, lit by a bare bulb, was still swinging.

5

TWO

Jimmy's next-of-kin was his father, Jim. His first-of-kin really, I thought as I watched the old man by the graveside. Short and slight like his dead son, a thick black coat engulfed him, protecting his pallid skin from the icy wind. His boots shone black in the snow. He looked on grimly as six jockeys fed purple cords through fingers that would normally be slipping reins on this last day of December. The lads lowered Jimmy into the ice-fringed hole and let the cords drop, knots drumming on the coffin lid. Mister Sherrick had wanted Jimmy buried before the new year began.

The cold snap had wiped out racing since Boxing Day, although there was a benefit in the freeze. Empty changing rooms and deserted racetracks meant all Jimmy's friends could be here. Most accepted Mister Sherrick's invitation back to the hotel to "celebrate Jimmy's life". But suicide and celebration are hard things to reconcile. And jockeys anticipating a quick resumption of racing dared not delve into the buffet, so it was a subdued affair, ending with empty goodbyes and full platters.

That night, at home, I went into the garden, leaving the door wide open behind me and the TV volume on high so I could hear the bells ring the dead year out over the frosty woods. I felt the old familiar tingle of hope in this thirty-third winter of my life.

Renewal.

Since childhood the thought of new days, new months, new years, new horses, new chances, had kept me going.

6

Lambourn village lay a mile north across the fields. I heard faraway music and laughter, and I silently told the party goers to enjoy everything while they could.

Perversely, I sat in the sun house, an expensive wooden hexagon I'd persuaded myself I'd use in my 'new life'. That life was supposed to have begun more than two years before when I'd found this piece of land and decided, finally, to try to put down roots.

I'd stumbled on the place by accident, out running one morning. Boredom steered me off my usual route, down a lonely road past a beautiful old Manor house then onward downhill, the tarmac giving way to a rutted track falling steeply, enticing me into a dancing hurtle as I dodged holes and jutting stones, my feet reacting almost before my brain, trying to keep me upright as adrenaline and gravity drew me down down down.

The hill gave out, though I needed a wooden gate to stop me, arms reaching for the top bars then a bump and a slump and panting laughter and relief that I hadn't broken a leg in the mad plunging run.

And when my breathing calmed I stood upright and turned slowly, surveying this pocket of greenery in the fold of three small hills, deep woods on two sides. Something made me hold my breath...and I heard silence.

Don't let anyone tell you that silence can't be heard. It can. Perhaps above all else it can. Pure. Clean. Peaceful. And for the first time in my life I knew I was home.

It took eighteen months of planning, saving, borrowing, paperwork and meetings. In February the money ran out and I recalled standing again at that gate, looking at the concrete foundations, but knowing that everything was going to be all right. And my mother made it all right. She died.

My father had died the year before and I had hoped his death would free her, that the ragged ruined strands of the supposed bond between mother and child could somehow be re-tied. But his memory and her guilt had done too much damage. The dry words in her will offered the only recompense she could find: "To our surviving son, Edward, we bequeath our share in Harborne Stud."

Surviving son. A final barb.

The other shareholder in the stud, my sister Marie, was living there. She offered to buy out my share and I told her she could have it for nothing.

'Why?' Marie asked, 'You're entitled to half the value.'

'Because it's blood money.'

'Don't be stupid, Eddie, for God's sake! It was her way of trying to make everything right.'

'I've found the place I want to live. I don't want to build it with their money, not a brick of it.'

Marie and I had seen little of each other over the years, but she knew me well enough to realize it wasn't worth arguing. We agreed that she'd lend me enough to finish the bungalow.

That's how far forward I had planned; a bungalow. No stairs. Nothing to hinder battered arthritic joints if I reached retirement age. I'd learn to relax, I told myself, do some gardening, sit in the sun house reading on summer evenings.

I'd known, of course, that the aptitude for relaxation had always eluded me. But this, this renewal, this home I had built would change things, wouldn't it?

I smiled as I sat swilling whiskey round my glass, trying to make it reach the rim without looping out. I'd spent no more than an hour in this sun house since I'd bought it, and here I was in the freezing darkness, the snow pale on the lawn except for the yellow rectangle lit from the picture window.

Oh, yes, that window was to be another relaxation outlet; my view of nature, of wildlife. I drank and washed the whiskey round my mouth, thinking back to the spring, to my mother's funeral. I stood at the grave, soil and turf barely settled over my father when they'd carved it open once more for his wife.

With both parents below me, I was conscious of taking a step forward in the mortality line, one rank closer to death. I looked around the icy sun house. Maybe if I lived to be as old as Jimmy Sherrick's dad I'd get the best of this place.

THREE

I lay awake in the dead silence. Since finding him hanging, I'd been unable to wipe the image, to blink it from my mind's eye. Anytime my thoughts were unoccupied, he came back. I even had a name for him now: Swinging Jimmy.

Swinging Jimmy. It wasn't meant to belittle him or his memory, it was just that he was with me so often, my mind had found a way of welcoming him. Not as a ghoulish suicide, but as a relaxed, peaceful, gently swinging Jimmy.

His body had been warm. I'd lifted him, half over my shoulder. Rust flakes from the chain fell into my hair.

I'd kept saying his name. He had wet himself and it seeped into my shirt. Supporting him with my right arm, I'd managed to pull my phone out with my left hand, intent on holding him up until an ambulance arrived. But there was no mobile signal in the cellar.

I had made myself count out a minute in silence, holding my breath to try and hear Jimmy's. I clutched his wrist, seeking a pulse. Nothing.

I let him go and ran upstairs to make the call and when I returned he was swinging in a small circle. I sat in his dangling shadow cast from the cobwebbed light-bulb, and when the police arrived I turned away, not wanting to see strangers work Jimmy through the cold practicalities of release.

A uniformed policeman, Sergeant Middleton, took my statement. I told him Jimmy had asked to see me, although I didn't know why.

'Were you close friends?'

'Not really. We'd known each other a long time, and I saw him two or three days a week on the racecourse, but we didn't socialize.'

'So you've no idea what he wanted to talk to you about?'

'He told me he was packing his job in. I'd helped get him it and I think he might have wanted to explain his reasons.'

'In what way did you help him get the job?'

I told him how Jimmy had saved my life fourteen years ago. 'I owed him.'

He nodded, finishing his notes. He got me to check and sign them. 'Is this a formal statement then?'

'For now.' I might need to ask more questions in the next few days.'

After New Year's day breakfast, I looked at the satellite picture of the UK on my PC.

White.

Sixty racecourses buried under snow and frost. I should have been on the road to Cheltenham for two rides, but my workplace was snowbound. The weathermen promised no relief in the coming days.

I put on my running gear and headed into the woods, imagining myself alone on the planet, breaking new ground through the whiteness. A mercenary thought crept in. I'd probably get the rides back for Bayley Watt's yard now that Jimmy was gone.

Bayley had offered me that position as stable jockey along with a small cash retainer. I could have used the job and the money. But balancing things on my imaginary scales, I found my wallet outweighed by my conscience.

Jimmy was clinging by his fingertips at the time. He'd split with his wife and was just trying to handle each day as it came. He'd needed the job more than I did, although he hadn't known it was on offer.

I persuaded Bayley to take him instead of me and they'd done okay together.

I crunched on rhythmically through the snow, trying to recall what Jimmy had said about warning me to be careful if Bayley Watt made an offer. I'd wait a day or two, then ring Bayley. Or maybe a week. For decency's sake.

FOUR

On the afternoon of January 3rd, my phone lit up with an unknown number. It was Jimmy Sherrick's father. He sounded surprisingly strong, given how frail he'd looked at the funeral. 'Eddie, I got your number from Jimmy's diary. I'm at his house trying to sort out his stuff. He left a letter for you.'

'Oh.' I searched for something to say.

He said, 'Do you want me to drop it in? You're not far away, are you?'

'I'm not, no. Ten minutes. But I can come to you. You'll have enough to do.'

'I'd... I'd rather be on my own here until this is done, if you know what I mean. No offence. It's a bit...hard.'

'Sure. Fine. I understand. Do you want to ring when you're leaving and I'll give you directions?'

Mister Sherrick arrived as dusk fell. His hand was cold, the skin loose and thin. 'Come in. The kettle is on, or I can offer you something stronger.'

He wiped snow from his shiny black boots. 'Tea would be fine. Heat me up. You're well tucked away down here, eh?'

We settled at the kitchen table, the room warmed by the stove and the bright lights. Mister Sherrick kept his jacket on. He wore a brown suit, black tie tight to his shirt collar. I knew from my childhood that the schedule of mourning was important to his generation. He took a pale blue envelope from his pocket and handed it to me.

11

"E. Malloy". Business-like. I could imagine Jimmy sitting alone, putting his affairs in order. We should all have done it by now, but jockeys, who have less chance than many of living out their full years, are no more disciplined than the rest.

Mister Sherrick watched me. I didn't know the protocol for this. Maybe there wasn't one. 'Should I open it now?'

He shrugged, open-armed and said. 'I read mine at the house.'

How many letters had Jimmy written? I opened it. One sheet of paper, neat, symmetrical writing in blue pen.

Dear Eddie,

I'd been meaning to talk to you for a while. If you're reading this, then I probably never got round to it. Don't think too badly of me. I was just trying to come with a late run. I doubt I'd ever have got up, and the stewards would have taken it away from me anyway.

Life is short. Health is precious. Spend no time trying to make your mark, because we will all be forgotten.

Best
Jimmy

Folding it I said, 'Sad. I wish I'd known he'd been struggling so badly.' I told Mister Sherrick about the job offer from Bayley Watt and how I felt Jimmy would have been better suited to it. He nodded. 'Did he mention suicide in the letter?'

'No. He didn't.' I felt obliged to hold the page out to him. He palmed it away with a raised hand. 'No. No. Thank you. I don't doubt your word. There was nothing in mine either. If only he'd given me some clue.' He bowed his head.

'You're not responsible for what Jimmy did, Mister Sherrick.'

He said, 'I'd thought at first it was a cry for help gone wrong. He knew you were coming to see him and I believe his body was still warm when you found him and, well I just kind of thought he'd tried to time things so you'd get there to save him. But the police told me he took cyanide too.'

'Cyanide?'

He nodded sadly. 'He was quite thorough, Jimmy. Attended to detail. He was the same when he was a boy.'

'Jeez, where would he get cyanide?'

He shrugged again and looked toward the stove. I watched his watery, bloodshot eyes. He turned to me and said, 'They asked if I wanted to listen to the message he left. The suicide message.'

'The note?'

'A note, I suppose, but he didn't write it. He recorded it. The police found it on his computer and on a, what did they call it, some kind of stick, a computer thing.'

'A memory stick?'

'That was it. I told them I didn't want to know what was on it. They offered me the memory stick anyway, said I didn't have to play it but that it was part of Jimmy's belongings. I told them to keep it.'

I nodded, 'Probably best, Mister Sherrick.' I could understand him not wanting to hear it but I wanted to, because the voice on it would not belong to Jimmy Sherrick. A murder message, maybe, but not suicide.

FIVE

On January 4th, the racing world was still hibernating. I waited alone in what the female PC who led me there had called the 'green room' in Newbury police station.

The door opened and Sergeant Middleton came in dressed in a short-sleeved white shirt and navy trousers. When I'd first met him in Jimmy Sherrick's cellar, he'd been burlier and more serious, though I realized now that he wore no uniform jacket or high vis waterproof. No need in here for a stab vest.

He held out his hand and I stood to shake it. 'Thanks for seeing me at short notice.'

'That's okay. All quiet on the western front. Sit down, please.' We sat facing each other. 'You mentioned Jimmy Sherrick?'

'I saw his father yesterday. He told me Jimmy had left a suicide message on his PC.'

He looked at me; no doubt weighing up the wisdom of confirming then realizing he could hardly imply Mister Sherrick had been lying. 'That's right,' he said.

'And he saved a copy on a memory stick?'

He nodded slowly, his look keener now.

'Jimmy couldn't even send a text. He was a technophobe, a digital dyslexic.'

He hesitated then said, 'How do you know that?'

'It was a standing joke in the weighing room.' He seemed puzzled. I said, 'The weighing room's where we all head for. It's where we get weighed before riding in a race then weighed again

14

when we come back in to make sure we haven't dumped a stone of lead in the water jump. The jockey's changing room is inside the weighing room.'

He nodded. 'Go on. About the texting.'

'Let me give you an example. About two weeks ago we were all laughing when Bill Kittinger came in and told us he'd sent Jimmy a text that morning and, for the first time ever, Jimmy had responded. He put "OK". Bill sent him another one saying "Who taught you to text?". A minute later Bill's phone rang. It was Jimmy. He said "Bill, I can only do OK so I had to call you."'

The sergeant thought about it then said, 'Some people claim to be technophobes just to make themselves stand out these days.'

'Jimmy wasn't like that. There was only one side to him. What you saw was what you got. A few of us had tried to teach him how to text but he just couldn't grasp it. Somebody brought in a laptop a few months back to show him how to use email and look at the *Racing Post* website.'

'Maybe he developed from there?'

I shook my head. The sergeant said, 'Well he developed enough to order cyanide online.'

I looked at him and waited. He said, 'We checked his PC and found the confirmation email and receipt for payment.'

'How did he pay?'

'Debit card.'

'Are you sure?.'

'Certain. Why?'

'Because all he used his card for was to withdraw money. Jimmy paid cash. He used to warn anybody who said they'd ordered stuff online that they'd end up in a fraud case.'

'Give me a minute,' he said, and went out. He returned with a black memory stick and thirty seconds later I was listening to Jimmy's voice.

"Every day I hurt from old injuries and from old memories. Something happens to a man when he turns forty. I've seen too many sad people. I don't want to be one of them. I want to make extra sure. That's why I did it this way. Hanging? It's no certainty. Goodbye."

Sergeant Middleton watched me. 'Would you agree that is Mister Sherrick's voice?'

'It sounds like him.'

'It is him. We compared it with two interviews he did on TV.' He checked his notes. 'The forensic speech analyst we use classified it a five, the highest score, which expresses as, "Exceptionally distinctive - the possibility of this combination of features being shared by other speakers is considered to be remote"'.

'How remote?'

'Enough to convince ninety nine percent of judges and juries, I'd say.'

'Sergeant, interview some of the guys who worked with him. To make that recording Jimmy would need to have downloaded software, installed it, and learned how to use it... just to record a suicide note, which he'd then go to the trouble of saving on a memory stick so it was easily found?'

'That's what we're left with, evidence. Add it to the fact he hanged himself and took a cyanide pill and ask yourself what the man in the street would say about the police if we came to any other conclusion.'

I nodded. 'Fair point. But I still think it's the wrong conclusion.'

'Why?'

'Look, I'm not going to say Jimmy wasn't the type to commit suicide, he might well have been. We weren't bosom buddies, but I knew him pretty well. I told you in my statement how he was unhappy riding for Bayley Watt.'

'You should speak to his father about this. He says Jimmy never really got over the break-up of his relationships. He was in pain much of the time. There's more I could tell you but it wouldn't be right to. I've seen his medical notes. Why do you believe he didn't commit suicide?'

'I don't necessarily believe he didn't. I came here ready to bet that wasn't Jimmy's voice on the tape but it sounds exactly like him. I just don't know how he did it, made the recording I mean. And I still don't think he did.'

'Sometimes people just aren't what they seem. The longer you've known them, the bigger the shock can be.'

I took out the letter Jimmy had left for me and passed it over. 'Jimmy's father found this yesterday.'

He read it. 'Sad.'

'It is. But what do you think of it, as a policeman, I mean?'

'In what way?'

'Forget the content, look at it. Check the date. Draw a conclusion about what kind of person would have written it.'

He looked at it, turned it over, placed it flat on the desk. 'Neat handwriting, even, unhurried. I'd say somebody fairly meticulous, a person who liked to plan things, keep control, somebody who didn't like surprises.'

'Jimmy wrote that for me more than four months ago. He wrote one for his father and a few other people, though you'd need to ask Mister Sherrick about that.'

'Go on.'

'Why didn't Jimmy leave recordings for us? Or a nicely typed note? Why would he take the trouble to record a suicide message when he could have written it in less than a minute?'

'Good question. I don't know the answer.' He picked up the letter. 'What is this about the stewards taking it away from him? Any idea?'

'It's just an expression. The stewards are judge and jury in racing. If they decide you've broken the rules in a race, they can disqualify you; take the race away from you.'

'Could Mister Sherrick have been hinting at something there?'

'I don't know. He'd had a few personal problems and they might have been coming to a head around the time he wrote that. He's obviously low, and trying to make plans, but there's no direct mention of suicide, and even if that was his intent, there can't be many who'd wait four months after writing it. Not if they were serious.'

'I think it's best if I take another statement from you. I need to pass this to the CID.'

On the way home I tried to talk myself out of this. Most of my troubles in the past few years had arisen because I couldn't walk away from something that was eating me. Without a fair bit of luck, my pride and pig-headedness could have got me killed.

And here I was, back on the same merry-go-round with the hanging corpse of Swinging Jimmy.

SIX

I rose at daybreak feeling irritable, edgy, indecisive. My bedroom window framed the dark wooded hill. Acres of snow told of unchanged temperatures and barren racetracks. The bedroom was warm, the bathroom chilly and I talked to myself under the shower and I talked to myself out of the shower, trying to decide what to do about Jimmy.

After breakfast I rang Bayley Watt. 'Bayley, Eddie Malloy. How are you?'

'Eddie, hello. I'm,..I'm all right. How are you?'

'Bored shitless in the snow.'

'We'll not be seeing much racing this week. That's global warming for you.'

'Global freezing, more like. You busy?'

He hesitated. 'Always busy with eight horses. You know how it is when you're a one-man-band.'

'I'd be happy to come over and help out. I'm doing nothing here. Only take me half an hour to reach you.'

'Best not chance it, Eddie. Plenty folk getting stuck in the snow round this way.'

'I've got a four wheel drive now. I'll get through.'

'Nah, I'll be fine, honestly, be done by noon.'

'How about me buying you lunch then?'

'Maybe some other time Eddie, thanks.'

'Listen Bayley, I need to speak to you about Jimmy. Something's come up.'

18

'What?'

'Best talk face to face, I think.'

'Okay. Well, let me sort a few things out. I'll call you later.'

'Fine. Speak to you then.'

A nervous man.

Watt surprised me by calling back within twenty minutes, inviting me to his place for a ride-out in the snow.

Mounted, we left Watt's yard on a track past the barn, cracking the blue-white crust around old hoof prints. 'Where are we going?' I asked.

'I thought we'd just hack around the roads for an hour.'

'Look,' I said, pointing south across snow-covered farmland dotted with copses. Bayley stopped and looked toward the ancient Ridgeway path, Britain's oldest road set on a chalk ridge once walked by Prehistoric man. 'Let's head for the Ridgeway,' I said, 'It'll be like walking across a Christmas card.'

'A Christmas card with gates. You can undo them.'

'Fine.'

Bayley expertly unlatched his gate without dismounting and I went through. A mile to the south, a hundred metres above lay our destination. I rode a bony, angular iron-grey called Sam Stone. He wasn't much to look at, but had a decent engine. I'd won on him at Stratford not long after my comeback.

We'd gone less than a hundred yards at a slow walk when Sam Stone jinked suddenly sideways, dropping me in the snow. Bayley heard me curse and turned, hands on the pommel of his big western saddle. 'Well, it's early in the year, but I think you've easily won the most embarrassing unseated rider award.'

I got up, dusting myself down. Instinctively, I'd kept hold of the reins, but my horse was still jittery, rolling his eyes till the whites showed. 'Hey, take it easy.' I talked softly, trying to calm him but he backed off ten paces before I could settle him enough to climb back on board. I looked at Bayley. 'You'll dine out on this one for a while. What the hell's up with him?'

'Doesn't care for getting cold feet, I suppose. Maybe the road would have been the better route.'

All this without raising a smile from Bayley. If it had happened among jockeys, they'd have been falling off their own mounts with laughter.

I knew little about this horse, other than how he was in a race. This was a reminder for me that jockeys only saw the finished product and sometimes forgot about all the prep work that's needed. We stroll into the paddock, jump aboard, ride our race then hand the horse over to the lad who looks after him twenty-four-seven. Or in Bayley Watt's case, he was the twenty-four-seven man. He had no full time staff.

Bayley moved alongside me as we crossed the wide white land. 'Did you never consider all those offers to get a full licence?' I asked. Watt had always resisted urging from owners to take out a full licence and train horses for other people.

Shaking his head slowly, he patted his horse's neck. 'I couldn't cope with the hassle. Never have been able to. People believe optimism and confidence and all the gung-ho "Let's do it!" bollocks is the way to get things done. But I'll tell you what's better, knowing your limitations. That's how you get things done. Know your limitations.'

I looked at him, at his sagging jawline which hid much of the thin black helmet strap. When I had ridden regularly for him, Watt had always been big and fit. At first glance you might have thought him twenty pounds overweight but he was a big-framed man. Now he seemed smaller, loose-fleshed and chubby, despite burning through calories at what must have been a high rate looking after eight racehorses. 'You lost weight?' I asked.

He glanced down at himself, blue fleece jacket paunching, almost resting on the horn of the old western saddle. 'A bit, maybe.'

'Dieting?'

'At my age?'

I smiled. 'How old are you now?'

'I'll be fifty six next month.'

'How old do you feel?'

'Seventy fucking six.'

I laughed. He didn't. His dark eyes narrowed. Grey hair curled out from the rim of his battered helmet.

'I get those days myself.' I said.

We walked on. I turned in the saddle, scanning the land. Nobody out but us. I smiled. 'Maybe the Indians are watching from the ridge. Spotted that saddle of yours, think you're the law in these parts.'

'The old Indians knew a lot more about horses than some of the chancers around here,' he said.

'No doubt.'

On we went, leather-creak and crunching snow the only sounds.

After a minute I said, 'Jimmy's dad came to see me the other day.'

I watched my riding partner carefully. He stared ahead, features set but seeming uncertain whether to turn and look at me, unsure if he should speak. 'Me too,' he said.

'About the letter?'

'Break your fucking heart.'

We covered a hundred yards without speaking then Watt said, 'A week before Jimmy died, I had to tell him he was finished here.'

I looked at him.

Watt said, 'He stared at me like...like I'd told him a firing squad was waiting outside for him. I tried to explain, laid out my reasons which were clear and logical to my mind. But Jimmy just kept staring at me. He never said a word.'

'Did he mention that in his letter?'

'He said he didn't blame me and that I wasn't to feel guilty and that he knew he was coming to the end of everything anyway.'

The horses were climbing more steeply now toward the ridge. I adjusted my balance, leant forward into the slope. Watt stayed loose in his big saddle, resting a hand on the ivory horn, gripping as the horse rocked.

'Did he say what it was that pushed him over the edge?'

He shook his head. 'Just said he didn't want me to feel guilty.'

'But you do?'

He looked at me. 'Wouldn't you?'

I shrugged. His story was the opposite of Jimmy's, but I played along. 'I don't know, Bayley. I don't know what the reasons were and I'm not asking you to tell me. Plenty jocks have had the same bad news without going on to...do anything drastic.'

He lowered his chin and I couldn't tell if he was nodding at what I said or if his head was bobbing to the stride of his climbing horse. He didn't speak again until we topped the Ridgeway and turned westward. For the first time that day I noticed a chill breeze on my face. Watt clicked his horse and mine responded too. They broke into a trot. We went about five hundred yards at that pace, me standing in the stirrups, Watt rocking and rolling in his deep polished saddle the colour of horse chestnuts.

Walking again, this snow covered chalk spine seemed endless against a sky the same colour. The fields fell away on both sides, a copse here, a farm there, frozen streams. A hundred yards on, Bayley stopped. I pulled the grey to a halt and did a half turn to face him. He said, 'What was it that you rang me about? You said something had come up about Jimmy.'

The breeze was keener now. His eyes watered. He wiped them. I said, 'He took cyanide.'

'He hung himself! I…I was told he hung himself in the cellar.'

'They found cyanide in the autopsy.'

'How do you know?'

'His father told me. The police told me.'

'You went to the police?'

'Yesterday.'

He wiped his eyes again while I was trying to read him. He was on the verge of something and a crazy thought came to me that if I'd been downwind of him I could have smelled what it was. But he squeezed his horse into a walk again and the moment passed. He said, 'Listen Eddie, I want you to ride one or two for me once racing's back on.'

'That's not what I came here for Bayley. I'm not saying it hasn't crossed my mind since Jimmy died, but it's not why I wanted to talk to you.'

'No matter. I'm offering. You don't need to accept.'

'I accept. Look, I'm not being ungrateful, I just don't want you to think I'm some kind of mercenary cashing in on Jimmy's death.'

He turned on me, eyes fully open and blazing. He shouted. 'We're all fucking mercenaries! What are you talking about, man! We're all in it for what we can get! That's how life fucking works!' It startled his horse who jinked sideways and almost lost its footing though Watt was unfazed by the slip, automatically gathering rein and, like a puppeteer, lifting the horse onto an even keel. He glared at me, daring me to challenge him. I held his gaze until the fire in his eyes went out and he said quietly, 'I'm sorry. It's been a shit week.' And he turned his horse on the right rein heading north again, downhill, hock-deep through unbroken snow toward home.

SEVEN

In Bayley Watt's bright kitchen we drank tea and he explained. 'You know me. I like to experiment. It's one of the reasons I won't train for anyone else. I read an article a month ago and did some more research on it and that led me to telling Jimmy he was finished.'

He seemed confrontational again. I waited. He sipped coffee, still looking at me, then he said, 'The Indians or native Americans or whatever you want to call them, knew nothing about horses until the Spanish shipped them into Mexico. The Indians stole them and experimented, and learned. Then the tribes started competing, especially on the Great Plains. Comanche Indians ended up owning about thirty five horses each.

'They discovered that a horse's spirit stayed more competitive the greater number of different riders it had. Most tribes believed that a horse would do its best for someone it knew. The Comanche went against that and they claimed they were right. I've decided to try it. That's why I sacked Jimmy. That's why I'm telling you I can offer you the odd ride but not all of them.'

I nodded and sipped tea. 'Fine.'

Still he stared at me, waiting for a challenge. He said, 'If Jimmy had told me he was going to do himself in because of it, I wouldn't have changed my mind.'

'Jimmy wouldn't have said that. Even if he was planning suicide.'

'I'm just saying.'

'And, I'm just saying, Bayley! What do you think I'm going to do, slag you off? Tell you you were wrong? It's your business. You were straight with Jimmy, you've been straight with me. I'm not making any judgements. Cool it.'

The stressed look eased. He lowered his head, massaged his face, a habit he had, and I was glad to see it back on display, although two things struck me as his fingers worked his closed eyes and his brow; the chubbiness of his hands, and his smooth hairless wrists. I'd known Bayley Watt for years. I'd watched him do the face rubbing routine a hundred times and the wrists stretching from his shirt cuffs had always had a noticeable covering of dark hair.

I remembered him telling me it was the main reason he did not wear a wrist watch. He carried an old silver watch in his pocket.

He stared at the table for a while. When he spoke again, the gritty edge had gone from his tone. 'I'm sorry, Eddie. Things have been building up. I'm getting paranoid, snowed in here, not seeing anybody.'

'I'd best not give you that DVD of *The Shining* I've got in the car, eh?'

He smiled. 'Sometimes I could make Jack Nicholson look like the soul of sanity.'

I raised my coffee mug to toast him. 'Heeeerrrre's Bayley!'

He smiled but he looked sad. He said, 'I've been an arse today. Apologies.'

'Forget it. We all have those days.'

I took my leave and headed home wondering why Bayley Watt had turned from a simple eccentric into a paranoid, unhappy man. Maybe the loss of muscle and hair signalled nothing more than the onset of old age, and that was affecting his mood too. I recalled his grim reaction when I asked how old he felt, and I wondered if he might be ill.

That evening I locked the doors, stoked the fire, poured whiskey over ice and settled at my PC with a notepad and pen.

Google produced plenty on losing weight and losing hair but I went with my earlier instinct that Bayley might be ill. The changes I'd noticed matched some side effects of chemotherapy.

Bayley was a private man. He'd never married. He didn't socialize on the race track or in the village. The rules of racing stated that, with eight horses, he should have at least two grooms working for him. Bayley registered a couple of names but he'd always believed he could do most of it himself. Even when he went racing, he just locked everything up and left the remaining horses on their own. So he had nobody to talk to on a daily basis. If he had cancer, I reckoned it would be highly unlikely he'd have anyone to tell, even if he wanted to.

I resumed my doodling.

One definite connection between Jimmy Sherrick and Bayley Watt: a trainer and his employee. Another very tenuous possible connection: Sergeant Middleton had told me he had seen Jimmy's medical records. Had he been seriously ill? Was Watt?

I found myself drawing a checkered cap and a blue light and writing "Police".

Why hadn't Watt asked me why I'd gone to the cops about Jimmy's death? That would have been a natural question, especially for someone so closely linked to Jimmy.

Supposing Jimmy had been lying to me about chucking it… maybe Watt was simply feeling guilty about sacking him and wanted to get off the subject. That might also have led to his sour mood and his outburst up on the ridge.

Watt had said he'd given Jimmy the news about his sacking a week before he killed himself. But I'd seen Jimmy a dozen times after that and he'd said nothing. Nor had I noticed any change in his demeanour.

The first time he'd mentioned anything was in that call in the car the day before he died.

I sketched a few small envelopes…what had been in Jimmy's letter to Watt? How many letters had Jimmy written and to whom? Had his father found them all? Maybe there were still some letters in the house? Jimmy had kept a diary. His father had told me he'd got my number from it.

I reached for my phone. I'd saved Mister Sherrick's number and I scrolled and found it, then stopped for a quick consultation with common sense. I'd need to be careful. Jimmy's dad would wonder why I was asking questions.

His phone rang out to voicemail. I didn't leave a message. Before my screen went off, he called back. 'Mister Sherrick?'

'Eddie. Sorry, didn't get to my phone in time.' His voice sounded shaky.

'How are you?' I asked.

'Ahh, not bad, Been laid up in bed since yesterday. Think I'm coming down with something.'

'Sorry Mister Sherrick, I've got you out of your sick bed. It's not important. It can wait. I'll let you go. Apologies.'

'No, no, not at all. I'm all right and stop calling me Mister Sherrick for God's sake! Call me Jim.'

'Thanks. Listen, I just noticed my Leatherman tool is missing. I wondered if I might have left it in Jimmy's cellar?'

'Your what?'

'Leatherman. It's one of those little multi-tools, screwdriver, knife, that sort of thing. It was in a black leather pouch. Be no bigger than three inches or so. I wondered if you maybe saw it when you were there tidying things up?'

'I didn't, Eddie, sorry.'

'No worries.'

'Do you want to pick the keys up and go and have a look? I'd meet you there but I-'

'No, no, not at all! Honestly. Don't worry. It'll turn up.'

'Well you're welcome to drop by and get the keys, more than welcome.'

'You sure?'

'Of course.'

'Well I will then, if you don't mind. I'll call over in the morning about ten if that suits?'

'Any time. Earlier if you want. I don't sleep late these days.'

'Do you need anything? Any shopping? A paper?'

'Nah, nothing. I'm well stocked up and I stopped reading the news years ago. It's all bad.'

'That's true, very true. Look, I'll let you get back to bed and I'll see you at ten.'

'Good. See you then. Good night.'

'Good night.'

I switched the phone off, put the pen down, pictured Mister Sherrick climbing wearily into bed to face a long night alone, old and unwell. Then I watched the dying log-embers and listened to the silence. I tried to picture myself in forty years' time and had an intuitive flash that I wouldn't live that long.

EIGHT

Mister Sherrick seemed healthier than he'd sounded the night before. He lived in sheltered housing near the centre of Lambourn in a neat, warm, ground-floor flat. We shook hands and he gave me the keys to Jimmy's house.

'You're looking dapper,' I said. 'Feeling better?' He wore shirt, tie, mustard cardigan and a jacket. The sharp straight creases in his trousers ended on the soft shine of brown shoes. 'Much better, thanks. Some bug going around the complex. There's been a few down with it. Can I get you some tea?'

'No thanks,' I said, and then thought how little company he probably got and quickly said, 'Yes, I will. Thanks. If it's not holding you back. You look like you're heading out somewhere.' I sat on a stool at the small breakfast bar.

He smiled as he filled the kettle. 'Just up to the Sacred Heart hall. They do breakfast for us every Friday.'

'Well, leave it. I'll have some tea later when I bring the keys back.'

'You sure?'

I got up. 'Yes. I'll drop you off.'

'That's kind of you but I'll walk, I think. It's a nice morning. They've cleared all the pavements. It'll give me an appetite for the black pudding.'

'It's years since I tasted black pudding.'

'I'd smuggle a slice out for you but there's some greedy old bastards always grabbing the platter and saying "Anybody mind if I have this last little bit?" in a voice that'd put Oliver Twist to shame.'

I laughed. 'Gannets,' he said, and buttoned his jacket.

Jimmy's place was in Upper Lambourn, a few minutes' drive from his father's flat. It had been a semi-ruin with half a roof when Jimmy bought it. A static caravan in the garden served as his home for more than a year while he'd made the house habitable.

The bad weather had left the windows dirty. Footprints on the old snow covering the path looked sealed and permanent, like fossils.

I pushed through a drift of mail on the mat then locked the door and stood in the cold silence.

Empty.

Finished.

Had I not known beforehand that the owner of this place had left for good, I would know now.

A story a prison warder once told me came to mind: "Sometimes a man will die in his sleep. When you close the door on him, the sound it makes is different. It's like shutting the door of an empty cell. The soul has gone."

I walked through the kitchen to the larder Jimmy had converted into an office. A pine table with two drawers took up most of the space. A small revolving chair stood in front of it. An A4 tray held a stack of blank printer paper. A handful of pens and three highlighters lay in an old cigar box.

A dark grey Toshiba laptop sat slightly askew, its cable and power adapter lay on the floor. I sat on the chair and raised the lid of the PC, hesitated, then pressed the power button. Nothing. I tried again. Dead. I reached for the cable to plug it in then decided I'd ask Mister Sherrick if I could take it home and have a look through it. What tale I'd tell him to justify it I hadn't yet thought up.

The drawers were empty. I turned slowly in the chair to face an alcove with five shelves. A few copies of the *Racing Post* lay on the bottom shelf. I picked up the newspapers, three in all. The dates were weeks apart; from early October to mid-December. Jimmy would have had the *Racing Post* delivered daily. It was the only trade paper. Why keep just three?

I opened the first one. On page 7 was a picture of Jimmy at Cheltenham on Watt's star horse Fruitless Spin. Jimmy was smiling and waving. December 14th.

Within two weeks he'd gone from waving happily to swinging lifeless in the cellar.

In the November 9th issue he was pictured again on another of Watt's winners, Stifles in Spur. It looked as though Jimmy was gathering stuff for a scrapbook. The October 12th newspaper had him smiling again on Watt's horse, Bantry Bay and I got to thinking how much prize money Watt had already won this season. He was ahead of some established trainers and his strike rate for an eight-horse yard must have been at record levels.

I folded the papers and put them back, then opened the drawers again in that stupid way you sometimes do when you are looking for something and even though you've already checked a certain place you do it another six times.

No letters. Where had they been? Where had he stashed them that allowed his dad to find them easily?

I wandered around, knowing I was delaying the moment. Finally, I opened the cellar door, clicked the wall switch and went slowly down the stone steps, my breath visible in the dim light.

My eye was only ever going to be drawn to one spot…the hanging point. The underside of the beam was lit by the bare bulb. The chair stood like a prop on a theatre stage. The chain was not there.

I went down the last four steps and across to the beam. A vertical line of small rips where the links had chewed the wood showed where the chain had been.

I was sure the chain had been there after they freed Jimmy. I remembered staring at it, while I waited for the sergeant to finish his notes. They must have lifted Jimmy and eased it over his head rather than untangle it from the beam.

It had been rusty. I remembered the gritty flakes in my hair as I'd tried to hold him up.

Squatting, I looked for rust flakes. None. Clean. Very clean. I wet a finger and put it to the floor; one or two specks of dirt, but much less than I'd have expected. I moved along below the beam, wetting, pressing, coming up clean. The next beam was six feet away. I hunkered below it, licked my finger and immediately felt the grit. My finger came up black, the spit turning the edges of the dust to micro-mud.

Someone had cleaned a long, straight meticulous path under the beam that had held the chain that had now gone.

If the careful cleaner had not been Jimmy's father, then it had been someone with keys to the house.

NINE

In the car park of the Sacred Heart Church I waited for Jimmy's father to finish breakfast and leave behind his black-pudding-eating friends. I was going to drive him home and ask questions and tell no lies. And I knew that when I left him, I would be in this for keeps.

Racing would start again soon. I'd curse myself for complicating my life once more with other people's problems, but I knew that walking away would leave me sadder in the long run. Guilt gnaws. Curiosity compels. Injustice incites. I'd learned I could never escape from who I was.

Mister Sherrick came out the side door, waving to someone. I have a dislike of horns sounded in quiet places so I got out. 'Mister Sherrick! Jim!'

We small-talked the few minutes back to Mister Sherrick's flat. I accepted his invitation for tea and when we sat down, I gave him the keys to Jimmy's house. 'Oh, thanks. Did you find your tool-thing?'

I'd forgotten about the lie. 'It was in my car. It had slipped under the seat. I didn't think to look until after I'd had a good root around at Jimmy's place.'

'Oh well, at least you found it.' He sipped tea. There was a vacant air about him, a hollowness, as though someone had cored his life and plugged each end of the husk. He seemed to be acting out his days, determined not to burden anyone with his sadness.

'Jim, can I asks you a few questions about Jimmy?'

He looked at me and nodded slowly.

'I've been wondering what it was he wanted to see me about, the night I found him. There was nothing in his letter, and that set me thinking. Can I ask you where those letters were, where you found them?'

'I didn't find them. His solicitor had them. He called me.'

'Oh. I'd got the impression when you rang me from his house that you'd just come across them.'

'No. I picked them up that afternoon.'

'Can I ask who else he left letters for?'

'Well, me, Jennifer, his sister, I don't think you've met her, she lives in York?'

'I haven't.'

'She wasn't at the funeral. She has cerebral palsy.'

'I'm sorry.' And this man whose wife and son were dead, whose daughter was afflicted, just raised his eyebrows and half-nodded and drank again. He seemed to have forgotten about the other letters. 'Was there anyone else?' I asked.

He looked confused. 'Jimmy's letters.' I said.

'Oh, yes. A couple of other jockeys, Bill Kittinger and Riley Duggan, and his valet, Fred Tibbetts. One for Bayley Watt and one for Gillian, my daughter-in-law.'

'Do you still see her, then?'

'Mmm, he swallowed tea. 'She's family. They were married a long time. She visits most Sundays.'

'Did Jimmy still see her, if you don't mind me asking?'

'No. No, he didn't.' He stared at the unlit fire.

'Nobody else?'

'Those were all I got. I hired a car for a couple of days and took them round myself. Don't really need a car full time, if you know what I mean. Not these days.'

'No, of course.'

'Limited parking here too. Doesn't help.'

Was he trying to steer me off the subject or was his mind wandering? I said, 'Did you see Jimmy much?'

He stared at the fire again for a long time then said quietly, 'No. No I didn't.' He held his breath for a few seconds. And he was perfectly still, a faraway look in his blue eyes. 'Jimmy felt he had let me down and that his mother would have been disappointed in him. Marriage was for life in our family, or maybe our generation is a better way to put it. Till death do us part was a big thing with Ann, his mother. When Jimmy and Gillian broke up it sort of broke something in Jimmy too. He'd ask my forgiveness.'

He turned to look at me. 'Daft, eh? What could I forgive? Jimmy asked if I thought his mother would forgive him, her spirit, at least, and I said sure, sure she would and what was there to forgive? Sometimes things don't work out. It's not always someone's fault. Not his alone, anyway. It's life, isn't it?'

'It is.'

'He was a man for the guilt was Jimmy. An old Catholic failing some say and maybe they're right. Even as a boy, he could never tell a lie. His mother would confront him, "Did you steal those sweets?", "Yes Ma, I did. I'm sorry." Didn't stop him stealing them in the first place though!' He smiled at that.

'I don't think Jimmy killed himself.' I said.

'Oh, he did.' Oddly, he was smiling, as though trying to reassure me that there was no need to protect his feelings or offer him hope. 'He left a suicide note recording. The police checked it against a TV interview and an expert told them it was Jimmy's voice. I thought I'd told you, sorry.'

'You did tell me. I've heard the recording. I went to the police because I knew Jimmy wouldn't have been able to make a recording himself. He could hardly use a mobile phone.'

He gazed at me now, concentrating for the first time. 'Wasn't it Jimmy's voice? On the recording?'

'I think it was. But I don't believe he made the recording, or if he did he did it by accident. Or somebody recorded his mobile calls and patched that tape together.'

'A tape?'

'Well, no, it was a recording on a memory stick which they said was also on his PC. By the way, I picked up Jimmy's laptop from his desk when I was there. I was hoping you wouldn't mind if I took a look at what was on it.'

'Not at all, but you'll have to get it repaired first.'

'It might just need charging.'

'The screen's broken,' he said.

'How do you know it's the screen? It didn't come on at all, didn't power up when I pressed the button, but the cable was on the floor. It's probably been lying for a while in the police station.'

'The screen's smashed. I dropped it in Jimmy's office when I was trying to pick it up by the lid to move it.'

'Hold on. I've got it in the car.' He followed me to the door. I took the laptop from the back seat and slowly opened it. The screen was intact. I turned it toward Mister Sherrick and moved it on its hinges like some big signal mirror so he could see it at all angles. He shook his head and frowned.

I went back inside and we looked again at the laptop. He said, 'The glass smashed. I had to sweep it up. Either somebody came in and fixed it or that's not Jimmy's computer.'

'Where did you leave it?'

'On his desk.'

'With the lid open or closed?'

'Closed. I deliberately closed it in case any dust got into the works through the broken glass.'

'When was this?'

'The day I went to clear up. The day I called you.'

'Were you there on your own?'

'Yes.'

'Did you go down to the cellar?'

'No. I wouldn't have done that.'

'You haven't paid for a cleaner to go in or anything like that?'

'No. It was too…personal.'

'Could anyone else have had keys?'

He shrugged, 'I don't know. Somebody might have.'

'What about the police? Did they mention anything about a return visit?'

'Not to me.'

'How would you feel about talking to them again?'

'When?'

'Today. Someone's been in the house between your visit and mine. They cleaned a strip in the cellar very thoroughly and it looks like they picked up Jimmy's laptop and left another in its place.'

'Why?'

'Good question. Very good question.'

TEN

The sergeant rang me as dusk fell and said he'd come over. Mister Sherrick heated soup and warmed brown rolls and we ate and we drank tea and I learned more about his life.

Jimmy had left him the house in his will but Mister Sherrick had no inclination to sell it. 'Maybe come springtime I'll consider it,' he said.

'Was there anything in his will which surprised you?' I asked.

'*That* surprised me. The house. I thought he'd have left it to Gillian. I'll give her half the money when I do sell it.'

'Maybe he thought Gillian was still young enough to make her own way in the world? He'd have been worried about you, getting a bit older, maybe.'

He nodded. 'But what do I need? This place will see me out. Seven eighths of my life is gone. Maybe more. Gillian still has half hers left.'

'Was she bitter about the break up?'

'No. She's not the bitter type. I think she felt sorry for Jimmy. She always said it was a mid-life crisis thing. She'd resigned herself to losing him for a year, maybe a bit more.'

'It didn't even last that long, did it?'

He shook his head. 'The girl was a new lease of life for him. He was like a teenager again. I remember him telling me, describing her "beauty" to me as though it was some kind of excuse, some acceptable explanation for leaving his wife. I can still see the intensity in his eyes. He was sitting where you are now.'

35

'How long had he been married?'

'Nineteen years.' He looked at me and pursed his lips in that way which says "What can you do?"

He said. 'I knew that would cripple Jimmy, that decision. If he was anything, he was loyal. That's what his character was and I don't believe he realized that. You can't change your character. You can't. And if you go against it, as Jimmy did, it eats away at you like rust.'

His eyes went to the fire again and he was quiet for a while then said, 'Are you cold, Eddie? It's gone chilly in here.'

'I'm fine.'

He moved forward in the chair, ready to get up. 'Mind if I light the fire?'

'No, of course not. Here, let me do it. You stay there.'

I had to hit the ignition button three times. The gas caught with a tiny boom that longed, one day, to cause havoc.

Mister Sherrick hunched forward, holding his hands out as though at a brazier in the street. 'That's better,' he said.

'What happened with the girl in the end?' I asked. 'I don't even know her name.'

'Amanda. It just fizzled out for her, I think. She was twelve years younger than him. He came home one night and she'd gone. Left a note saying it was good while it lasted or some other throwaway line. He brought the note here, like a child, as though he was hoping it would read different to me than it did to him.'

'How did you feel?'

'Sad. Sad and sorry that he wasn't a kid again in short trousers so I could take the poor bugger in my arms and hug him. He told me that even though he knew it had been wrong to leave Gillian, that once he'd met Amanda, he said, "You might as well have asked me not to breathe again as not to see her again." That's how bad he had it and that wasn't for poetic effect or anything. It was just Jimmy's way of trying to explain.'

'And was that why you kind of accepted, if that's the right word, his suicide?'

His eyes went again toward the fire but his look was tunnelling down through the years. He nodded very slowly, 'I suppose it was…I suppose it was.'

'Did Gillian hope he'd come back to her after Amanda left?'

He made a face and tilted his head as though weighing up his thoughts. 'She hoped he would, but she knew the same as me that the damage was done.'

'Too proud to admit he was wrong?'

'No. No, I don't think it was that at all. It was the loyalty thing again. It's like the old saying, you can't be a little bit pregnant. With Jimmy, you couldn't be a little bit loyal. He'd blown a hole in his own character and he knew he couldn't board it up or fill it in or whatever way you want to look at it, by going back to Gillian. And she wouldn't have scarified him. Wouldn't have cast it up…No, it wasn't pride, it was making your bed and lying in it, another old saying of his mother's. He was a lot like her. A lot.'

I watched him. He watched the fire. The burbling hum of the blue flames the only noise.

'More tea?' I asked quietly, reaching for his mug on the floor. He turned, smiling. 'Please.'

Sergeant Middleton arrived as the kettle boiled and Mister Sherrick welcomed him and took his jacket and pulled another chair to the fireside where we sat in a semi-circle.

'A long day for you sergeant?' Mister Sherrick asked.

'Always seems longer in winter,' he replied, resting the mug on a ledge on his stab vest.

'Must be a relief to get that off at night?' I said.

He smiled. 'Positively float up the stairs to bed.'

'What does it weigh?' I asked.

He looked down at it as though a label held the information. 'About three kilos, I think.'

I thought about carrying my saddle and weight-cloth loaded with lead plates. 'Can't help when you're chasing villains.' I said. He smiled, 'The utility belt and the boots and the hi vis jacket don't either. Not to mention the spare tyre and forty five birthdays.'

'You should have joined the mounted section,' I said.

'Not for me. Those big buggers kick at one end and bite at the other. Best left to nimble sorts like you.'

'Well I'll be glad to be back riding when the thaw finally comes.'

He turned to Mister Sherrick. 'Mister Malloy was saying on the phone that you have some concerns about the formal verdict on your son, Mister Sherrick?'

'Well somebody swapped his computer by the look of things, and Eddie said they did a big clean-up in the cellar.'

I told the sergeant what had happened. He asked about other keyholders, cleaners, window locks, and came up blank.

'Did you take the chain as evidence?' I asked.

'What chain is that?'

I glanced at Jimmy's dad then said. 'When you got Jimmy down, did you take the chain down at the same time?'

'I didn't, personally, but another officer would have. The ligature is seized in all suicides.'

'What about Jimmy's PC?' I asked.

'That is a strange one,' he said. 'We definitely took that but I returned it to Mister Sherrick. Well, I tried to. You wanted it put back in your son's house, didn't, you Mister Sherrick? I don't think you were quite ready at the time to, well, deal with things.'

'I wasn't. I wanted to get everything planned for one day. See Jimmy's solicitor, sort out the will, go to his house and do a final check there. That's when I saw the computer on his desk and dropped it. Or thought I did.'

'I've got it here,' I said. 'Are you happy for us to try and get it working?'

'You've already handled it, obviously?'

I nodded. He turned to Jimmy's dad, 'Mister Sherrick, have you touched that PC today?'

'I don't believe I've ever touched it unless it is Jimmy's and somebody came and fixed it or unless I've lost the plot altogether and cleaned up broken glass that was never there. I'm beginning to wonder myself now.'

The sergeant said to me, 'Let's see if we can get it booted up.' We plugged it in above the breakfast bar and hit the power button. The disk whirred. The screen glowed. We waited through the start-up routine which seemed to take forever. A dozen icons dotted the desktop; one was for the *Racing Post* site. I clicked on it: no Internet connection.

'Have you got Internet here, Mister Sherrick?' I asked.

'I don't. It is in the complex, I'm sure, with some wireless thing.

'

'Wi-Fi?'

'That's it. I don't need it. I read, mostly.'

I tethered my phone and got a connection. I clicked again on the *Racing Post* icon and the home screen requested a login. The panel came up with JSherrick in the username box and the password already saved. The sergeant said, 'Try the email.'

Jimmy's dad took a soft glasses case from his cardigan pocket and put on gold-rimmed specs.

I clicked the icon. Jimmy's Hotmail feed appeared. His Inbox had a line of unopened mails. The sergeant said, 'Put cyanide in the search box.'

I did and Jimmy's online order for cyanide capsules came up. Jimmy's dad stared at the screen. I watched him, the bright rectangular PC panel reflected in his glasses. He began blinking as though trying to wipe the confusion from his eyes. Slowly he reached out a hand and ran his fingers over the screen, back and forth, back and forth, lost in another world.

ELEVEN

On my way home I eased off the gas as I passed Rooksnest, the Manor house that marked the edge of Lambourn civilization and the end of tarmac below the Subaru's wheels. Moving on to the rough road, the car trundled down the rutted track, headlight beams bouncing on the sparkling snow which lay hard and clean on the woodland border.

I held Jimmy's laptop for fear of it hitting the floor. Mister Sherrick had handed it over to me with a finality that said he'd no wish to see it again. He'd been subdued, almost shocked as he had closed the unbroken screen and looked at Sergeant Middleton. 'You okay with me taking this and having a look through the stuff on it?' I'd asked the sergeant.

'It's Mister Sherrick's property. I've got no problem with it.' I'd felt sorry for Jimmy's dad. We'd spent much of the day together and I had learned more about Jimmy than I knew when he was alive.

I was sure Jimmy hadn't made that recording. And I was certain he hadn't bought cyanide, or anything else, online; pigheadedly certain. But Mister Sherrick's story had thrown me. Had grief somehow confused him when he was at Jimmy's place? His insistence the screen had been broken, that he'd swept up glass didn't hold out. So had he cleaned that strip in the cellar too?

I gripped the steering wheel tighter with one hand as we bumped over the worst section of the track, headlights showing glimpses of the white walls of my bungalow and glinting on the glass of the sun house.

The security light flooded the garden catching millions of frost motes. I carried the laptop inside and locked up.

Over a thin mushroom omelette and a mug of tea, I searched the files on Jimmy's laptop. Compared with him, I was an expert, but compared with a friend of mine who called herself Maven Judge, I knew nothing.

I'd first met Mave in early summer at Bangor races in North Wales. I was to learn that this was a rare outing in daylight for her. She usually came to life at dusk and stayed up all night.

That day, she had been waiting in the car park for me after racing, sitting on the roof of my car in the late afternoon sun, her chestnut ponytail healthy looking against her pasty complexion. She had a big nose and small eyes and her ears stuck out. At first I wasn't sure if she was male or female. She was slight as a child though I judged her to be in her thirties as I approached, trying to look as cool as she did about the fact she was sitting on the roof of my car, knees to her flat chest, hands round the shins of her blue jeans, her face expressionless and brown eyes intense as she watched me.

I stopped and looked up. 'Did you fall out of a plane or did you just climb up there the old fashioned way?'

'I'm an angel.'

'Where did you leave your wings?'

'They're retractable. You're thinking of the old angels. They went out with the ark.'

'Retractable wings, eh? That'll be handy when they come with the straitjacket.'

'You're a funny man, Eddie.'

'I'm a funny man with a long drive in front of me. What are you, animal rights?'

'I couldn't give a toss about animals. I don't even like humans.'

'I bet you didn't put that on your CV when you were applying for the angel job.'

She smiled. Her teeth were crooked. 'You're a cool dude,' she said.

'Thanks. Now get off my car.'

'You want to be rich?'

'Nope. I want to go home.'

'I can make you rich.'

Maven had been working for years to develop software for betting on horses. She spent half an hour that day trying to persuade me to team up with her to help complete her programme. 'Why me?' I'd asked.

'You're straight.'

'How do you know I'm straight?'

'Because it's my job to know things.'

'In that case you'll know it's against the rules of racing for me to offer information for financial benefit.'

'I worked that out. You won't get anything until you retire.'

Mave had kept chipping away at me since then and I fended her off with 'maybe someday'. I could have ignored her calls and emails but I enjoyed the banter. I had no close friends, nor had Mave. We were loners with no sexual interest in each other but with something in common - a sense of the ridiculous, of how crazy the world was.

I finished eating and switched on my own PC then hit the Skype video connection against Mave's name. She accepted. All I could see were her fingers working the keyboard by the light from her PC screen.

'The Man from La Rancha,' she said.

'What?'

'How's it going on that sprawling ranch of yours?'

'Mave, it's not a ranch. It's a bungalow on an acre of land.'

'That's forty four thousand square feet of prime real estate Mister Malloy.'

'That big?'

'That big. What can I do for you this winter's night?'

'You heard about Jimmy Sherrick?'

'I did.'

'I've got his laptop. I wanted you to take a look at it.'

'In search of what?'

'Clues. You'll find a recording on it, of his suicide message. I don't think he made the recording.'

'Okay.'

'I'll mail it to you tomorrow.'

'No need. You got it on just now?'

'It's right beside me.'

'Type this into the address bar.'

Five minutes later, I watched the mouse move around on the screen. Mave was controlling it from her tiny cottage on the tip of the Lleyn Peninsula in North Wales, almost two hundred miles north west of where I sat.

'You seeing that?' Mave asked.

'The wonders of technology. Can you get into the guts of it with this remote access?'

'I can do anything I could do if it was sitting in front of me but I'm busy until about midnight. I'll take a look at it after that.'

'OK. Thanks.'

'Want me to wake you if there's any scary shit on there?'

'No. I need my sleep. It's not as if I'll be able to do much anyway. I want to see if you can work out how that recording was done.'

'Okay.'

'Thanks Mave. I'll ping you in the morning.'

'Am I correct in saying there's nothing in this for you?'

'In what?'

'In finding what you're looking for.'

'It lets me scratch my itch.'

She sighed. 'I offer you a million to do stuff for me in your spare time and you'd rather ferret around a dead guy's PC. For nothing. Can you feel my frustration?'

'Remotely.'

'Piss off.'

'Good night, Maven.'

I ended it smiling, as I almost always did after speaking to Mave. I called Mister Sherrick and it rang half a dozen times. I checked my watch, in case I'd misjudged and might be getting him out of bed. Then he answered.

'Jim, it's Eddie.'

'Hello. Hello Eddie.' He cleared his throat.

'I hope I didn't wake you. I just wanted to make sure you were okay. It's been a long day.'

'Thanks. I don't know if I'm okay, to be honest with you. That carry on with Jimmy's computer earlier knocked me back on my heels a bit. Do you think I could have dementia?'

My instinct was to say no, to reassure him, but if I did, he might delay a visit to the doctor. 'Are you asking because of the stuff with Jimmy's laptop?'

'Mostly, I suppose. But I was thinking there might be other things. Maybe I've been forgetting more than that and not realized it. When you live on your own you've got nobody to tell you that you already did something three times, or that you keep telling the same story over and over. Know what I mean?'

'I suppose I do. It could be stress over Jimmy's death. You'd be amazed how stress can affect you.'

'Mmm.'

'Why don't you call your doctor tomorrow?'

'I will.'

'You'll get some reassurance then.'

'You're right. Thank you. I enjoyed your company today. Jimmy always spoke highly of you.'

'He was a good man. And it was a good day today…in its way. You know what I mean.'

'I do. Yes.'

'I'll let you get settled.'

'All right, Eddie. Nice of you to call, to check. Thank you.'

'No trouble. Good night.'

'Good night.'

TWELVE

I was up before six. Early rising was a habit in the racing business, where horses are seldom more than a tongue-click away from wakefulness. Within a ten mile radius of my house, two thousand thoroughbreds would be stirring, awaiting breakfast, grooming, dawn, exercise. None would be travelling to a racecourse on this day, although the radio brought news of a coming thaw.

I showered, dressed and headed for the kitchen and the coffee pot, pressing the power switch on my PC as I passed the table. Sunrise was still two hours away when I sat down and opened Skype to see if Mave was still awake. She was. I clicked. She accepted, then immediately ended the call and typed a message telling me to call her landline number. I scrolled through my contacts and found it.

Mave answered on the third ring, 'Eddie.'

'What's up?'

'Maybe nothing but don't Skype me for now. I'll give you a link. Download the software on it and install it then ping me through that. It's secure.'

It took me five minutes to do it and connect with Mave. 'You found something on Jimmy's PC?'

'Everything there is a copy, a mirrored image of a hard drive. The image was installed on December twentieth.'

That was three days before Jimmy's death. 'Tell me what this means in layman's terms.'

'All the files on the laptop have been copied from another PC and pasted onto that one you've got, which is eighteen months old and has had all its previous content deleted before the current stuff was put on it.'

'What about the recording, the suicide note?'

'It was recorded with a programme called Audacity, which is pretty common. The files were imported to the PC, extracted from an email which came from an account which was closed on Christmas day.'

'So no recording was made directly onto the PC?'

'No.'

'Not even on the original PC the files were copied from?'

'Nope. It was recorded elsewhere and edited elsewhere and I'm pretty sure it isn't a contiguous piece of speech.'

'Contiguous?'

'Well, it's contiguous now since somebody put it together. Each part connects logically with the previous one, but those are sections of speech from different conversations.'

I dragged my notepad and pen across. Doodling helped me organize my thoughts. I said, 'Would you say it's the same person who made the recording?'

'The same person in that it's the same guy speaking?'

'Yes.'

'It's the same guy. But the variations in the sound wave patterns suggest that sections were spoken at different times. If you listen really closely to the pitch and the tone you can hear the tiny variances. You are not talking to me now in the same pitch as you were last night. Time of day will change the tone and pitch, the person you're talking to, the subject matter, how tired you are, what your emotions are like.'

'Okay. Could you break it down into sections for me, tell me which you think were recorded at another time?'

'How big a hurry are you in?'

'As soon as?'

'I need to sleep, Eddie'

'Sleep's for wimps.'

'People whose brains actually work need sleep. Knuckle-draggers like you don't.'

I smiled. 'Midnight tonight?'

'Cool.'

'One more question; the cops said they had a language expert verify this. Should he have spotted what you spotted?'

'You're assuming language experts are male, why?'

'All right, he or she.'

'Not necessarily, I suppose. Was the sample being compared with a known recording?'

'Yes.'

'Well, concentration would be on the comparison rather than this individual one. Also, the content scores high on emotional pull so whoever is listening will be distracted by the message rather than how it was being delivered. You heard it?'

'The cops played it back to me.'

'What did you think as you listened?'

'I was concentrating on trying to prove it wasn't Jimmy's voice.'

'

'Listen to it again. Forget what he's saying and concentrate on how he says it.'

'Okay. Thanks, Mave. If something comes up during the day can I disturb your beauty sleep?'

'No.'

'Thank you for your cooperation.'

'You're welcome. Goodbye.'

'Mave!'

'What?'

'Why didn't you set me up with this secure link before?'

'Because I thought all you were doing was riding horses for a living.'

'I was.'

'Well, whatever you're into here, your opponent is pretty smart on the tech side. You ought to review your security, online and off.'

'My opponent?'

'Adversary, enemy, whatever.'

'Let's call him, or her, "this guy" or our conversations are going to end up like Batman comics.'

'Fine. I'm going to bed. Good luck. I'll speak to you tonight on this link ... If you're still alive!' She cackled theatrically and closed the connection.

I drew a smiley face on the notepad. Jimmy Sherrick hadn't made that recording. It seemed less likely that he'd committed suicide.

My first thought was to call Jimmy's dad and reassure him that he wasn't suffering from dementia. The laptop he'd dropped was not the one that sat in front of me. This had been doctored on Christmas day when Jimmy's was locked up in Newbury police station.

But telling Mister Sherrick what Mave had told me meant giving him information someone wanted kept quiet. I needed to know who that someone was, and I needed to know how dangerous he was. Assuming it was a he, as Mave would have reminded me.

I'd assume that. Most murderers were men.

But why had he killed Jimmy?

I found the recorded file and listened again to Jimmy's voice:

"Every day I hurt from old injuries and from old memories. Something happens to a man when he turns forty. I've seen too many sad people. I don't want to be one of them. I want to make extra sure. That's why I did it this way. Hanging? It's no certainty. Goodbye."

Mave was right, there was a slightly different tone to each sentence, a bit like the shading in a pencil drawing; tiny subtle changes. I ran it three times more. Each of those sentences, on their own, could have been taken from any conversation. "It's no certainty." That could easily have been a response to a question about the chances of a horse he was riding. "Hanging." That was a term in common use in racing. Horses would hang during races as their balance was affected by tiredness or attitude.

What if this guy has been bugging Jimmy's phone and recording the conversations? He'd need to have a few to pick from, so it was reasonable to believe he knew Jimmy, maybe knew him quite well. Well enough to have a set of keys for Jimmy's house? Or did he have access to Jimmy's gear to grab the keys and get copies cut? Was it another jockey taking advantage in the changing room when Jimmy was riding in a race? Was it a valet?

Whoever it was, why had he done it? What did Jimmy have on him? What could be serious enough to kill for? I sketched and doodled until daybreak then did what I usually do when I'm trying to figure something out, I got my running gear on and headed into the woods.

I'd gone a hundred yards through the thawing snow when I turned back. Routine can be comforting, but it makes you predictable. It had been a while since I'd had to watch my back. That, and moving in here to this silent hideaway had made me complacent. I went inside, logged off my PC and put Jimmy's laptop in the floor safe.

I tucked my phone into the small zipper pocket in my jacket and, for the first time since moving in, locked my front door to go out running. A final check before leaving the driveway was to stand and listen for anything in the woods. All I could hear was the irregular plop as the thaw released slabs of snow from branches.

I set out with the feeling I was being watched.

THIRTEEN

In the last two hundred yards of my usual four mile circuit, I could see my house appear and disappear through the dense trees as the path snaked toward its end. I slowed to a walk to cool down. My phone beeped.

It was a text from Bayley Watt: "If Taunton passes inspec, will u ride 1 in the 1st". I knew a couple of racecourses were planning inspections in the afternoon with an optimistic view of staging meetings tomorrow.

I showered, changed and rang Bayley Watt. 'Thanks for the text. What have you got in the first?'

'Newcomer called Spiritless Fun. Doesn't show much at home but he's a lazy bastard and he's probably good enough to get placed. '

'Fine, happy to ride him. The ground'll be a mess if they do race.'

'That won't bother him.'

'Okay. See you there if it's on.'

'Eddie, I've another runner there. I've booked Barry Copland. No offence but you remember what I said to you.'

'Oh, yes. The Indians.'

'You taking the piss?'

'Not at all. That's what your theory was based on, wasn't it? Different riders each time. The Comanches did it.'

'Comanche. Plural.'

'Bayley, you're getting touchy, my friend. I like riding for you but I don't want to be tiptoeing around you every time we talk.' He paused and I got the impression he was trying to calm himself. 'I know. I'm sorry. I need to get out more. Should be better when the thaw comes.'

'No worries. See you tomorrow.'

I sat in what I called the Snug. I like small cosy rooms. The only thing big about the Snug was my picture window showing the garden at the rear of the house, the lawn stretching fenceless into the dark wood. Staring out of the big window at the garden, I saw small maps of green emerging through the snow as the temperature climbed.

I'd almost stopped myself having a go at Bayley Watt but he would have expected me to do it. If I'd kept quiet he would have been uneasy and I didn't want him thinking I had him under suspicion.

Watt had failed to ask me why I'd gone to the police about Jimmy. He'd been close enough to him these past few months to have access to his house keys. He said he'd sacked Jimmy and maybe he had. Jimmy might have been trying to shore up his pride telling me he was packing the job in. That wouldn't be unnatural for anyone. But Jimmy might have been telling the truth, which made Bayley Watt a liar. And he'd been very jumpy lately. And patronizing...*Comanche. Plural.* Cheeky bastard.

I googled "Comanche or Comanches?" An online dictionary told me either was acceptable. So Watt was a patronizing, *wrong* bastard. Five years ago I'd have been grabbing the phone to correct him, but I told myself I'd mellowed.

Among the search results were links to a few articles on the Comanches. I decided to find out just how effective these rider changes had been for them back in the old cowboy days. Half an hour later I had not come across a single reference to this theory of Watt's.

Maybe it was another tribe? I spent an hour trawling and querying without finding anything to support Watt's claim.

Either Bayley Watt had found some great secret document that had never been catalogued online or he'd been lying. If he'd lied about it, what was the real reason behind him wanting different jockeys for each horse? What had Jimmy Sherrick found out from riding Watt's horses? Something that cost him his job? Something that had made him decide he wanted out? Something that had got him killed?

But if the trainer was running a scam, why ask me to ride for him again?

It made no sense. If Bayley was crooked, he knew I was not only straight but that I was also suspicious enough about Jimmy's death to go to the cops about it. Logically, he should have wanted to keep me as far away from his yard as possible. Unless he thought he'd be better having me inside the tent pissing out than outside pissing in.

My mobile rang, startling me. Jimmy's dad. I answered, 'How are you Jim?'

'I'm all right, Eddie, thanks. You?'

'Fine, thanks. Racing should be back tomorrow.'

'So I hear. Listen, Sergeant Middleton has just come back from Jimmy's place. He called by for the keys earlier. He wanted to check that what he'd said about the chain having been taken by police at the time was right and it wasn't still there.'

That seemed odd. Why couldn't he check at the station? Someone must have signed it in. Unless … 'Was it still there?'

'No, they'd picked it up as he thought.'

'Listen, do you mind if I drop by?'

'You're welcome. You're always welcome. When suits?'

'Now?'

FOURTEEN

Mister Sherrick's old kettle was whistling over the gas flame. He made tea and brought it to the fireside. He said, 'I'm going to push the boat out and turn this fire on for a bit. Rarely light it through the day but I was thinking I could pay the bill when I sell the house.' He bent and clicked it on.

'You're a wizard with that ignition button.' I said.

He smiled and settled in the easy chair, reaching for the yellow mug from the small table between us.

I drank some tea and we watched the reddening racks of elements in the fire. 'Jim, I've been wondering whether to tell you some things. I don't want you put in any kind of danger. But I don't want to treat you like a fool either.'

'Well if it's about Jimmy, I've got a responsibility to know, haven't I? Don't worry about what might happen.'

'I will worry. And I've got a responsibility too, to do the right thing. Well, I should say, the safest thing.'

'Ahh, your responsibility is to your conscience then?'

I sighed. 'I suppose it is.'

'I absolve thee.'

We smiled at each other. 'In advance,' he added.

I told him what Mave had found out. 'So I was right about the screen being broken?'

'Looks that way.' I said.

'At least that makes me feel a bit better.'

'But it also means that Jimmy might not have committed suicide.'

He nodded, staring at the fire in silence for what seemed a long time, before he looked up at me. 'Eddie, will you read the letter Jimmy left for me?'

'Of course.'

'Jimmy asked me in it not to tell anyone about it, but I think you're getting yourself deep into this. If you know what happened with Jimmy, it gives you a chance to walk away. You've no commitment to me or anyone else.'

I nodded. Mister Sherrick went to another room and came back with the letter.

I opened it.

Dear Dad,

Where do I start? You're reading this because things didn't work out for me. I was hoping they would, and I've done some stupid things to try and make everything better. Last month the doctor told me I had pancreatic cancer and that it was too far gone. I didn't want to tell you at the time because all it would do was cause you worry. Worry about something you couldn't do anything about. You had enough trying to cope with Mum's illness.

Anyway, I tried a new treatment that I was told had a good chance of working. That was another reason I never told you. If it had worked, you'd never have needed to know because I'd have got better. Well, it didn't work, but at least I didn't give up without a fight.

I don't know what else will have come out by the time you're reading this, and I'm not all that bothered about what others think. But I wanted to tell you that whatever I did, it was for Amanda and me. It was to try and give us a real chance of making everything work. You'll be in no doubt how I felt about her, God knows, I was like a kid blabbing it all out to you. But she came into my life at a time when everything was going downhill. I realize now that a lot of the way I was feeling was to do with the cancer, and I wish I'd gone for a check up sooner. But I was too scared of being stood down. Anyway, Amanda gave me something to live for again. Except I didn't. That's how the cookie crumbles as Ma used to say.

The one good thing is that by the time you're reading this, I'll be with Ma again. If she's forgiven me. I'll give her your love.

Please don't tell anybody about this letter or what I've said in it. Those who judge me won't be changed by any of it. They don't matter anyway, and I'll soon be forgotten by the outside world.

There was never anything you did that made me unhappy, Dad. The older I got and the more people I met, the more I realized how rare men like you are. Decent, good, honest, no sides or angles to you - a fine man and a fine father and I loved you always and I know you loved me. I wish I could say I was like you and that nothing I did was for myself. But in the past couple of years, everything I did was for myself. Everything. But the more you want something, the further away it seems to move. I tried to reach it and pull it back. It just didn't work. Forgive me.

Love, Jimmy.

I folded the letter and looked across at Mister Sherrick. 'Jim, I don't know what to say to you. You didn't fail Jimmy in any way. He doesn't mention suicide. He could have expected to die from the cancer. That's the impression I get.'

He reached for the letter. 'That's what I thought. That's why I asked you if he mentioned suicide in his letter to you.'

'He didn't. Only hints of what he seemed to be trying to get across there. That he was doing something others wouldn't approve of, but that could have been anything. Complementary medicine, hypnotists, some kind of off the wall treatment. Have you spoken to his doctor?'

'I didn't see much use in it.'

'Maybe you should. Maybe he'll have some idea what it was Jimmy was trying.'

'The main thing for you, Eddie, is that it looks like it might not all have been above board. It could have been costing a lot and he was having to...to duck and dive a bit to get the money.'

'Even if he was, there's somebody else involved in his death, isn't there? There has to be.'

He looked at me. 'At least it wasn't me. I didn't fail him. It must sound awful to you to hear a father saying he'd rather his son was murdered than he committed suicide.'

I reached to clasp his arm. 'I know what you mean. I'd feel exactly the same in your position.' He put his hand on mine and held it, staring once more into the fire.

'Did Jimmy ever talk to you about Bayley Watt?' I asked.

'Not in any detail. Nothing outside of the fact he was riding regularly for him.'

'What do you think of him?'

'Watt? I only met him at the funeral, then again when I dropped Jimmy's letter off.'

'Any idea if he might have had access to Jimmy's house?'

'Keys, you mean?'

'Yes.'

'I haven't a clue. Do you think Watt's been in the house?'

'Somebody has. No forced entry, so whoever it was had a key. Watt probably saw Jimmy more often than anyone else so I'm just putting two and two together and probably getting five. I need to do some more digging.'

'Watt had some stuff of Jimmy's. He gave it to me at the funeral.'

'Stuff from Jimmy's house?'

'Well…I'm not sure. He had a coat Jimmy had left at his place, so he said, and a pair of riding gloves. And this.' He held his left arm up and pushed his shirt cuff down to reveal a stainless steel watch. 'It was in a gift box. Jimmy had bought it for me as a Christmas present from one of the market stalls at Cheltenham, and left it in Watt's car … A Christmas present.'

His voice went shaky and I looked at him. But he was smiling. He said. 'Watt was actually quite apologetic that Jimmy hadn't had a chance to wrap it and write a card. He said he'd been tempted to do it after … afterward, but he didn't think it was right. '

'At least you got it.'

'Better late than never, and all that.' He pushed the bracelet round. It looked too big for him.

He sipped tea and watched me over the rim of the mug. 'Eddie, listen, you owe me nothing. However Jimmy died, he's gone and I can't get him back. Leave it to the sergeant now. I don't expect you to be investigating what happened. It's important to me that you're clear about that. I don't want you to feel even the smallest obligation to me. You have none.'

'I know. I'm just a pig-headed bastard. Jimmy was going to tell me something that night and I'd like to find out what it was. He might have been trying to help me and if that's what got him killed then I owe him. I owe Jimmy. It sounds a bit like a sentimental old movie script but he saved my life too when he barely knew me, when it was hardly worth saving, I was so much of a dick at the time.'

He smiled. 'An honest dick, though.'

I laughed, 'You're supposed to say, "Oh don't be so hard on yourself, you were a fine young man"'.

'I've been around a fair few years and I've yet to meet a mature nineteen-year-old. Listen, Jimmy would have done that for anybody. He wouldn't have held you to anything or expected a favour.'

'I know he wouldn't. Maybe, if I can't come up with a concrete reason to carry on, I'll let it go.'

He nodded slowly, looking at me. 'Maybe pigs'll fly.'

FIFTEEN

I followed Sergeant Middleton upstairs to his office. Bright lights overhead and the deepening dusk made mirrors of the windows and I watched our climbing reflections, the sergeant looking weary. He'd been very patient with me and it made up for some of the arrogant, stupid cops I'd come across in the past.

We settled at his desk and he leant back and ran his fingers through his grey hair.

'Another long day?' I said.

'They're supposed to be short, aren't they? January. Anyway, what can I do for you?'

'This time.'

'Pardon?'

'You forgot to add "this time" through gritted teeth.'

He chuckled and seemed to relax a bit. 'When does your shift finish?' I asked.

'Eight.'

'I'll buy you a drink if you fancy?'

'That's kind of you but I've got to get home.'

'Maybe some other time? You've been very patient with me.'

'That's my job.'

'Patience?'

'Partly. Mister Sherrick told you I'd visited?'

'He did.'

'Standard procedure.'

I looked at him. His cap was on the table, He reached for it, fiddling with the rim. 'Checking for something that should have been here in the station?' I asked.

He pushed the cap to the side and looked at me. 'Listen, we ballsed it up. A Detective Sergeant should have visited within twenty four hours, ideally. Any suicide, even one that looked as obvious as that, is treated as a suspicious death, which means a detective should attend. Also, I passed on the information you gave me when you were last here about Mister Sherrick being a technophobe. I thought everything was in hand, and when I left you last night, I checked, just in case, and found that no detective had attended. My report had slipped through the net and nobody could find the chain. There'll be a Soco team out there within the next day or two and we'll get things back on track. Apologies. And the chain and my report have now been found.'

I nodded. 'Are you planning to tell Jimmy's dad about this?'

'Yes. He's entitled to an apology too.'

'Sounds like you weren't to blame.'

'No matter. I should have stayed on top of it.'

'Don't take the fall for them, sergeant. Because they rank higher, it doesn't mean they can shift the blame.'

He smiled. 'Thanks. Anyway, does that put your mind a bit more at rest?'

'Well, I'm glad it's being taken seriously, because that laptop at Jimmy's wasn't his.'

I told him what Mave had found on the laptop.

'Our guys wouldn't have checked it to that level,' he said.

'Your guys had a different PC anyway. Whoever cleaned that floor beneath the beam took Jimmy's laptop and left a replacement. Jimmy didn't record that message which makes it highly doubtful he committed suicide.'

'So somebody gave him cyanide then hanged him?'

'And forged the recording.'

He sat looking at me, probably wondering if he'd been too open, too honest in the past five minutes.

'Would that chain have been checked for prints?' I asked.

'I don't know.'

'Would prints be easily left on a rusty chain?'

He shrugged. 'Probably, partial ones, at least. But if a murderer takes the time and trouble to make a pretty elaborate faked suicide message, wouldn't he wear gloves?'

'I suppose he would. What about the autopsy? Did that say whether the cyanide had killed him, or asphyxiation from hanging?'

'Cyanide poisoning was the cause of death.'

'Wouldn't the pathologist have thought twice? He, or she, assumes suicide, as everybody did.'

'Except you.'

'All I was sure of was that Jimmy hadn't made the recording. I was open to suicide, if you see what I mean. But think about it, Jimmy's timing would need to have been spot on. If he takes the cyanide before he climbs onto the chair and tries to organize the chain and kick the chair away etcetera, how can he be sure the poison won't kill him before he gets everything done?'

'He could have set it all up, swallowed the cyanide, then kicked away the chair.'

'Or somebody could have given him cyanide, waited until he was dead, then strung him up.'

I watched him. He'd need to be careful now because there was a PR side to this and maybe a negligence aspect.

I said, 'Do you believe Jimmy having cancer is still a big factor?'

I watched him try to run through the implications of the question. Was I suggesting that the police weren't treating it seriously?

He batted it back to me. 'You've seen the medical reports?'

'Jimmy's dad told me Jimmy had terminal cancer.'

'And what do you think? Has it changed the way you look at it?'

'Whatever I think, it doesn't alter the fact that the message was faked and his PC stolen and doctored.'

'But those factors don't mean he was murdered. What strikes me is that Mister Sherrick died before he could tell you what he had called you about the day before. Who else could have known about the meeting you'd planned?'

'Well, I told no one. Jimmy could have told a dozen people.'

'Could he just have changed his mind about talking to you? Or perhaps he wanted to be found quickly.'

'Maybe. But why cyanide as well as hanging? One or the other, yes, but not both. I daresay nobody's lived to tell what it's like when cyanide gets to work on you, but I'll bet it's not a pleasant death.' As I finished saying that, it dawned on me what Jimmy might have meant in his letter - "I tried something new. I don't know what else will come out by the time you read this."

'Sergeant, this is probably going to sound like a very stupid question. Is there any way of knowing if the cyanide was taken all at once? Could it have built up from very small doses?'

'It's possible, I suppose. Why? Do you think someone had been trying to poison Mister Sherrick gradually?'

'I'm wondering if he was taking tiny amounts of cyanide in the hope of killing the cancer.'

'Why do you say that?'

'A sudden hunch, probably wildly wrong. What would be the chance of getting the body exhumed?' I asked.

'On the basis of a hunch?'

'On the basis of a double check to confirm exactly how he died.'

'That would be a tough one.'

'Well, given the incompetence of your colleagues in this, losing files, losing the chain. You know what I'm saying.' I didn't feel too guilty about pulling this on him, given he hadn't been directly to blame.

Still, his look hardened a bit as he took in the implications. 'Let's see what Soco get, and maybe then I'll speak to the pathologist. I believe we still have the memory stick so I'll ask for another analysis on the recording.' He straightened and made to get up, reassert authority.

I stood and said, 'Will you be able to let me know what you find out?'

He made a face which reinforced what he then said, 'That could be tricky. The inquest date hasn't even been set yet. We had to push things a bit just to allow the funeral. Mister Sherrick senior was in a, was, . . anxious to have his son buried before the new year. He, Mister Sherrick senior, is next of kin, so let's see how things go. You seem pretty close to him anyway, no doubt he will keep you informed.' We shook hands and he saw me all the way downstairs and out.

Walking through the rain to my car, I reflected on his hesitation when talking about Jim Sherrick. He'd been going to say that he was "in a hurry" to get Jimmy buried. He knew Jimmy had left his father a neat bundle of letters. I suspected he also knew Jimmy had left him the house. And with my suggestion that whoever had swapped the PC and cleaned the floor had easy access to Jimmy's place, I wondered if, in the sergeant's mind, Jimmy's dad was becoming something more than next of kin.

SIXTEEN

I always enjoyed the drive to Taunton. If you picture the right leg of England kicking out into the Atlantic, Taunton sits about mid-thigh, in the county of Somerset. The course lies just off the M5 motorway, and soil from the dig for that road had been used to lengthen the straights and ease the bends on this tight little track at the foot of the Blackdown Hills.

On most of Britain's sixty tracks, horses race anti-clockwise. At Taunton, they go clockwise, or right-handed, and some horses enjoy racing that way. I hoped my ride in the first, Spiritless Fun, would be one of them.

In the small changing room there was more hilarity than usual as we celebrated our return after more than a week of frozen ground.

Jockeys working a particular region, in my case mostly the south and the midlands, saw each other almost daily. When we weren't riding in a race, this was our haven, the changing room. Only jockeys and valets allowed. Track officials could come in but seldom did. Here we were safe from frustrated trainers, boorish owners and the odd angry punter.

We each had a 'peg' where our clothes hung below saddle racks. Some jocks carried three saddles. The lightest consisted of little more than strips of fabric or leather strong enough to support stirrups. These were reserved for those horses allocated a low weight by the handicapper. The heaviest saddle was kept for the luxury of riding a horse carrying more than eleven stones.

Pegs, benches, heaters, showers, sauna, deep sinks for valets to plunge muddy silks and breeches into, wood floor, tables and the smells of liniment and leather.

The top jockeys got the best peg. I was about halfway down the pecking order and I'd long ago stopped thinking of the days when the best peg had been mine.

We trooped out, a snaking line of colour among the dark winter clothing of those in the paddock.

Normally, the groom will be walking your horse around while the trainer chats with owners on the lawn. But Bayley was groom, owner and trainer. He led number 7, a compact bay gelding.

Bayley nodded to me. I went to the edge of the lawn and waited for the mounting bell.

Bayley legged me into the saddle and I settled, feet in stirrup irons, Spiritless Fun already belying his name with a springy athletic jog. Bayley looked up and said, 'There's not much of him but he's fit and ready and he's been schooling well.' He took hold of the rein, leading me out onto the track where the wind was cold. He said, 'You'll find him straightforward so I'll leave it to you.' With that he released the rein, and the horse launched immediately into a canter.

Many trainers give instructions to jockeys on where and when to take certain positions in a race. Some horses pull hard and need settling, some stop trying when they hit the front and must be brought with a very late challenge.

But Bayley would know little about this one's racing style as the horse hadn't raced before. For a debutant, he seemed remarkably composed. Normally, they'll be looking around, pricking ears at the PA announcements, acting curious, like a child on a first trip to the funfair.

But this fellow just put his head down and moved determinedly toward the start, his gait relaxed but powerful. You don't need to be going fast on a horse to tell how good he might be, and although five others were shorter in the betting, horses from the big yards, I'd never sat on a first-timer who felt so good. We started on the far side, opposite the crowded stands. Behind us lay the snow-clad Blackdown Hills, ahead of us ten hurdles. Fourteen horses set off, a big field for this tight little track but Spiritless Fun went anywhere I asked, responding immediately. Tactical speed they called it; the ability to accelerate very quickly at any point in a race and grab a gap or avoid being boxed in.

Many horses need stoking up to reach full speed, and some have only one pace at the gallop. But this bay gelding was special, and as we glided to the front coming to the last hurdle, I felt two quick stabs of regret. One for Jimmy, who should have had the thrill of sitting on this. The other for myself when I remembered that Bayley Watt would want a different jockey next time he ran.

Spiritless Fun beat the others as though they were a different, short-legged, clumsy species. Bayley was smiling as he came to meet me. 'I thought he'd go well,' he said, shaking my hand. 'Bayley, this is the best horse I've sat on since my comeback. He'd be in the top ten of anything I've ridden, ever.'

'That good?' Bayley Watt knew I had three Cheltenham Festival winners to my name.

'He'd be a Cheltenham horse.'

'That's a thought, Eddie.'

'Let me ride him next time.' I rarely begged for rides and I'd never have dreamt of doing so with Bayley, especially as he'd told me what his supposed policy was. But I knew the Comanche stuff was nonsense. I'd no idea why he'd spun me that crap. But I didn't want to lose the ride on this horse.

'Eddie -'

'Bayley, I know what you told me and I believe you're a genius mostly, but this horse doesn't need a change to find more speed. My granny could win on him. He is a tailor-made, fresh out of the mould, proper fucking horse and I don't want to lose the ride.'

We walked into the small winner's enclosure to growing applause. I looked down on Bayley's hat. He didn't respond. I jumped, off, undid the girths and slid the saddle off. The horse hadn't broken sweat. I glanced at the runner-up, his big ribcage heaved. Spiritless Fun wouldn't have blown a candle out. I looked at the trainer, 'Bayley ...'

'I'll think about it. Go and weigh in.'

I stamped back toward the weighing room feeling a fiery mixture of frustration and excitement and, I realized, nostalgia. In my brief spell as Champion Jockey, horses like this would be something for me to ponder: which should I ride. Fuck! Damn!

What a stupid complacent bastard I'd been.

I sat on the scales, clutching my saddle as the clerk watched the needle bob to ten twelve, confirming that I had carried throughout the race the weight officially allotted. 'Okay, Eddie,' he said.

'Thanks.'

I went into the changing room. Riley Duggan sat on the bench, next to my peg. He said, 'That looked a piece of piss.'

'He wasn't out of second gear.'

'So what's the problem? You look like a man who just flushed his lottery ticket down the pan.'

'Nothing.'

'Watt not pleased? Not supposed to be off today?'

'No, he's fine.' Many horses that show promise at home are given 'educational' rides first time. "Not off", as Riley had said, was a euphemism for a non-trier. Few things upset owners and trainers more than one of their horses winning when they hadn't had a decent bet.

'Well cheer the fuck up, Eddie. Racing's back, all your old mates are still around. A new year awaits.' He slapped my back.

I tried to smile.

I had two more rides and found myself stupidly resenting their slowness, their inability to keep up, their tired slog up that Taunton straight. At least Bayley Watt's other runner lost. That was some compensation on the long trip home in the dark.

Even as I pulled into my driveway, an arrival that always calmed me, I couldn't settle myself, the irritability goading me to slam the car door so hard it echoed into the cold, dark woods.

The security lamp lit my angry, frowning, teeth-grinding face and I marched inside and half-filled a glass with whiskey and kicked the wash-basket over and bawled every swear word I knew until I ran out of curses and ended up half-laughing, half-crying at my ludicrous behaviour.

By the time I'd finished the whiskey and lit a fire, some stability had returned.

Some.

I sat in the dark, watching the flames. My head remained full of regrets, but they were weary regrets now, having been kicked and cursed for hours. Tired, old, self-pitying regrets.

I even wished I hadn't ridden that horse today. My tumultuous time was supposed to be behind me. This place had been built for a fresh beginning, to lay the foundations for a new life, a life in the middle lane, my cruise control into old age. Now a horse had blown a hole in that road. He'd rebuilt a burnt bridge and offered me a route back. Back to the glory days when all was young and new and everything lay ahead. And all my years of practised self-analysis, of determined acceptance of a lost career, of trying to keep some mental stability, had been shattered by the simple exquisite motion of a galloping horse, each hoof-beat cracking that careful path I'd laid across the years.

Whiskey sedated me for two hours in bed, then I woke and tossed and turned and tried to open once more the logical part of my brain. But dark rooms in the dead of night encourage doubts and fears, not rational thinking. I got up, reached for my dressing gown and went to the kitchen.

Nursing a hot lemon drink I stared at my blank PC screen, then remembered that Maven Judge would be storming through her working 'day'.

Unable to quiet my own brain, I decided to pick at hers. Booting the PC I hit the secure link she'd set up for me.

She answered right away, her small thin face lit from the side by a desk lamp 'Nightmares again?'

'Night geldings if there were such a thing. How are you doing up there on the edge of the world?'

'I'm doing okay. What's wrong?'

'I'm upset.'

'Aww.'

'I rode a horse today that opened me up from belly to brain and hauled out my entrails and spread them like fucking trophies and said, "come and see what you could have had"'

'Multi-talented horse, that. What's its name?'

'Spiritless Fun. If it gets beat this season I'll show my arse at midnight Mass.'

'I preferred your previous image, the entrails and stuff. Who trains this mighty beast?'

'Bayley Watt who is fucking madder than you are with his tales of Comanche jockey changes.'

'Didn't Jimmy Sherrick ride for him?'

'He did. Jimmy told me he was packing the job in. Bayley Watt told me he sacked him a week before he died.'

'Who do you believe?'

'I don't know yet.'

'Why would Watt sack him?'

I told her what the trainer had told me about the Comanches and that I could find no trace of it online.

'Want me to check it out?'

'I spent an hour on Google.'

'There are other ways.'

'Okay. See what you can find.'

'So do I guess right when I say that Mister Watt would like to stick with his new policy, ergo you are jocked off the next time this potential superstar runs?'

'He says he's thinking about it.'

'You begged him.'

'I wouldn't put it … Yes, I begged.'

'That's what's keeping you awake. A traitor to your principles, Mister Malloy. How do you plead?'

'Guilty. '

'Tut tut.'

'A fool to myself, my mother used to say.'

Her fingers worked the keyboard, as they had since we'd started talking. 'Who isn't?'

'What?'

'A fool to themselves, Edward.'

'Are you?'

'I don't believe so. Others will.'

'Does it matter to you?' I said.

'That others think me a fool? No. I have two things in common with Lester Piggott: I want money, and I don't care what people think of me.'

'I don't believe that. I don't believe any person does not care what other people think of him, or her.'

'Only because you're so fragile about your image.'

'It's not an image, Mave, it's not some PR thing, it's me.'

'It's low self-esteem, my friend. Pure. Simple. And very common.'

'Oh, I'm not getting into some philosophical debate with you halfway through the night.'

'What news on J Sherrick? Are the plods going to re-open the case?'

'Re-open his grave, maybe. I asked them if they'd consider exhumation.' I told her what I'd said to Sergeant Middleton, that he might have been killed by cyanide before being hung on the chain.

'Think they'll agree?'

'No. Not yet. Maybe after they analyze that recording again.'

'The faked one?'

'Yes.'

'What does Bayley Watt think?'

'About Jimmy's supposed suicide? I don't know. I don't want to ask him too many questions just now. If there was a way of knowing if he was lying about sacking Jimmy that would give me a steer.'

'Why say he'd sacked him? That puts Watt on the spot as a potential contributor to suicide. It would have been easier to play dumb.'

'But if he was trying to throw someone off the trail, it would push people more toward the suicide theory.'

'You believe Watt could have been involved in his death?'

'Maybe. I don't know. No. I've known the man for years. He's not a killer.'

'You knew Jimmy Sherrick for years. He saved your life. Jimmy says he chucked it, Watt says he didn't. Gun to your head, who would you believe?'

'Jimmy.'

'So what is your man hiding?'

'Rule out this Comanche stuff for me and I'll make a serious start on him.'

'And say farewell to this fine horse of his who stole your heart?'

'Maybe.'

She continued working, never looking at her webcam as I watched. 'Maybe is a weasel word, Eddie. You'll never find peace with a head full of maybes. All decisions are better than maybes, even wrong decisions.'

'How old are you, Mave?'

'Does it matter?'

'You talk with the certainty of a woman who's seen everything.'

'You don't have to be old to do that, Eddie. A dispassionate view of life for one year will tell you all you need to know about human nature. It changeth not and never will.'

'Do you ever have nightmares?'

'I work nights.'

'Like vampires?'

Finally her fingers stopped and she turned to the webcam with that detached, knowing look I was becoming familiar with. 'Eddie, there's only one sucker around here.'

I smiled. 'Touché.'

'Good night.'

Before going to bed, I searched online trying to find out if cyanide had ever been used in micro amounts to try to kill cancer cells. It didn't take long because there wasn't the slightest hint it had ever been tried. Still, I didn't discount it. Jimmy had said it was something "new". And what did he have to lose?

SEVENTEEN

Next morning's *Racing Post* carried a nice picture of me and Spiritless Fun jumping the last at Taunton. The report said the horse was as short as ten to one for the Supreme Novices' Hurdle at the Cheltenham Festival. I looked streamlined in the saddle, head motionless, perfectly balanced; I was still pretty stylish over a hurdle, I thought. That brought a smile for the first time in twenty four hours.

Some mental stability had returned. If I kept the ride on the horse, fine. If not, no point going crazy over it.

Also, trying not to upset Bayley Watt would have driven me mad. He was probably already thinking he could use the horse as leverage. I decided to go on the attack. I called him. He was abrupt. 'Eddie. I still haven't made up my mind. I'll call you toward the weekend,'

'That's not what I'm ringing about.'

I let that simmer for a few seconds then said, 'Had Jimmy sat on that horse?'

'Why?'

'Had he?'

'Why are you asking?'

'How long have you had him?'

'Eddie, I've got four fucking horses still to muck out. What's with the twenty questions all of a sudden?'

'Put it like this, Bayley, if I'd been thinking of suicide, and I had that horse to look forward to, I'd need to have been almost comatose with depression to do what Jimmy did. I'm not making light of it and I'm not trying to be a smart arse, that's just how I see it.'

'The way you see things isn't always right, is it? How can you put yourself in Jimmy's shoes over one horse considering what the poor bastard ended up doing?'

'I found Jimmy dead.'

'I know that. So you ought to show a bit more respect before saying a horse should have made a difference to him.'

'I knew him well enough to believe it would.'

'You did? So you think if he'd sat on that horse he wouldn't have killed himself?'

'That's what I think.'

'Well, you're wrong. Jimmy did all his schooling.'

'What did he say about him?'

'Jimmy didn't big things up.'

'What's that supposed to mean?'

'Exactly what it says! Everything with you is shit or bust, Eddie. Always has been.'

'Sometimes that's the way it needs to be.'

'Sometimes, Eddie, not every fucking time. Know your limitations, remember?'

'I'd better let you get on, Bayley.'

'I think you had. You're not the most diplomatic guy in the world considering you want that ride so badly. You need to engage your brain before reaching for your phone. It's like a sixgun for you in a fucking holster and you think you're in High Noon.'

'That's pretty rich coming from the man with the big western saddle and inside knowledge on the Comanches.'

'Comanche!'

'Fucking Comanches! Look it up!'

Call ended.

I laughed. I looked at myself in the mirror above the fireplace and laughed at having committed my own suicide with a trainer, not for the first time. Jimmy's dad had been right, you can't change character. I couldn't change mine and whatever Bayley Watt or Maven Judge thought of me and my flaws they could go and take a flying fuck at a rolling donut.

I zeroed the odometer on the Subaru as I set off for Leicester racecourse. I always did this when driving to Leicester. It fascinated me that it was exactly one hundred miles from the pillars on my driveway to the entry gate at the course.

I had three rides booked. None looked that promising but you never knew. At a hundred and fifty quid a ride, I'd clear maybe three hundred after expenses. A winner would be a bonus. And there was the chance of picking up a spare if some poor sod got injured.

At dusk I pulled out of the racecourse car park, watching the odometer click toward 101. I was winnerless, but had ridden a second and a third when neither had any real right to be placed so I reckoned I'd done a good day's work.

An hour into my journey, Jim Sherrick called, his voice sounding weak and shaky through the speakers. 'Eddie, are you able to talk?'

'Sure. I'm heading back from Leicester. Nobody with me. Are you okay?'

'I wondered if you might be passing on your drive home? Sergeant Middleton just left. I could do with having a chat with you.'

'I can be there about half six if that suits?'

'That's fine. Good. I'll put the kettle on.'

Mister Sherrick opened the door a few inches, then unhooked the security chain. He offered his hand, 'Sorry, I don't usually use that chain but I've been getting more and more shaky since the sergeant left. They want to exhume his body.'

I hesitated. 'Did he say why?'

'They've been through his phone records and had another fella look at that recording.'

'What did they find?'

'He didn't go into detail but he seems pretty serious about it now. I was kind of relieved when we talked last night, you and me, but now I'm thinking, why would anybody want to kill Jimmy?'

'Did the sergeant mention ruling out suicide now?'

'He was ducking and diving. Didn't really say anything outright and that hasn't helped me, I don't mind telling you.'

'Should we sit down?' I said.

He smiled wearily, 'Sorry. Yes, sit down please. I'll make some tea.'

We settled by the fire with the now familiar yellow mugs. I said, 'You might find the police a bit less, well, helpful for a while at least. They'll be conscious of maybe not doing their job properly first time.' I was thinking too of Sergeant Middleton and my impression he had some degree of suspicion about Mister Sherrick.

'What did you say when he told you they wanted to exhume?'

'Why? I asked him why. He told me about you telling him how Jimmy couldn't really handle technology. He said you mentioned something about Jimmy texting "OK" to somebody?'

I recalled the story where Jimmy had phoned Bill Kittinger to explain that was all he knew how to text. 'That's right.' I said, wondering if the sergeant had also told him of my visit yesterday.

'Well that was the only text they found on his records. And he said there were some inconsistencies now with the recording Jimmy left.'

'And did he actually ask your permission to exhume?'

'He said it would make it easier. Quicker.'

'What did you say?'

'I told him they should do what they felt was best.' He put the mug on the hearth and began rubbing his brow.

'When are they going to do it?'

'I don't know. He said there were arrangements to be made with the council and the church.'

'Did he ask if you wanted to be there?'

'Yes.'

I waited. He was staring into the fire. 'Do you?' I asked.

'I don't want to be, it's a matter of whether I should be. He's still my son.'

I watched him. 'Jimmy wouldn't want you distressed.'

He nodded. 'I know. It's a matter of whether I'll be more distressed being there or not being there.'

'If you decide to go, I'll be more than happy … Well, not happy, that's the wrong word, but you know what I mean. I'll come along with you if you want me to, if you believe it would help.'

He turned his gaze from the fire and looked at me. 'You were a good friend to Jimmy. You're a good friend to me. I appreciate it.'

I nodded and smiled. I thought about the police. The sergeant had gone from an admission of sloppy procedure to sudden action. Even on the back of my veiled threat about police negligence, he'd acted much quicker than I thought he would. I wondered if they'd discovered something other than what he'd told Mister Sherrick. 'Would you mind if I go back to Jimmy's place tomorrow for another look around?' I asked.

'The Sergeant took the keys. That's what they're doing.'

'When?'

'He didn't say.'

They hadn't treated it as a crime scene, now the Scene of Crime Officers were being sent in, as the sergeant had mentioned. But Jimmy had been dead for over two weeks and somebody had already reorganized the evidence.

Jimmy's PC had been replaced, and a long section of the cellar floor had been well cleaned.

'They might be closing the stable door an awful long time after the horse has bolted.' I said.

'You definitely believe Jimmy was killed then?'

I felt uncomfortable, awkward. 'I don't think he recorded that message and I'd bet he didn't order cyanide online. Somebody went to a lot of trouble making that recording. The only way they could have done it was by bugging Jimmy's phone and recording everything he said.'

'Maybe they bugged the house?'

'Maybe. But he lived alone for what, the past year or so? He'd not have much to say at home.'

'Depends who his visitors were.'

'True. Did he have many?' I asked.

'I don't know. I'm just trying to look at it from a different angle, if you see what I mean.'

'Fair comment. Maybe his house was bugged, and his phone.' I said.

'Should I ask the sergeant about that when he brings the keys back?'

'It would do no harm. Once you get the keys, I'll have another look around the house.'

'Do you want me to call him tomorrow and ask when he'll be finished with them?'

'Best not. My relationships with the police tend to head rapidly downhill when I start poking my nose in. They'll want to go there sooner rather than later and do everything they should have done the day Jimmy died.'

He nodded slowly, his gaze back on the blue and yellow gas flames. 'They might find something.'

I stopped myself from saying that I doubted that very much, and I was proved right. Mister Sherrick told me next day he'd been awakened in the early hours by two fire engines and how odd it had felt to find out they'd been on their way to his son's blazing house.

EIGHTEEN

It wasn't big news, the burning of an empty house. I didn't hear about it until I got to Fontwell where I had two rides booked, and I wondered why Mister Sherrick hadn't rang me. I left the weighing room and returned to the car to call him.

'I heard about the fire,' I said.

'Yes.'

'Are you all right?'

'Yes. I'm okay.'

'Is there somebody with you, Jim?'

'No.'

'What's up?'

'I think it would be better if you took no more to do with this, Eddie. I've not been fair with you. I shouldn't have rang you yesterday. It's not your problem.'

'I don't see it as a problem, Mister Sherrick. Jimmy was a friend. You're a friend.'

'I know, and I'm glad to be, but I think I've overstretched that friendship by making you feel obliged to do something about all this. '

'I don't feel obliged to anybody, believe me. I feel pissed off at the police taking everything as done and dusted just because it looked neat, and because it meant they didn't have to do much work. And I'd still like to know what Jimmy was so keen to tell me that night. It's beginning to look like somebody wanted it kept quiet. Don't feel you need to cut me off now to protect me. I'm into this and I'm staying with it.'

'You sound pretty definite.'

'I am. What did the police say to you? Are *they* asking you to get me to back off?'

'No. The sergeant wasn't too pleased that I told you I'd given him the keys, but, well, he didn't ask me to warn you off or anything. I think he wants to talk to you himself.'

'He'll be wondering if it was me that torched Jimmy's place. If he'd done his job properly at the start he wouldn't need to be talking to me. Or you. And what about the house now? What are you going to do? You were planning to sell it, weren't you?'

'That doesn't matter. I kept the insurance up.'

'Well you can bet they'll give you a hard time when they find out it was arson.'

'Probably. I'll worry about that when I have to.'

'Okay. Want me to drop by on the way home from Fontwell?'

'No. Thanks. I'm fine. I'm supposed to be playing dominoes tonight. Best to try and stick to some sort of routine.'

'It is. Forget your troubles for a while.'

'That's it. *My* troubles. Remember that.'

'I will. They're not troubles to me Mister Sherrick. Puzzles, frustrations maybe but no troubles. None at all.'

My first ride was in a three mile steeplechase on Fontwell's unusual figure of eight track. The ground was sticky and tiring for the horses and we went very steadily, just six of us, trying to make sure stamina would hold out.

We chatted among ourselves on the way round, going quiet in the final few strides before each fence to mentally count our horses into the take-off point. Barry Copland was alongside me on a mud-speckled grey, his red and black silks fluttering in the breeze. Barry had ridden that loser for Bayley Watt at Taunton. I asked him if Watt had booked him for any more rides.

'Not a jot. That was my first ride for him. He didn't look delighted with the result.'

'I wouldn't worry. He's never been predictable. Probably offer you a retainer out of the blue.'

'Ha! I doubt it.'

'Have you done any schooling for him or ridden out?'

'Nothing. Never been asked.'

'I wonder who's helping him now Jimmy's gone? He's got eight horses. He can't be doing everything himself, especially exercise and schooling.'

We were pretty closely grouped in the mid part of the race and I called out to the others asking if anyone knew who was helping Watt. It was common for jockeys to ride exercise or school for different trainers. Many did so in the hope of picking up the odd ride for a yard, but jockeys would often help just as a favour.

Even though Watt had only eight horses, he'd want to work them in pairs at the very least. Bill Kittinger said he'd heard that Blane Kilberg was riding out for Watt.

I moved my horse alongside Bill's. 'Blane Kilberg, the vet?'

'That's the man. That's what I heard.'

'Who told you?'

'Pete Cheaney.' Pete was a farrier based in Lambourn. He was popular, and would be shoeing and fixing feet in a number of yards. Bayley's was probably one of them. As we turned into the straight and my horse began tiring, I wondered why Bayley Watt was using a local vet as a work rider when there were plenty willing jockeys within twenty minutes of his yard.

Pete Cheaney would be in The Malt Shovel pub in Upper Lambourn. If he didn't have a horse's foot in his hand, he filled it with a Guinness glass. I headed back via The Malt Shovel where Pete told me he had seen Blane Kilberg schooling a horse at Bayley Watt's yard three days earlier.

When I reached home, I called the man who used to be Bayley Watt's vet, Stewart Lico.

'Long time, no hear.' Lico said

'Well, like everybody else, we only call our old friends when we need a favour.'

'You're a credit to your much maligned profession Mister Malloy, a non-beater about the bush. What can I do for you?'

'Are you still working for Bayley Watt?'

'Watt. Not. I am semi-sorry to say. It was good while it lasted but he's a fucking fruitloop.'

'Did you jump or were you pushed?'

'Pushed very clumsily with some daft story about Indians making sure that a different medicine man always attended their sick horses or some such bollocks. I can't quite remember the detail as I was too busy wondering if your man was losing it altogether.'

'Apparently he gave Jimmy Sherrick the same kind of nonsense a week before he died,' I said.

'He sacked him?'

'So Bayley says.'

'Did he sack you too when he took Jimmy on?'

'Funnily enough he didn't. I recommended Jimmy to him so you can have three guesses about how I'm feeling.'

'You think Jimmy killed himself because Watt sacked him?'

'No. Bayley put me up on one of his at Taunton the other day and spun me the same Indian story he gave you and Jimmy. I'm just trying to figure out what's happening with the guy. Isn't Kilberg a bit of a weirdo himself?'

'With his lycra and his ballet and his "passion for animals"!' Lico did a passable skit of Kilberg's American accent. He said, 'Passion is one of the most overused and annoying fucking words of the century. Everybody's "passionate" about what they do and nobody has things happen to them anymore, do they? They go on a "journey". Bring back the old Jockey Club is what I say. At least you knew where you were and nobody was getting a "heads up" or "facetime". Honestly. Kilberg's a classic example. Big Chief Bullshitter.'

'He was assistant trainer to, who was it, Jeni Chipman?'

'That's right. When he first came to Lambourn. Then he was supposed to have won a right few quid at Cheltenham. Spent some of it on a hair transplant, new teeth and lasered eyes then a fair lump on his wedding to that Romanian kid who worked for Jeni.'

'I remember now. She was just sixteen, wasn't she?'

'Correct. And like any sensible teenager, she rapidly spent the rest of old sugar daddy's money and pissed off back to Romania.'

'And didn't he follow her and run into a family of gypsies or something over there?' I asked.

'Her family, apparently. He was on the next flight home, wifeless and potless.'

'Jeez.'

'I know. Can you imagine him and Bayley?'

'I hear Kilberg's schooling for Watt,' I said.

'You're kidding? Bayley Watt has lost the plot. There's a bit of verse for you. No charge. Fucking hell…this place goes from mad to worse.'

NINETEEN

I had breakfast before daybreak, the *Racing Post* open on the table. A quiet Thursday. No rides booked, and I couldn't be bothered driving east to Huntingdon in the hope of picking up a spare. Hanging around the weighing room like a vulture was a shit part of the job. Getting a spare ride usually meant one of your friends was heading for hospital after a bad fall.

I was due on the schooling grounds at ten anyway, to help with education of three young horses trained by Ben Tylutki.

It would probably be busy up there on the downs, on the grass gallops laid out like long, wide, three-lane green highways. Miles of white plastic rails criss-crossed a thousand acres, channelling strings of horses on long slopes. Tarmac roads and parking areas were used by vehicles to bring trainers and owners to the low roof of this small world where no opponents waited, no crowds bayed, no bookmakers huddled. A morning place. Above the towns and the jobs and the bills and the worries. A land of hope. And, sometimes, glory.

As I set off for the gallops, I reminded myself it was also a place where stories were swapped and gossip was born and I resolved to ask no more questions about Watt or his new vet Blane Kilberg.

There was no doubt in my mind now that Bayley Watt had gone beyond eccentricity. He might have nothing to do with the death of Jimmy Sherrick, but Watt was doing something he shouldn't be. Changing jockeys, a new vet, no pros riding exercise or schooling. He was hiding something.

Also, it had dawned on me that within hours of Mister Sherrick telling me that the police planned to visit Jimmy's place again, the house had been torched. Who else knew of the planned visit? If Jimmy's phone had been bugged, was his father's bugged too?

Ben Tylutki had asked me to meet him on the gallops. He'd have the horses ridden up by lads who would then take a break while I schooled their charges over a line of fences. These were horses who'd raced over hurdles, the small jumps. Now it was time for them to learn a new technique.

As I pulled in to park, Ben waved to me, the corner of his sky blue jacket flapping in the wind. I raised a hand and smiled. As I switched off the engine, my phone rang. No caller ID came up.

I answered.

'Mister Malloy, it's Sergeant Middleton.'

'Good morning to you.'

'Good morning.'

'Are you busy?'

'I'm on Mandown gallops, just about to do some schooling,'

'I'm not far away. Do you mind if I drive up?'

'Can you say what it's about?'

'I'd rather not. Until I see you.'

'How long will you need me for? I've three horses to school.'

'Five minutes. And I'll be there in under ten.'

'Are you in uniform?'

'Yes. Why?'

'It's best if I come to you.'

'Okay. Would you like to meet at your house?'

'Fine. Noon?'

'See you then.'

'Sergeant, is Mister Sherrick okay?'

'As far as I know. I'll see you at noon.' He hung up.

I could see the roof of the police car as I trundled down the track, wipers working noisily in the misty rain.

The sergeant got out as I turned into the driveway. He pulled his cap on and I remembered someone telling me that a cop had to have his hat on before he could arrest you.

Coming toward me, he didn't look that serious.

We shook hands. 'Nice hideaway down here,' he said.

I looked around at the woods and rising meadows. 'Not quite the hole-in-the-wall gang, but it's peaceful enough. Come in out of the rain.'

He drank black coffee. I had tea. He nodded toward the picture window, 'Must take some cleaning.'

'It does. When I get round to it.'

I waited. He'd seemed pretty anxious on the phone. He blew ripples along the surface of the coffee.' Mister Sherrick told you we planned to visit his son's house.'

'That's right.'

'Did you mention it to anyone?'

'No.'

He watched me. I held his gaze. He said, 'Did he tell you we spoke to him about exhuming his son's body?'

'Yes. And I didn't mention that either.'

He nodded once and looked down, his hair misted with fine rain.

'What's happened?' I asked.

He looked up, hesitated, then said. 'I got a call this morning from the local authority. They'd sent someone to check that the memorial stone had not yet been erected. Their man said the ground had already been noticeably disturbed. We've got a team out there now, working behind screens. The corpse has been stolen.'

I watched him. He sipped coffee. When he realized I wasn't going to speak he said, 'They took the coffin too.'

'When?'

'Best guess? In the last forty eight hours.'

'Does Mister Sherrick know?'

'Not yet.'

'And that's why you're here?'

'Partly.'

'Mainly.'

He nodded slowly. I said, 'You want me to tell him?'

'I'll tell him. I thought it would ease the blow if you were with me. He told me…well, he speaks highly of you, put it that way'

'Okay.' I said.

'Is it convenient now?' He reached for his hat.

'Yes.'

He pulled out his notebook. 'I'll ring to check he's in.'

'Don't.'

'Why not?'

'Because his phone is bugged or his house is bugged.'

'You know that or you think it?'

'Mister Sherrick tells me you're exhuming the body. The body's gone. He rings me to say you're going to check the house. The house is gone. Jimmy Sherrick's recorded suicide note has been patched together from snippets of his conversation, probably taken from his phone.'

He looked at me and said quietly, 'I think the wrong man is wearing the uniform here.'

'I think you've got a murder inquiry on your hands.'

TWENTY

We drove to Mister Sherrick's flat in my car. When he answered the door, I put my finger to my lips, trying not to be too theatrical. I pointed to my car, and gestured for him to follow me. I helped him into the back seat and got in beside him. The sergeant turned, forcing a smile. Mister Sherrick was wide eyed.

I said, 'Sorry for the hush hush stuff. We think your flat or your phone might be bugged.'

'What's happened?'

Sergeant Middleton said, 'I had a call this morning from the local authority telling me that your son's grave had been disturbed. The soil.'

'I've ordered a stone, maybe the contractor was doing some work or something.'

The sergeant hesitated then said, 'We sent a team down to check. I'm afraid your son's body has been removed.'

He stared at the sergeant. 'Not by you, you mean? Not by your people?'

The sergeant shook his head. 'It's been taken. The coffin too. We're treating it as a crime scene.'

Mister Sherrick seemed stunned. He turned to me but said nothing. I said, 'Remember you told me about the plans to exhume Jimmy's body, and that the police intended to visit the house again?'

He nodded. 'Did you mention that to anyone else?' I asked.

'Nobody. No. Not that I can remember.'

'There has to be a fair chance that your conversations are being monitored,' said the sergeant.

'How?'

'We don't know yet, but hopefully it shouldn't be too difficult to find out.'

Mister Sherrick seemed to deflate, to slump slowly. His head went back, resting on the seat-top until he was looking at the roof. We watched him. A tear crossed his temple and ran into his right ear. The sergeant pursed his lips. Mister Sherrick said quietly, 'I'm done.'

I got Mister Sherrick's mobile phone from the flat, and locked the door. He agreed to come to my house.

The sergeant used my PC to type a note requesting permission to inspect the old man's flat for 'listening devices'. Mister Sherrick signed it. I followed the sergeant to his car. 'When do you plan to do it?'

'The sweep?'

'Yes.'

'As soon as I can get it arranged.'

'He'll want to get home.'

'I know.'

He looked stern, tired. It seemed to me a thankless job he had and I wondered why he did it. I said, 'Have you considered leaving the bug in place if you find it?'

'It crossed my mind. I'll need to speak to DS Wilmslow.'

'Who's he?'

'CID. This is his case.'

'What about Mister Sherrick's mobile phone?'

'I'll have the guys check that first. Can I call you when they are on their way?'

'Sure. And they'll go from here to the flat?'

'That's the plan,' he said.

'What if whoever planted the bug is watching the flat?'

'Will it matter? The damage is done, isn't it?'

'I suppose so.'

'I'll call you,' he said.

An hour later, two men in plain black overalls arrived at my house. They showed ID before I asked for it and were gone within five minutes.

Mister Sherrick sat looking at his mobile phone. 'Feeling any better?' I said.

'At least they didn't bug my phone. I'd rather they'd bugged the flat than the phone. It seems kind of less personal.'

'I know what you mean.'

By nightfall there was still no word from Sergeant Middleton. Mister Sherrick was beginning to fret. Just before six I saw the bumpy rise and fall of headlight beams through the window and went outside. It was a liveried police car. Mister Sherrick came and stood at my shoulder as Sergeant Middleton approached.

'Did you find it?' Mister Sherrick asked, sounding eager now.

'Your flat is clean Mister Sherrick. They swept it twice and found nothing.'

The three of us stood in the wide bright spot of the security light like stage actors who'd forgotten their lines. Mister Sherrick looked at me. The sergeant looked at both of us then took off his cap and asked if we could talk inside.

I made hot drinks. We sat at the big pine table in the kitchen. The sergeant had unbuttoned his jacket, perhaps to help ease the tension. He said he wanted us just to talk as three men, to forget he was a policeman.

'Informal, off the record, whatever you want to call it,' he said.

'Fine by me,' I said.

Mister Sherrick nodded. The sergeant said, 'My name is Geoff.'

On some sort of autopilot, Mister Sherrick reached to shake his hand. 'Jim,' he said.

I shrugged. 'Eddie.' We all smiled.

Geoff Middleton ran a hand through his thick greying hair. 'We need to work out how this fella is getting the information. There's no bug in your flat Jim, nothing in your phone. You don't have a car, do you?'

'I don't need one. I hire one if ever I need one.'

Geoff nodded and turned to me. 'There is a possibility that it's your phone that's been bugged.'

'They'd need to have broken in here or got into my car at the racecourse.'

'Unless they're monitoring your calls remotely.'

'In which case, maybe it's Jim's calls they been monitoring,' I said.

'Maybe. We need to get yours examined all the same.'

'Okay.'

He checked his watch then said, 'I can get the guys back out here now, if you want?'

'Sooner the better.'

He stood to make the call, pacing the kitchen, buttoning his jacket as he spoke, as though his superiors could see him.

'About half an hour,' he said as he sat down again and drank coffee.

'We're pissing in the wind here,' I said. 'Even if they don't find anything in my phone, somebody could still be listening in, couldn't they?'

'Very possible.'

'How do they do that? Do they hack the line or something, or the computers at the phone company?'

'I don't know. I'll ask the guys when they get here.'

The guys turned out to be one technician who used a headlight with a magnifying glass on it and told me my phone was clean. He said there were numerous ways of eavesdropping on calls and the best protection was use pay-as-you-go sim cards and change them regularly.

'That's not an option for me,' I told him.

'Best be pretty careful what you talk about on the phone then.'

That triggered something. I turned to Mister Sherrick. 'Remember when you told me Jimmy's body was going to be exhumed?'

He nodded. I said, 'It was in your flat you told me, wasn't it? You didn't mention it on the phone, you just asked me if I could call in on the way home from Fontwell.'

'That's right.'

I turned to the sergeant. 'So it has to be in the flat,' I said. The technician was closing his bag. He didn't look up, he just said, 'The flat's clean. We did two runs.'

'You might have missed something,' I said, trying not to sound as annoyed as I felt.

'We didn't.'

'What, you swept every inch?'

He stopped and stared at me. He'd have been about my age. I guessed by his attitude that he believed in his skills as much as I believed in mine, and it looked like he didn't report to Geoff Middleton.

'Every *relevant* inch,' he said, unblinking.

'So you checked down the toilet?' My temper was rising.

He glanced at the sergeant as if to say "Who is this guy?", then said, 'No, we didn't check down the toilet. A listening device needs a power source. You don't find too many of them down toilets.'

'So you only checked sockets and stuff in the kitchen?'

'We swept the flat. Twice. And no, we didn't check just the sockets, we checked everywhere a battery-powered device could have been left.'

'Everywhere?'

'Everywhere. Now I've got three more jobs to do. Do you mind?'

I sipped tepid coffee and held my tongue. The sergeant thanked him and showed him out. When he returned, I said, 'Sorry, Geoff. It's been a long day.'

He smiled. 'It'll do him good. Cocky little sod.'

Mister Sherrick said, 'Do you mind if I go home now?' He looked at his watch, turning the bracelet to see the face which glinted under the light and ignited my tired brain.

The watch Bayley Watt had given him. The watch he'd have been sure Mister Sherrick would always wear as a last present from his son. The watch with a power source.

I grabbed my notepad and quickly wrote, 'Don't speak. Go outside and call your tech guy. Tell him to get back here now.'

TWENTY-ONE

Impulsive behaviour. I'd regretted it before and I knew, as I lay awake, I would this time. The bug was in the watch. The watch was on the wrist of Jim Sherrick. The ball was in the court of the cops and I was in limbo.

I should have kept my mouth shut and got Mave to find me someone to check the watch. But I'd been set on showing off how clever I was, determined to put the hotshot technician in his place. Now I couldn't confront Bayley Watt. I'd have to let the police handle it. The sergeant was a nice guy, but he wasn't the brightest.

He'd said he would visit Bayley in the morning along with a detective. I hadn't asked if he would tell me what Watt said, because it wouldn't be 'call me Geoff' anymore. It was formal now. Maybe he wasn't so simple after all.

I lay listening to the silence and tonight it wasn't comforting, not in the least. I'd stupidly cut myself off, and put more strain on poor Jim Sherrick. He too would be lying awake, wearing a watch that was sending every sound to Watt or whoever the trainer was involved with.

The sergeant had told him just to carry on doing what he always did, stick to his routine. Easy counsel to give in his position, not so easy to carry out when you're old and tired and scared and alone. I'd been warned to stay away from Mister Sherrick until 'advised otherwise'.

I ran through my extensive list of curse words aloud, but felt no benefit. Dawn seemed an awful long time away.

At 2 a.m. I admitted defeat. I got up, pulled on a dressing gown and went through to boot up my PC. Mave Judge clicked to accept my video call on the secure link.

'More nightmares?'

I told her what had happened.

'That was pretty slick thinking, Eddie.'

'That's what I thought. Trouble is I couldn't do the sensible thing and keep my trap shut.'

'Don't be too hard on yourself. Ninety nine percent of people would have done the same.'

'But you'd be in the one percent?'

'Depends. What's the objective?'

'The objective is not to let the police waste weeks and weeks trying to find Jimmy's body and the people who took it.'

'Leave them to it. They'll blunder around in their own sweet way as all workers in large organizations do.'

'Mave, forgive me if I don't get into one of your discussions on management efficiency.'

'You're forgiven. What do you want me to do? Oh, by the way, the Comanche stuff Mister Watt was on about seems to hold no water.'

'I'd kind of guessed that by now, though it hasn't stopped him spouting it to all and sundry as an excuse for sacking people.' I suddenly felt the need for coffee. 'Mave, will you hold? I'm going to put the kettle on.'

'I'm holding.'

I called out as I walked to the kitchen, 'What are you working on anyway?'

'What am I always working on?'

'Your betting programme.'

'Correct. '

'Never ending.'

'That's the way it was built. Every day you learn a tiny bit more. Tweak, tweak, tweak.'

The sound of the kettle heating made it pointless shouting across the room, through the double doors. I spooned instant coffee from a jar then tore a banana from a bunch and peeled it.

Back at my desk I saw Mave's fast fingers busy on the keyboard. I chewed banana and said, 'How many words a minute can you type?'

'You're eating.'

'A banana.'

'Don't talk to me when you're eating. It's fucking irritating.'

'Sorry.' I smiled. I watched her work, finished the banana and reached for the coffee. 'Can I talk to you when I'm drinking?'

'So long as you don't gulp. The sounds of humans consuming or kissing or copulating are among the most slaveringly unwelcome to the ear, especially amplified through a set of speakers.'

'I'm passing on the kissing and copulating tonight, you'll be glad to know.'

'Copulating is a very cold word for the activity it describes, don't you think? Mechanical. Utilitarian.'

'I've not given it that much thought, Mave.'

'You are a thirty-three-year old healthy heterosexual male. You should be thinking of copulating about every nine seconds.'

'I doubt I'd get much done at that rate.'

'What do you do by way of a sex life then?'

'Mave. Would I ask you a question like that?'

'No. You're a prude. And you respect women too much. You're too gallant.'

'Listen, the only part of copulating I'm interested in at the moment is the first syllable. I need to find a way of getting to Bayley Watt without upsetting the sergeant.'

'Why worry about him? Think he's worried about you? Ignore him and do your own thing. It's not against the law for a jockey to talk to a trainer, is it?'

'I suppose not. How easy would it be to track the tracker? If I got hold of the watch could you tell from the transmitter where it was transmitting to?'

'I'll tell you now. It'll be to a PC somewhere the owner of which will be some poor John Doe who hasn't a clue it's been hacked. It'll be the end PC on a network of thousands your man's hijacked so he can't be traced. He'll be scraping the recordings from it once an hour or something. You won't catch him like that. Can't you set him up?'

I sipped coffee, quietly. 'I've been thinking about that, but the easy way is Watt, isn't it? Whoever gave him the bugged watch for Mister Sherrick is the one we want. This fella's smart. Watt is not. I want a crack at him first.'

'Then you'd best figure out what this guy has got on him or how much he's paying him. Start with money. Money. Sex. Revenge. Three horse race. Trust me.'

'And money's favourite?'

'Odds on.'

'Except I've got not a single thing to go on.'

'Tell him you know the Comanche stuff is bullshit. Ask him why he really sacked Jimmy or if he really sacked him. Somebody killed Jimmy Sherrick. What did Jimmy do? He rode horses for Bayley Watt. Jimmy was either doing something he wasn't supposed to or he wasn't doing something he was supposed to. Watt was pissing him off or he was pissing Watt off, or, more likely, whoever's controlling Watt.'

'Yeah, yeah, yeah. But when I lay all that out to Bayley Watt you know what he's going to say, don't you?'

'I can guess.'

'So can I.'

I finished the coffee and returned to bed.

With little more than a couple of hours sleep, I was in a foul mood as I looked in the bathroom mirror and prepared to shave. I glared at myself, still pissed off with my grandstanding last night. If I could have taken the guy in the mirror outside and thrashed him I'd have done it. That sudden thought made me smile. 'You daft bastard,' I said aloud. 'Get shaved, get showered, and get on with it.'

TWENTY-TWO

I listened to the ten o'clock news in the car, bound for Warwick. I resisted calling Mister Sherrick. I knew he'd be nervous enough now about any calls, about acting naturally while the police tried to track down whoever was bugging him.

I had three rides at Warwick, a left handed track with tight turns and tricky fences. I'd seen some bad falls here. Walking from the car park to the weighing room with my kitbag, I saw Bayley Watt leading a heavily rugged horse toward the stables. I stopped and watched until he was out of sight.

I usually read the racecard the night before to get a handle on the opposition and start working out how to exploit their weaknesses during a race. But with all the hassle last night, I hadn't checked. Unless the sergeant had turned up early to interview Watt, he'd have missed him. That gave me a chance.

In the changing room, I joined in the usual banter as I walked to my peg. Franny Scotton was reading the *Racing Post*. 'Franny, what's Bayley Watt got today?' I asked.

He riffled through. 'Er ... One in the first, against you. Newcomer, Fissure Splint. You'll be hoping he's got a splint, give you a chance of riding a rare winner.' He smiled, unembarrassed by pink gums no longer serving any purpose after numerous kicks in the face from flying hooves. 'A rare winner.' He repeated.

'Put your teeth back in Franny, you'll scare the horses.' I said. Splints are small bony growths which can cause lameness. A fissure splint I'd never heard of and I wondered if Bayley had named the

95

horse or bought it already named. I unpacked my bag. Doubtless he'd spin some tale about a fissure splint being to the benefit of Comanche horses.

I was riding Helios against Bayley's. It was trained by Ben Tylutki, the trainer I'd schooled for yesterday. He'd given me a good feel on the way to the start, and Ben was pretty confident he'd win. Like Watt's horse, Helios was having his first race in this Novice Hurdle.

We lined up at the tape, pulled our goggles down against the strengthening January wind and twelve of us set off. The next four minutes or so galloping through this sticky ground would be important for most of these horses. For the debutants, their experience here would colour how they approached future races.

My job was not just to win if I could, but to teach this young horse that racing would cause it no anxiety. If I was lucky, Helios would enjoy this, and the next time he was led toward the horse box from his stable, he'd be excited about racing again. A nicely made, well balanced gelding, black except for a white star between his eyes, he was favourite to win.

Halfway through the race Helios was traveling well and had jumped the first four hurdles slickly. But Watt's horse, Fissure Splint was just ahead of us, simply cantering on a loose rein. That's very unusual for a horse on its debut run. Many young horses pull and race keenly, carried away by the excitement and the galloping herd.

But Fissure Splint had an impressive, smooth action, he reminded me of the gelding I'd ridden for Bayley Watt at Taunton, less than a week ago.

And he won like him too.

We finished second, a long way back. In the unsaddling enclosure I took a close look at the winner. He was very similar in size and colour to Spiritless Fun, the horse I'd been begging to ride again. The only difference was a white sock on his near fore. Spiritless Fun was a solid colour with no markings.

Now, it's not at all unusual for a trainer to favour a certain type of horse. Quite a few will go for those which, to their eye, make an ideal model. Some admire big rangy horses, the type that another trainer might avoid in the belief that the bigger the horse the more likely it is to suffer an injury.

This one of Watt's was sixteen hands, compact, more solidly put together than you might think if you only glanced at him. He'd probably weigh as much as some horses who were a couple of inches taller. Spiritless Fun had been exactly the same make and shape and colour, bar the white sock. Bleaching six inches of hair on a horse's leg would be simple. I watched Watt wash the horse down. He was frowning, grunting as he reached underneath with a long sweep of the sponge. The jockey, Jack Morrin, seemed bemused, smiling and shaking his head in what looked like wonderment, as he slung girths over saddle and headed for the weighing room.

I finished talking to the owners of Helios and to Ben Tylutki, and I followed Jack, but I stopped beside Watt's horse. The trainer saw me and hesitated until he realized I wasn't going away. Slowly, he turned toward me, bucket still in hand. I looked into his eyes and he looked into mine and we knew at that moment that the game had changed.

TWENTY-THREE

I set the phone on hands-free and dialled Sergeant Middleton's number. As it rang, I pulled out of Warwick's car park and headed south in the dusk.

'Mister Malloy, what can I do for you?'

That was interesting, he'd added me to his contacts. 'Sergeant, hello. I just wondered if you'd managed to interview Bayley Watt yet?'

'I went there this morning. He wasn't at home. His assistant said he was at the races. I'm hoping to speak to him tomorrow.' That suited me, but I didn't want to show it. 'Sergeant, forgive me, but this guy looks like he could be implicated in Jimmy Sherrick's death. Is it normal to let something like this drift across a couple of days?'

During the pause that followed I tried to picture the look he was framing. He said, 'What Mister Watt appears to have done is passed on a watch from Jimmy Sherrick to his father. It could be more than that, but I'm fairly sure that is what he will claim. And he might even deny he had anything to do with the watch. It would be Mister Sherrick's word against his.'

'So what's the next move if he does deny it?'

'I think we'll wait and see what Mister Watt has to say tomorrow.'

'We?'

'Detective Sergeant Wilmslow and myself.'

'What about Jimmy, his corpse? Anything on that yet?'

'No.'

'Any CCTV at the cemetery?'

'None. In any case it would need to have had infrared capability.'

'It was done at night?'

'I'm not certain, but I think it's a reasonable assumption.'

His tone was hardening. There was no point in antagonizing him. 'OK. Fair comment. I'll let you get on.'

'Mister Malloy...You've been helpful, more than helpful. But as I said to you last night, I'm limited in what I can tell you as this progresses. You have no legitimate interest, in the informal sense of the word, but you know what I mean. I'm sorry.'

'That's okay, no worries. Best if I go through Mister Sherrick from here on then, I suppose?'

'I think so. Unless you get information that could help in the investigation then, by all means give me a call.'

That sparked me. A couple of years earlier I'd have lit up with a tirade about the police giving nothing but wanting everything, but I counted to five and realized that what the sergeant might be doing was giving me some sort of informal wayleave to do a bit of nosing around myself. 'I will, of course.'

'Thanks. Goodbye.'

'Sergeant, one last question. It won't compromise you.'

'Go on.'

'You said you spoke to Bayley Watt's assistant.'

'That's right.'

'What did he, or she, look like?'

'Male. Late forties, early fifties, North American accent, five ten, about twelve stone, dark brown hair, almost certainly dyed, very white teeth.'

'And did he introduce himself as Watt's assistant?'

'Assistant trainer.'

'He's a vet. His name is Blane Kilberg.'

'You think he was lying?'

'Not necessarily. There's nothing to stop vets becoming assistant trainers.'

'It would seem a sensible secondary occupation.'

'It would. But not many trainers with a handful of horses need an assistant trainer. And knowing Kilberg, his ambitions would run to working with one of the big guns. I'd have thought he'd be embarrassed to admit he was working for a permit-holder like Watt.'

'Interesting. Anything else?'

'That's it. For now.'

'Have a safe drive home.'

'Thanks.'

So Kilberg was not only schooling for Watt, he was his assistant. Things were beginning to stack up, and hold steady.

If Watt's horse today was a ringer, if it really was Spiritless Fun, my Taunton winner, running in another name, then Kilberg would fit very nicely into the deception.

Every racehorse has a computer chip implanted in its neck. That chip carries the horse's details, its colour and markings. The chip is scanned by security staff at the track and compared with the details in the horse's paper passport. How difficult would it be to remove the microchip from Spiritless Fun and replace it with the chip assigned to Fissure Splint? Apply dye or bleach to get the markings to agree with the passport, and a very nice betting coup could be landed.

Stopped at a set of traffic lights, I found Stewart Lico's number. It rang a dozen times before he answered. 'My my, Malloy, I don't hear from you for months then two calls in a week. What do you want this time?'

'I won't insult your intelligence with small talk Stewart.'

'Well that's good to hear because I am staring at the winking vulva of a very valuable mare. Another minute of it will see me drop into a trance. Can I finish what I'm doing here and call you back?'

'Never let it be said that I kept you away from a winking vulva. I'll wait.'

'Call you soon.'

I was still smiling when he called me back five minutes later. 'Vulva sorted?'

'For now. It's an odd one. She's not in oestrus but frequently appears as though she is.'

'Can't help you there, mate.' I said.

'Well how can I help *you* this evening?'

'Tell me about microchips. Did you implant any when you were working for Bayley Watt?'

'Two or three, maybe. They're mostly done at foal stage.'

'But there's no problem implanting in a mature horse? Well, a three-year-old or four-year-old?'

'Not really, no.'

'Run me through the procedure.'

'We get the chip from Weatherbys and insert it in the Nuchal ligament, halfway along the left side of the neck, about two inches down from the mane. Injection with a bigger than normal needle but a simple job. No anaesthetic.'

'And the chip carries details of the horse's conformation and markings etcetera?'

'Nope. All it has in it is a fifteen-digit number which is then copied into the horse's passport. The passport holds all the markings and stuff and, if a horse has any injuries or surgery which leaves scars, the passport should be updated to show them.'

'What about removing a chip?'

'There shouldn't be any need.'

'If there ever was?'

'Simple incision, a pair of tweezers and a steady hand, I'd imagine.'

'Good. Thanks. I owe you a drink.' I said.

'I won't ask you any questions.'

'Very wise,' I said.

'And you, as ever, will be the soul of discretion should my name ever come up in conversation.'

'The heart and soul my friend. You know that.'

'I do know it. I do. The number of people I trust in this world could be counted on the fingers of one foot. But you are chief among them.'

'Likewise, Stewart. Tell me one more thing, do you recall when Watt stopped using you? He'd been your client for a few years, hadn't he?'

'About four years, I'd say, going on five. He gave me the medicine man bollocks in August, just before I went on holiday.'

'Did he have any new horses in when you last did any work there?'

'No. Same handful as last season.'

'Thanks. That's all for now.'

'Be careful,' he said.

'I will. You be careful. A large winking vulva might swallow you up. You'll stick your arm inside and it'll be like equine quicksand. Sound about the same too.'

'Horizontal equine quicksand.'

'The muddy soles of your boots the last thing to disappear. Then the winking stops.'

'That's all folks!'

We laughed and said goodbye.

I switched the radio off. My mind was working, processing plans, moving fast, inspecting, rejecting, mulling and finally deciding I should resort to what I did best. Wing it. Kick off and see what happens.

Don't pre-plan. Don't go home. Head for Watt's yard. Now.

TWENTY-FOUR

Watt's place in the valley was on an unlit road. He'd be at least half an hour behind me, driving his box from Warwick. I rolled two hundred yards past the entrance to his yard and turned, parked on the verge, nosed up to the hedge so I was almost concealed, and switched off the lights.

Blane Kilberg would be minding the place and the horses. I'd wait until Kilberg had gone. I wanted to confront Watt on his own.

I found Gerry Waldron's name in my contact list and called him. Gerry was a PR man for one of the big bookies.

'Eddie, good to hear from you. What do you know?'

'Not much Gerry. How are you?'

'Passable. Passable. What can I do for you?'

'I rode a winner at Taunton last week, a horse called Spiritless Fun. Can you find out if there was a run of money for him or any unusual laying of the others?'

'Give me ten minutes.'

'Check the first winner at Warwick today too, will you? And maybe get me a general impression from your guys of Bayley Watt's punting habits.'

'Will do.'

I waited in the dark, watching the narrow road. Gerry Waldron had been in the game a long time. A lot of PR guys for bookies only lasted a year or two. A few bookies were employing women now in that role; young, photogenic as well as very knowledgeable. But Gerry was an old hand. He had a few people in racing on his payroll. If the favourite for Saturday's big race stepped on a stone, or coughed in his box at midnight, Gerry would get a call before anyone else.

He'd been around when I'd had my first bite at fame and he'd offered me sound advice regarding the company I was keeping. I decided not to listen because I knew better, didn't I?

When I got warned off, Gerry never said "I told you so", he just rang to offer help. I never forgot that.

I'd help him when I could. I might assess a race or tell him if I thought a new young jockey might make up into a champ. I took no payment and I never broke the rules.

I'd thought that turning thirty would set me on a steady slide to oblivion but one of the advantages of aging in this business is that you get to know who you can trust. There weren't many, but they were all the more valuable for that. Gerry Waldron was one. The vet, Stewart Lico was another.

A light went on upstairs in Watt's house. I saw Kilberg in the room, passing the window. My phone rang. I answered, keeping my eyes on Kilberg. 'Gerry. Any luck?'

'It depends what you were hoping for. There was nothing untoward about either horse on the betting front. Normal betting patterns in both races. And Watt's not a punter.'

'Okay. Thanks. By the way, I should have asked, how is your wife?'

'Stable. She's doing all right, thanks. Bad period around Christmas but mostly she's fine. We're happy.'

'That's good.'

'How've you been?'

'I'm okay. Settled in the bungalow now. Quiet life. Come down when the weather's better, see my summer house.'

'Get you and your summer house!'

I smiled. 'Thanks for the info Gerry. Give me a shout if you need anything.'

'Take care, young man.'

His glowing name died on the screen. Dark again. While we'd been talking, Kilberg had switched off the light in the upstairs room. What kind of relationship did he have with Watt that let him prowl around up there?

How was Watt getting money on those horses? It was pointless running ringers if you weren't profiting, and there were just two ways to do that in a race: bet the winner or lay the favourite. Everybody could be a bookmaker now with betting exchanges. If you didn't think a horse was going to win, you could lay it, taking bets from others who thought it would win.

And where had he found the horse? What was its true identity? Horses of that quality don't go unnoticed. Spotting raw talent was big business. Good horses never stayed under wraps for long, and this one of Watt's was high class. He'd raced somewhere before, I'd bet on that.

At the junction, three hundred yards ahead, I saw beams of light at right angles to the road; they grew brighter then bounced and swung toward me as the horsebox turned left then indicated right to go into the yard.

I jumped out and hurried along the hedge line. Vaulting a gate, I jogged across a field toward the rear of the house as the yard lights came on and reflected in the window at the top of the horsebox as it slowed and stopped.

My shoes and trousers got wet moving through the grass. I'd been hoping to find a gate in the hedge running parallel with the yard, but there was none. The blackthorn was bare and thick, barring my way. I stopped. Watt was speaking. Kilberg answered in his higher pitch, almost effeminate, his accent recognizable even though I couldn't quite pick out the words.

Sounds of hooves on the ramp, on the old cobbles. A door sliding shut on squeaking rollers. The yard lights switched off. I waited. The lights came on again. An engine started. I hurried toward the end of the hedge to see what I took to be Kilberg's car pulling out. I went back to the gate, onto the road, thought about picking the strands of grass from my trousers, heard my socks squelch, cursed, and headed for Watt's door.

He had no spyhole. 'Who is it?'

'Eddie Malloy.'

Decision time for Bayley Watt.

The door opened. It led into his kitchen. My eyes had adjusted to the night, and the light almost blinded me, making Watt a silhouette. He opened it fully and stepped back. I went in.

He closed the door slowly then turned to face me.

'What's the horse?' I said.

He just stared at me. Not threatening or aggressive. Not confused. Just unsure. He was very still. His brown suit hung baggy, a noticeable gap between his throat and the collar of the pale blue shirt, yellow tie not yet loosened. His grey beard-shadow framed a gaunt face and I wondered if he too had cancer. I glanced at his wrists and he saw me and he turned his hands up thinking it was them I was watching, then he did that old face-rubbing thing with weariness and surrender. His wrists were still hairless. He dragged a heavy kitchen chair across and sat, elbows on knees. He stared at the grey tiled floor for a few moments then looked up at me. 'What do you want?'

'What's the horse?'

'Does it matter?'

'Did it matter to Jimmy?'

He just blinked, and kept blinking.

'Was that what Jimmy wanted to know? Did he ask the question?'

'What do you want, Eddie? Do you want the ride back?'

'On a ringer? For a bent trainer? Are you fucking mad?'

He rubbed his face again then said, 'Money?'

I shook my head. 'Who killed Jimmy Sherrick?' I asked.

'Jimmy killed himself.'

'Why?'

'He had cancer.'

'Who told you that?' I said.

'Jimmy did.'

'Was his watch bugged too?'

'I don't know.'

'You know he didn't make that recording.'

He stared again at the floor, almost bent over, elbows on knees. 'Who made the recording Bayley?'

'I don't know.'

'Do you know anything? Who burned his house down? Who stole his body?'

He shook his head. I moved toward him, pulled out a chair and sat down. He wouldn't look up.

'The cops have proof you gave his father a bugged watch.'

No answer.

'Bayley, they were here this morning. Kilberg told you that, didn't he?'

Nothing.

'You're fucked, Bayley.'

106

No response. No Comanche stories. No idea how to get himself out of this.

'Who's got you by the balls? Maybe I can help you.'

He looked up, but without hope. 'You can't.'

'You are not a well man, are you? You look more like a cancer victim than Jimmy ever did.'

He went back to gazing at the floor.

'Is that what this guy's got on you, he knows you're dying? What's he doing, collecting terminal cancer patients, doing deals?'

No answer.

I got off the chair, hunkered, tried to look up into his eyes but he wouldn't turn his head. 'Bayley, if you're dying, tell me what you know. What's the horse? What's happening? Who's behind all this?'

Blank.

'Can't you even tell me to go away?'

Silence from the condemned man. I'd expected a raging argument, denials, bribes...he'd made a half-hearted attempt at that. Maybe because he knew me. But I knew him too, his tantrums, his flare-ups and this wasn't Bayley Watt. Threats...I'd expected them. But all I faced was a beaten man.

I stood up. 'Time for the sixgun Bayley.' I pulled out my phone and pointed it at him.

'Who do you want me to call first? Sergeant Middleton? Peter McCarthy?' McCarthy was head of integrity services at the BHA. Watt would be warned off for life for running a ringer.

I got McCarthy's contact details on my phone. No signal. 'I'll call from outside. You'd better concentrate on coming up with some kind of defence other than the fifth amendment.'

He did. As I opened the door and stepped out, he grabbed something very heavy, and all I remember was a moment of surprise at the blinding pain of the blow that shut me down for the night.

TWENTY-FIVE

I came to in the dark, wondering where I was and what had happened. I realized I wasn't at home. The floor I lay on was cold and hard and I had a serious headache.

My memory returned.

Before trying to rise, I touched my face and head lightly, searching for blood...none. I bent my knees, dragging my heels along the tiles, then raised my hips, flexed my arms, stretched them.

No pain below my neck. He must have hit me once and left me. I reached up into the blackness, checking that I wasn't beneath a table or something. I'd been downed on the threshold. Watt must have dragged me inside.

Slowly, I sat, then turned and got to my knees. I didn't want to risk standing up in the dark in case I keeled over.

I half crawled until I touched a skirting board then used the wall to help me up. I rested against it. The moon showed briefly giving me a fix on the kitchen window and the big table Watt had been sitting at. I moved and felt along the wall for the light switch. Found it. Closed my eyes before clicking the light on. My head felt bad enough without risking a sudden flash.

My eyelids opened a millimetre at a time. The kitchen was empty. A cast iron frying pan, Watt's weapon, sat on the stove. I cursed myself for complacency. I'd been certain he was a beaten man. I had eased down before the winning post and got caught on the line. Painfully.

I reached for my phone…gone. Car keys. Gone. I closed my eyes and cursed. My watch. Still there. Ten minutes to twelve. At least I knew by the darkness outside which end of the day I was at. I went looking for Watt's house phone. The wire had been cut.

I leaned on the door handle. Locked. The back door too was locked. I knew by then that Watt had gone. All he'd wanted was to buy time.

I climbed through the kitchen window and set out to walk home against a rising wind, under deep cloud and a full moon that played frustrating peek-a-boo in the rural blackness.

My house keys were safe in my jacket and I fingered them as I passed Rooksnest and headed downhill on the rutted road, tiny rain streams bubbling in the narrow gullies. I slowed. I'd been walking a long time, nursing a pounding headache.

I sat at my table with a lamp burning. A search in my laughably sparse 'medical box' came up with a paracetamol hot lemon drink. The warmth of the mug in my hands was comforting. Two thirty. That had been a slow walk. What now? It was pointless dialling 999. Watt could be out of the country by now. I switched the PC on and pinged Maven Judge and told her what had happened.

'You got auto-wipe on your phone?'

'Yes.'

'Best log on and wipe it.'

'He'll have dumped it in a field or something Mave. There's nothing on there he can use.'

'If he's dumped it, all the more reason to wipe it.'

'Okay.'

'Do it now. And report it stolen or someone will run up twenty grand on your sim. I'll be here. Gimme a shout.'

I did as she said, then topped up my drink and returned to the PC.

I reopened the window that showed Mave's left profile, monochrome, lit only by her screen, shadows under her cheekbone, darkness below her chin as though her head floated there. Her webcam was offset tonight. She'd need to turn about seventy degrees left for me to see her face properly. But she seldom looked at the webcam. I was used to watching only her fingers and skinny arms, or her heavy black keyboard or her T-shirt logo. You never knew where the camera would be.

She turned and glanced at me, stern. 'Done it?' she asked.

'Yep.'

'Now what?'

'I'll finish this drink. Try and get some sleep. Call the sergeant in the morning.'

'I'd have thought you'd have had enough sleep.'

I smiled. 'I prefer the type that comes on naturally through weariness after a long day's work.'

'As against the instant repose that results from being whanged on the nut with a skillet the size of a bin lid. You're never happy, Eddie. Usually when we're talking at this time, it's because you're moaning about not being able to sleep. Somebody offers you a solution and you're bad mouthing him. Poor Bayley Watt.'

'He's a worried man. It's not just me he's running from. I'd bet on that.'

'Did you check his PC?'

'Shit! No, I didn't.'

'Was it still there?'

'I don't know. Never thought to look. I was trying to find keys to get out.'

'Can you go back to his house before you phone the cops?'

'I suppose I could.'

'I take it all the horses were still there?'

'They were. The horsebox too.'

'A lot of bloodstock to abandon.'

'He's scared.'

'Must be. What about Kilberg? Maybe he'll call him and tell him to get round there?'

'Depends how much Kilberg knows.'

Mave was concentrating. Her frown had deepened. The click rate on the keys had increased in volume and speed. Then she slowed and said, 'Why don't you drop out of this now? There's nothing in it for you but hassle. Nobody knows you went to Watt's place, do they?'

'No.'

'He's legged it, leaving behind a fortune in assets if you add the house to the horses? You said you thought he might be dying anyway, and he's so scared he won't even stay there to die in peace? Whoever he's afraid of must score pretty high on the terror scale. You ought to hand in your dance card at this point Eddie, and bow out.'

'I know.'

'Listen. Seriously. I know what you're like and you feel for old Mister Sherrick and you were Jimmy's pal and you don't like people to think he killed himself and all the rest, but apply logic for once. Drop all the white knight crap and apply some hard logic. It is worth nothing to you. Absolutely zero. If you were up against some amateur or some knucklehead, okay. But this guy is serious shit. Whoever he is, he is serious shit. Don't you think?'

'Probably.'

'Probably! I can tell by the way you said that one word you're already working out how you're going to try and nail this guy. You're as mad as he is only you're soft mad, crazy. He's hard mad as in psychotic. P-S-Y-' she hesitated, 'C-H-O-T-I-C.'

I smiled and sipped the hot lemon. 'Had to think then, didn't you? A brain the size of the moon and you can't spell psychotic without a breather.'

She wouldn't look at me, but she smiled wide and worked on. 'Okay,' she said, 'head over there in a taxi. You got a dongle? A memory stick?'

'Somewhere.'

'I'm going to email you a file, save it on the stick then put the stick into Watt's PC.'

'He'll have a password on it.'

'Doesn't matter, this programme will break it and pull some info in for me. You put the memory stick in yours and send me the file. I'll have a look at his PC from here before the cops take it.'

'Okay.'

Half an hour later I was in a taxi, telling the driver my car had broken down and I was heading back to it to wait for the recovery service. I had my spare car keys and a pay as you go phone I kept for emergencies.

Watt's place was as I'd left it. But it was much tougher getting in through the window than it had been getting out.

His PC was a big old unit with the dusty cobwebbed USB ports on the rear. I used a shirt from his wardrobe to handle the PC box, turn it round without leaving any prints. I put the stick in and hit the power button.

Five minutes later, the machine closed itself down. Mave had told me that's what would happen. I wished I could check that everything had saved to the stick but I couldn't. Before leaving by the window again, I checked the ledge and the kitchen floor for my footprints. My shoes had been soaking when I'd first arrived at Watt's place. The prints were easy to see.

I considered cleaning up because it was in my mind not to contact the police at all, to let them find out in their own time, keep myself out of it.

But that would have meant making sure I'd left no trace. It would also mean the horses being left unattended. I didn't know what the arrangement was with Kilberg.

Maybe he only turned up to mind the place when Watt was away racing. Best call the sergeant come daybreak.

Sitting at my PC, I sent the file to Mave. 'Okay. Leave it with me.'

'How long?' I asked.

'Depends what's on it.' She stopped typing and stared at her screen. 'You look like shit.'

'Feel like it.'

'A couple of hours sleep might be a good idea before a trip to hospital.'

'I'll be fine.'

'You were out for a long time, Eddie.'

'I'm okay. Just need a day's rest.'

'Go to A and E. I'll have this done by the time you're home.'

All right. I'll call you.'

She closed the link. I had no intention of getting a formal medical check. If the racing authorities found out, they might not let me ride for a while. A fall on the track that resulted in loss of consciousness, even for ten seconds, would get you stood down.

I still had a headache but no nausea, no dizziness. Tired and sore and somehow back to square one. I lay awake trying to find gaps in the gonging headache in which I could think. Why call the police? What good had that done so far?

If I called in Peter McCarthy, the director of racing's Integrity Department, there'd be a shitstorm of panic in case the word got out to the betting public. Mac would try and shut me up for months.

I had to find out where Watt had gone. The only one likely to know would be Blane Kilberg, his so-called assistant trainer. That would never sit right with me, or anyone who knew about racing.

An experienced vet, acting assistant in a yard with just eight horses?

No way.

Kilberg was in on the ringer scam. He had to be. Fissure Splint was also Spiritless Fun. Each had a passport, each had a microchip in his neck confirming his identity against the passport. Kilberg's job was to implant and remove the chips, it had to be.

Could Kilberg be Mr Big? Had Bayley Watt feared him so much he'd risked killing me, then bolted, leaving behind a yardful of horses, a house and land worth upwards of a million pounds? A business he'd spent years building?

Blane Kilberg was nothing to look at. Well nothing that would scare you. He was something of a fitness freak. At dusk he was often seen on the gallops, without a horse. He'd be wearing lycra, and carrying silver dumbbells as he ran up the steady slopes of the all-weather strip, like running on sand dunes. Then he would jog down again, backwards. He was fit and fox-like, light on his feet and fancied himself a dancer. There were stories of him doing ballet moves in the gym at Oaksey House, working at the Barre, close enough to steam up the mirrors, black headphones over his buzzcut blonde hair he'd paid thousands for.

Hair transplant, lasered eyes, new teeth, everything above his collar bone must have cost close to fifty grand. Some would do that to boost confidence, but a man that was happy to do ballet in full view of stable lads and jockeys, didn't need much of a confidence boost. He'd been the butt of enough jokes last year when his teenage bride had taken off in her three litre wedding present, all the way home to Romania.

Kilberg had bet some people he would bring her home, but her gypsy family had circled the wagons and the vet was soon home complaining about "Third world gangsters".

So, that was what I knew of Blane Kilberg. Narcissist? Definitely. Delusional? Probably. The man who had terrorized Bayley Watt? I doubted it. But I had seen stranger things.

Anyway, Kilberg was the first port of call. Not the sergeant. Not McCarthy. I had one advantage: I was the only one, apart from Kilberg, and whoever Watt was running from, who knew what the trainer had been up to. Why surrender that advantage at this stage?

I'd go to Watt's yard on the pretext of doing some schooling for him. If Kilberg wasn't there, I'd call McCarthy, to make sure the horses were looked after, and play dumb. If I told Mave that was the plan, playing dumb, she'd have said "You won't find that difficult, Edward."

TWENTY-SIX

Kilberg's black Mercedes was at the yard when I drove in, it was parked at an angle, nose-up to the sandstone gable end of the house, as though he'd roared in and pulled a handbrake stop.

I parked alongside, at the same angle.

Kilberg was in the feed room, filling a battered old black plastic bowl with feed. His parking suggested he'd arrived in a hell of a hurry, but his boots gleamed as black and shiny as his Mercedes. He was clean shaven and I could smell his cologne through the sweetness of oats and bran.

He glanced up at me, as though I was the hired help. 'Morning' he said.

'Good morning, you landed breakfast duty then?'

'And lunch and dinner,' He continued to scoop feed.

'Where's Bayley?'

'Dead.' He shook the bowl, looking into it.

I waited, watching him being Mister Cool, wondering where he was at in whatever script he'd prepared in his head. He marched out, obviously expecting me to follow like some apprentice, eager to discover the secret of becoming a full-fledged cool dude.

I stayed in the feed room, listening to him snapping the bolt on the door of a box, slapping the hungry horse, knocking the plastic bowl against the manger to get the last few flakes out. Then his leather boot heels on concrete, as he came back and my nose took over from my ears as that sweet scent he'd rubbed on his shining jaw came at me like the jet stream.

115

His manicured hand gripped the door, then his short spikes of blonde hair appeared as he peered in at me, round the edge of the door. 'Coffee?' he said.

'Fucking powdered shit.' Kilberg said, spooning coffee from a jar into pale blue mugs, 'Why would a man spend a hundred grand a year running a yard, and not buy a decent coffee maker?'

I looked around the kitchen I'd been in last night. My dried footprints were still on the tiles. The weapon Watt had used sat on the stove, looking harmless in the daylight.

I was sitting where Watt had sat, unwilling to wait for Kilberg's invitation, to sit down.

He brought the coffee, then opened the fridge door and rooted around, tutting. He closed the door. 'No cream either.'

'Listen,' I said 'Quit the Cool Hand Luke stuff, will you? I'm not impressed, and as far I can see, there is nobody else here. Sit down and tell me what's going on.'

Coffee mug in his left hand he reached in the back pocket of his black jods and pulled out some paper that had been folded into a square. He handed it to me.

It was a copy of an email from Bayley Watt:

"I'm done. Malloy came to the house just after you left. He knows everything, so we're fucked. Do me a favour and see to the horses. Then you do what you think is best for yourself. If you decide to run, make arrangements for the horses first, please. I panicked and thought I'd get out of the country. I'm on a ferry to Ireland, but I've been sitting in this cabin asking myself where I'm running to with whatever time I've got left. Running's for horses and young men. I'm going Jimmy Sherrick's way, poor bastard. No hanging. That still fucking haunts me. But I've got enough Cyanide. When they find me at Cork, it'll be the worst case of seasickness in history. I've emailed my last wishes to my lawyer, there's something in it for you so long as you look after the horses. Good luck."

The final line was "Sent from my android phone" It was timed 3.37. I checked my watch: Watt had sent it while I was here rooting around his PC.

Kilberg was sitting now, hands clasped on the table. He raised his eyebrows when I looked at him but his eyes told me nothing. He seemed determined to play the part all the way through, and it dawned on me that this wasn't some act, it was no bold facade. Blane Kilberg saw himself this way. In his own reality, he was some big time star or hero or gangster or something. Anything but a middle aged vet in a village rabid with ambitious people, many delusional, like Kilberg.

I lay the paper flat and drank some coffee. 'You were moving the microchips then, on that horse?'

He nodded, 'That was me.'

I had been trying to pin down his accent. It had something of that Boston twang I recalled from the newsreel footage of J.F.K. Maybe he'd lived in Boston or gone to college there. 'What's the horse?'

'I don't know.'

'Bayley wouldn't tell you?'

'I never asked.' His eyes said "I was too smart to ask" And he was expecting me to press him on it, but I denied him the pleasure.

'How much did you make?'

'Not enough.'

'It's never enough, is it?'

'We needed it. We had plans.'

'And Jimmy Sherrick was about to scupper those plans?'

'Jimmy Sherrick killed himself. Bayley was there to help him.'

'How?'

'Jimmy arranged a meeting with you. He wanted to be sure he was found quickly so his Dad wouldn't suffer so much.'

'So why did Bayley need to be there?'

'Jimmy had asked Bayley to be there. He told him he was scared of getting it wrong, scared of hanging kicking and choking for ten minutes. Bayley told him where he could get cyanide and helped him order it online.'

'Sounds like Bayley was hardly rushing to talk Jimmy out of it.'

'Jimmy had cancer. Pancreatic cancer. Bayley had leukaemia. He tried a couple of courses of chemo, but he couldn't hack it. He wanted the money from betting to go abroad and have all his blood replaced.'

I thought back to last night, to what I'd said: "What's he doing, collecting terminal cancer patients?" Now it seemed as though there was no "He," no mister big. Watching Kilberg, and listening to him, and thinking of Watt's email, I knew Kilberg wasn't in charge of anything.'

'What about you?' I said 'What's your angle?'

'Liver. I need a new liver in the next three months or I'll be joining Jimmy and Bayley.'

'You on the list, the waiting list?'

'Here? No, what's the point? Ninety two percent of people waiting for a transplant die. My plan was to go overseas and buy my way to the top.'

I watched him, unable to make my brain work quick enough to sieve all this stuff about cancer and cyanide and suicide. Incapable of filtering my instinct to sniff out inconsistencies.

My head hurt.

Kilberg unclasped his hand and put his thumbs in the waistband of his jods, then sat back until his nose pointed at the ceiling, he tilted his eyes, looking at me through the narrow slits. And I noticed a jowly flabbiness about him, a softness, similar to the way Bayley had looked these past few weeks.

'What are you going to do?' He said.

'I don't think I'm going to have to do anything. They could be opening the cabin on that ferry as we speak. If Bayley's sent a note to his solicitor like he said, it's a matter of time before the police turn up, then the BHA'S Integrity guys. The question is what are you going to do?'

'Bayley won't have given them any details, he's left the yard and horses to me. That was part of the agreement if he died first. He wanted me to have the chance of saving myself.'

It was slowly dawning on me. 'You want me to keep quiet so you can carry on with this ringer scam?'

He looked straight at me now, thumbs still stuck in his waistband. 'If you stay quiet, I swear I'll run the horse straight for the rest of the season. That's assuming the BHA grant me a licence. I believe Fruitless Spin can win the Supreme in March and I think you already know he can. I'll run him straight. I'm not saying I won't bet him, because I have to or I'm a dead man. He runs straight, and you ride if you want to, I'll understand if you don't.'

'Bayley tried to bribe me. Now you.'

He just watched me.

His story about Jimmy's death had been told with conviction. Bayley had told him and Kilberg had swallowed it. 'Did you know Jimmy's taped suicide messaged was faked?' I said.

He shook his head, 'The opposite,' he said 'Jimmy was afraid that if he left a note, people might say it was forged. Bayley told me Jimmy had asked for his help to make the recording.'

I shifted in my chair and it screeched on the floor tiles. 'Did you believe everything Bayley told you?'

'Why would he lie?'

'Why did he give Jimmy's father a bugged watch? Did Jimmy get one too? One that disappeared that night in the cellar after Bayley had patched together a so called suicide message from it?'

'Who told you that?'

'I know it. Bayley didn't deny it. Did you get a watch from him?"

He raised his right hand and a thick black leather strap slipped half an inch down his wrist. He turned it to let me see the silver chunky face, 'I've worn this since I was twenty-one. My father gave it to me on my birthday.'

'So why would Bayley Watt give Jim Sherrick a bugged watch?'

'Who knows? Bayley was with Jimmy when he died. He helped Jimmy kill himself. That's a pretty serious crime. Maybe he just wanted to make sure Jimmy's Dad wasn't suspicious about anything.'

'But he found out he was, and Jimmy's house burned down. Then his corpse was stolen. What did Bayley do with Jimmy's body?'

'How would Bayley Watt have dug a grave and hauled out a coffin?'

'Maybe someone helped.'

'You mean me?'

'There was no one closer to Bayley.'

'Not guilty, Eddie.'

I finished the coffee and got to my feet. 'I'll tell you what, if I find out where Jimmy Sherrick's body is by this time tomorrow, I'll ride that horse for you and keep my mouth shut until the end of the season.' Kilberg stayed seated, looking at me. 'I don't know where Jimmy's corpse is, and I'm pretty sure Bayley doesn't, or didn't, either. So it looks like I'm in trouble.'

'Think about it. About what you're asking me to believe. I can just about swallow the cancer story, but if you and Bayley didn't steal Jimmy's body it means somebody else was involved. Somebody with an awful lot to lose.'

He just kept staring. I noticed again the loose flesh on his jowls. I said 'I'll hold until noon tomorrow.'

He nodded. No shrug of ignorance No final plea. A nod, which told me he knew where Jimmy was.

TWENTY-SEVEN

I rode a winner at Stratford in the afternoon, finished last in the novice hurdle, then had a lucky fall in the novice chase. The fall to rides ratio in our business is about one in ten. You get straight to your feet from most of them. The occasional tumble results in an ambulance trip, and once in a while somebody dies.

On firm summer ground I might have ended up in hospital rather than in the showers trying to remove the mud stain from my thigh with a scrubbing brush I'd borrowed from Vernon Siddal, a valet.

As I dried off and got dressed, Vernon was the only person in the changing room. Through the window, the last of the winter light was fading. I was amazed that the racing grapevine hadn't yet picked up on the death of Bayley Watt. I watched Vernon work away at the deep sink, grinding the worst of the mud from several pairs of breeches, before putting them in a washing machine.

I walked over and nodded at the dirty pool of tangled legs, 'Didn't someone once call mud glorious?' I said.

He glanced at me, smiling, then back into the swirling mass 'For hippos I believe that was,' he said.

'I shouldn't complain, I suppose, it was a nice squelchy cushion for me in the novice chase.'

'Aye, I saw that. You lot should have the longest slide competition. You know, the way golfers have the longest drive competitions?'

I laughed 'I think I'd have won today's'

'Definitely.'

'I'm getting too used to riding in the ambulance, the only walking I seem to do these days is to and from the car. I might start doing the early morning runs up the all-weather like Blane Kilberg.'

'There's a few doing it now. Always were. It was just that Kilberg was the only one in lycra.'

'I think I'd draw the line at the lycra, keen as I am to get fitter.'

'They must have embarrassed Kilberg out of it too, he's been in baggy cotton gear this season. More like a mad monk now.'

'That won't do much for his free flowing style. Still, there's always the ballet.'

'I suppose.'

'Maybe he's getting more sensible since he got that assistant trainer's job with Bayley Watt,' I said.

'I doubt it, old Bayley's on the eccentric side himself, isn't he? They'll make a good pair.'

'I better get dressed and head for home. You got much more to do?'

'Another hour should see it finished.'

'Plumpton tomorrow.?'

'Aye. Drive, wash, polish, sew, wash, drive, sleep, drive…Groundhog day.'

'But you love it?'

He laughed 'Most of the time.'

It was dark when I got in the car, I took my phone from the glove box. Jim Sherrick had left a message, using the coded sentence we'd agreed if he wanted to see me: "Eddie can you pick me a few things up from the shops?"

I called him. We small-talked. He asked for milk and eggs.

His television was on when I arrived. We chatted about racing for a few minutes, then he asked me to stay for tea.

'I won't, if you don't mind, Jim. I need to do ten stone at Plumpton tomorrow.'

'Ah, who'd be a starving jockey?'

'I often ask myself the same question.'

'Take care, Eddie. See you soon.'

'And you. Goodbye.'

He eased off his watch and laid it softly on the chair, and followed me out.

We sat in my car. 'Did you hear about Bayley Watt?' he said.

'Blane Kilberg told me this morning. Who told you?'

'The sergeant called by this afternoon.' Mister Sherrick told me that Watt's solicitor had contacted Thames Valley police who called the police in Cork. The Irish cops found Bailey's body in his cabin. Time of death was estimated at 4a.m., not long after his email to Kilberg.

I told Mister Sherrick about the email, although I mentioned nothing else Kilberg had said to me. I wanted to wait for that deadline of noon tomorrow. Kilberg knew where Jimmy Sherrick's body lay. I was sure of that. But I wasn't so sure he'd admit to it, so I didn't want to give Jimmy's dad false hope.

It was one of those rare decisions I got right. Blane Kilberg took the deadline literally. By the time it expired, so had he.

TWENTY-EIGHT

Driving up the single track road from my house next morning, I met a rolling police roadblock coming downhill. They stopped. I stopped and got out. Sergeant Middleton stepped out, His passenger made to do the same, but the sergeant waved him inside.

We looked at each other, and I knew the game had changed.

I could see a curtain of rain approaching from the far southwest. The wind gusted through the old trees, rattling the branches.

The sergeant walked toward me … ten paces. 'Eddie.'

'Sergeant.'

He gazed down at me from his uphill stance.

I said, 'I'm trying to find the word for how you look, sergeant. Grave is the first one that comes to mind. What's up?'

He gestured at the police car. 'DS Wilmslow is with me. When he joins us, he'll caution you. I asked for a minute first.'

'I'm listening.'

'Blane Kilberg is dead. Another suicide. He sent an email to us claiming you were harassing him and Bayley Watt…and Jimmy Sherrick. That you'd driven them all to suicide.'

'Harassing? How?'

'Threatening them because you lost the rides on Watt's horses.'

'I didn't lose the rides on anybody's horses, least of all Bayley Watt's. It was me that gave them up for Jimmy.'

'I know you did. That's why we're standing here talking…just you and me. But you're going to have to go through the process; formal questioning, statements. At the station or at your house.'

I checked my watch. 'How long will it take?'

'We'll try and do it in an hour.'

'I'm supposed to be at Plumpton.'

'Look, let's get it done. It'll be quicker at your house.'

I sighed and shook my head. 'Okay. I'll reverse.'

DS Wilmslow was much younger than Sergeant Middleton. He looked about the same age as I was. I offered tea or coffee and he asked for boiled water and did I mind if he added a touch of cold from the tap. I turned it on and was about to move the steaming mug under the running water when he stood up quickly. 'No! Please. I prefer to do it myself, if you don't mind.'

I handed him the mug. He adjusted the flow to a trickle then passed the mug below in a smooth movement. I glanced at the sergeant. He raised an eyebrow.

We settled at the kitchen table. Wilmslow moved the mug on the coaster until it sat dead centre. A man of precision or one with OCD. Yet his tie knot was askew, his brown hair untidy. His hazel eyes had a vacancy about them, suggesting his thoughts were elsewhere, despite staring at me while I talked.

Few things throw me, or make me feel uncomfortable, but DS Wilmslow's way of using his eyes was unsettling. Whether I was answering his questions or Sergeant Middleton's, Wilmslow would scan different parts of my face like he was looking for a route into my skull.

He asked questions in the style of a doctor, as though trying to diagnose rather than convict. He read from what I took to be Kilberg's email.

'Can I read that?' I said.

'Not at the moment. Do you keep a diary?'

'Only for rides.'

'You have notes of your conversations with Jimmy Sherrick or Bayley Watt or Blane Kilberg?'

'Why would I have kept notes?'

'Could your conversations, any of them, have been interpreted as threatening?'

'Yes.'

'In what way?'

'In the way that I told Bayley Watt that he had the choice of me calling you guys first, or the BHA's integrity chief.'

'Did you seek a reward from him for not calling in the authorities?'

'Well, I sought the use of his front step to get a phone signal so I could make the call. Then Bayley sought a wok weighing half a stone before seeking a spot on my head to whang me with it.'

Middleton smiled. Wilmslow just made a note and said, 'Did you offer Blane Kilberg a deal due to expire at noon today, promising not to expose him, so to speak, if you could ride a horse called Fruitless Spin in its remaining races this season?'

'I offered him a deal in exchange for information about what he and Bayley Watt had done with Jimmy Sherrick's body.'

'And what was his response?'

'He nodded.'

'Did you construe a meaning from that?'

'I construed that he'd give it some consideration.'

'Did he say anything else?'

I went through everything Kilberg had told me. Wilmslow wrote it all down, occasionally saying 'Hold!', while his writing hand caught up. He used block capitals for everything.

While Wilmslow was writing, I was stacking things up in my head…many questions.

The rain reached us, coming at the big window straight on, causing the only noise in the house as Wilmslow conducted a check of what he'd written, his silver pen moving from line to line. I signed it as my statement, and walked them to the door.

The sergeant asked where I'd be for the rest of the week. 'Racing every day. I can email you my schedule.'

'I don't think that will be necessary,' he said, glancing at Wilmslow then back at me, his mouth and eyebrows contorting in some kind of blame-shifting semaphore that was meant to keep me on his side.

It wasn't working, and he knew it. 'Am I allowed to know how Kilberg killed himself?'

The sergeant turned to Wilmslow, who said, 'We're awaiting the autopsy results.'

'I don't think I'll need three guesses,' I said. 'Have you checked Watt's place for a stock of cyanide pills?'

Wilmslow walked away. Sergeant Middleton said, 'We'll be in touch, Eddie.' He raised a hand as he left, half a goodbye, half an apology from a man who'd reached the limit of his competence.

On the long drive to Plumpton, I had time to take in the fact that another person had died. When the sergeant had told me, he must have thought me callous. All I'd been interested in was saying 'It wasn't me.'

Wilmslow would have been watching from the car for my reaction. At least I hadn't staggered in a dead faint like some ham actor. But I'd shown zero surprise, so where did that leave me in the suspicion stakes?

It was only now, alone in the car, heading for east Sussex that I realized the news about Kilberg had come as no shock. Nothing in this crazy case was shocking anymore. Yet, it should have been. Because I was becoming used to deaths, didn't mean I shouldn't question them.

Kilberg was a relatively young man. Why commit suicide within twelve hours of me asking him some questions? He was implicated in betting fraud not some child sex ring. Many in racing had been guilty of much worse crimes than Blane Kilberg or Bayley Watt.

Suicide made no sense here, however you looked at it. Kilberg's story about Bayley's leukaemia and his own liver could be grouped in the 'possible terminal illness' category that had loomed in my mind with Bayley and with Jimmy.

But Jimmy hadn't committed suicide, had he? Someone had tried to make it look as though he had.

So if Jimmy had been killed, why assume that Watt and Kilberg had not been killed too? If someone was capable of putting together a recorded suicide message, it wouldn't be beyond him to hack the email accounts of two men and send fake suicide notes from them.

A triple murder? Over a ringer fraud. A fraud where no unusual betting patterns had been found? That made no sense either.

Had they been killed for something other than being involved with the ringer? No. I couldn't go there. Things were complicated enough. I had to stick to this line. It was all I had and I was on my own.

I liked the sergeant, but he was little more than a beat Bobby. Wilmslow wouldn't be giving me help anytime soon.

Picking the brains of Peter McCarthy would be worthwhile, and Mave would help me. But that was it. I slowed and found McCarthy's number and counted the rings. I'd never known him to pick the phone up until at least the sixth ring. Seven this time. 'Eddie.'

'Mac.'

'The *Racing Post* tells me you should be at Plumpton.'

'I'm on my way.'

'You're running late.'

'I was delayed by a corpse.'

'A hearse?'

'Kilberg hasn't reached the hearse stage yet.'

'What are you talking about?'

'Blane Kilberg is dead. Haven't the police been in touch?'

'Hold on.'

I heard footsteps and muffled conversation, which told me Mac was in his London office at the British Horseracing Authority. He was head of security there. I heard a mild curse from him then his voice, clear again. 'Eddie, who told you this?'

'Sergeant Middleton of Thames Valley police, about an hour ago.' I filled in the rest of the story and told Mac there were eight horses at Watt's place with nobody to look after them.

'I'll call you back,' he said before I could tell him about the ringer. Two hours later, as I sat on the scales to weigh out for the handicap hurdle, I saw him standing just inside the entrance to the weighing room. He touched his hat brim and I nodded acknowledgment. On the way to the paddock, I slowed as I approached him, but he frowned and said, 'Keep walking. I'll meet you in the car after your last ride.'

My mind was not on the job. The south coast was ten miles distant and I could smell the sea in the cold wind, as I crouched sheltering on a tough old bay gelding called Supermaster, his mane flowing and swirling, and me wishing I could climb into it and get warm and get away from the bloody world for a while. And he won. With little assistance from me, powering clear from horses he'd raced against season after season, many of them getting their turn at least once a year if the handicapper took pity and reduced their mark enough.

It remained a small wonder to me that many veteran jumpers had an uncannily exact level at which they could win. Each was given a handicap rating which was reconsidered after each run. A horse who won when rated 115 might be raised to 120 for winning. That meant he would have to carry five pounds more in his next race. Often, such a horse would not win again until his mark slipped back to 115. These animals weighed half a ton. They'd galloped hundreds of miles on Britain's tracks for years, yet a pound on their backs could make the difference between winning and losing.

Supermaster was my third and final mount of the day and I posed for pictures with the delighted owners, Jan and William Cuthbert, an aged couple who'd bred the horse and raised him and, I'd heard, sold their house so they could afford to keep him in training. Jan Cuthbert proudly held his reins with one hand and her pale blue hat with the other as the wind strengthened. Then she hugged me and gazed at me with such happiness in her wet eyes that I saw how she'd been as a young woman, and how age had done nothing to her spirit but strengthened it.

Her image stayed with me as I returned to the changing room under darkening skies. It reminded me why I'd come into this sport, this world of hope, this Never Never Land. Only optimists survive in racing, and that fact was exhibit A in the prosecution case against the suicide of Jimmy Sherrick. And Bayley Watt, and even Blane Kilberg.

Mac was in his BMW in the corner of the car park, his big face and brown wavy hair blurred by the steady rain on the windshield. The clouds sailing in from the coast now were big and dark. Lights were on in all the buildings. The wind carried parts of the final race commentary over the stands and into the car park as I approached Mac's car. He leant across and pushed open the passenger door. I got in and the wind slammed it shut.

'You're wet,' he said.

'Rain tends to do that to me.'

'You should get a hat.'

'Time enough for hats and slippers when I'm your age.'

'I could never see you in slippers, Eddie.'

'You're probably right. Riding boots and running shoes. Anyway, what do you know?'

Mac tried to turn toward me but his bulk made him grunt and he settled for lowering the arm rest and leaning on it. 'You said there were eight horses at Watt's yard. Our guys counted seven.'

I'd have bet my life on knowing the one that had disappeared. But I was in a spot. Was there any advantage in not telling Mac about the ringer scam? The removal of Fruitless Spin or whatever that good horse was, had just sent a spool of information at me. The horse had been taken by whoever was running the racket. He'd done it or arranged in the short time between Kilberg dying and the cops getting there. Or had the horse already gone when Bayley sent his email?

That was another thing…three men commit suicide, supposedly. None leaves a written note. All 'communications' about the deaths are electronic.

I recalled Mave's warning about how smart this guy was. Smart enough to persuade three people to kill themselves? Or was he giving them the cyanide himself? Had he been on that ferry with Bayley Watt? Was Watt supposed to meet him there and try and plan a way out? Had the horse been taken to move him to another trainer and carry on the swindle?

'Eddie?'

Mac was watching me while I tried to process all this and decide whether to tell him everything. What had I to lose?

For once in his life, he didn't interrupt me. But as he listened, those facial giveaways I'd become so familiar with worked through their repertoire; closed eyes, chin droops, head shakes. The audio kicked in at the end with a deep sigh. 'Who else knows?'

'The cops,' I said.

'Jockeys?'

'No. It would have been mentioned.'

'Do you think the bookies suspect Watt was running ringers?'

'I'm pretty sure they don't.'

Mac nodded. He knew of my friendship with Gerry Waldron, the PR rep for the biggest bookmaker.

'You won't be able to keep this quiet, Mac. The cops have nothing. They'll be appealing to the public etcetera, etcetera.'

'I can probably wrangle a week or two out of it. I know a superintendent at Thames Valley quite well.'

'But can you find who's behind it in a week or two?'

'We can try.'

'*We* being?'

He pushed his hair back. 'Come on, Eddie. You've been in the thick of it, and that's where you're happiest.'

'Maybe. But I haven't the faintest idea who's behind this and I've even less of an idea of where to start trying to find out.'

'Is Mister Sherrick still wearing the bugged watch?'

'It doesn't matter now, does it? The horse has bolted. The horse. Literally. All I had was Watt and Kilberg. I thought they were running this between them. Whoever the top man is, Watt was shit scared of him.'

'Has Watt's autopsy been done?'

'I doubt it. He's dead less than forty eight hours.'

'I'll go and see Sara Chase in the morning.'

'Who's she when she's at home?'

'Superintendent at Thames Valley. Nice woman.'

'Appropriate name.'

He smiled. 'It'll be a while since Sara chased anyone down a street.'

'Let's see how she does in blind alleys.'

Mac flipped his wipers on and they opened the watery curtains for long enough to let us see the crowds hurrying out, many making for the train station next to the racetrack. He turned to me: 'What's your next move?'

'I'm going to try to find out the identity of the missing horse.'

'How?'

'I haven't worked that out yet. Can I take it you'll be putting your resources at my disposal with your usual generosity?'

'Softly, softly. Through me only.'

'I never talk to the monkey when I can reach the organ grinder, Mac.'

'Does anybody?'

'True. Anything else?'

'Nope. Just call me when you've got something.'

'I will. Listen, ask Sara Chase for a copy of the files on Jimmy and Watt and Kilberg.'

He nodded. 'Okay.'

'That was easier than I thought.'

'I know her well.'

'Do I detect a tone of romantic longing there, Mister McCarthy?'

He smiled slowly and laid his head back on the rest, the courtesy light reflecting in his eyes as I opened the door. 'I'm a happily married man, Mister Malloy.'

'I never doubted it. No harm in dreaming. Many folk get by on dreams.'

'You being dreamer-in-chief.'

'That's me, Mac. See ya.'

TWENTY-NINE

On the stroke of midnight I pinged Maven Judge and saw the lamplight on her left jawbone, sharp as a shelf below sunken cheeks. Her eyes, as ever, were on her screen, fingers rattling the keyboard. 'Edward. What ails you?'

'Where should I start?'

'Anywhere. It needn't be the beginning. I can usually piece together your ramblings.'

'Your brain being fresh at the start of another working day?'

'The dead of midnight is the noon of thought.'

'Shakespeare?'

'Anna Letitia Barbauld. Had there been a Cheltenham Festival in 1825, she'd have died the week before it.'

'An interesting piece of trivia.'

'It might be trivial to you, my friend, not to me. The woman was inspiring. "The most characteristic mark of a great mind is to choose some one important object, and pursue it for life."'

'Like a betting software programme.'

'Correct.'

'Good. I could use some help from your great mind and from your programme.'

'Shoot.'

'How far back does your video archive go?'

'Seven years three months.'

'Could some software be written to trawl all those races for the identity of a horse, on looks alone?'

'Possible, but it would take a long time.'

'How long?'

'A year. Maybe longer.'

'What about by winner only. By clear winner only.'

'You'd be as well doing a form book search with the term 'drew clear' and checking by eye. I assume it's this hurdler you rode for Watt?'

I told her about Kilberg and the horse going missing. She said, 'Well restricting it to hurdlers, and assuming the horse is no older than four, maybe five, my guess is there will be fewer than a hundred races involved, and you'd probably only need to watch the finish of each.'

'Could you run that query for me tonight?'

'What's the name of the horse you rode?'

'It doesn't matter, does it? It was a false name.'

'But you'll want the video clip of that finish for comparison with the others.'

'Duh! of course. It was at Taunton, he was called Spiritless Fun. He came out at Warwick the week after and won as Fissure Splint.'

'Anagram. Your man has a sense of humour. Running a ringer and he names it with the same letters.'

'Mave, you could shave with the edge of your brain.'

'You trying to say I should start shaving?' She rubbed her jaw and stroked her top lip.

I laughed. 'I meant, I could shave with the edge of your brain. Fruitless Spin. That fits too, doesn't it?'

'It does.'

'That was Watt's star performer for Jimmy Sherrick. The busiest guy in the yard must have been Blane Kilberg moving microchips in and out of this horse.'

I gazed at Mave in admiration. Not once had her keyboard gone silent. She processed multiple streams of thought without pause or glance at her webcam. A very unusual woman.

'You could have half a chance now, you know,' she said. 'Your man obviously thinks he's much cleverer than anyone else, to take the chance of using anagrams. Complacency. Never a good idea. I'd have bet against you up to this point, but you just might have a squeak. You got that email?'

I clicked. The list of winners of hurdle races in the past two seasons who'd earned the comment 'drew clear' in the official form book totalled 77. Every name was there. 'Thanks, Mave.'

'Scroll down. You'll find a link to my video vault. Search by name and date. Happy viewing.'

'Okay to ping you if I need anything else?'

'Ping away, my friend, ping away.'

I made coffee and settled at my PC. My first choice was to discount everything but bays. Bay was his natural colour, that reddish-brown coat you see in so many horses, with black mane and tail. Adding the odd patch of white would be fairly simple. Changing the whole body colour would be a major challenge.

I reviewed my Taunton victory a few times, then his win at Warwick. Horses can be as distinctive as humans in the way they move. This one had the type of action not uncommon in classy horses in that he tracked very straight. His hind feet followed his front ones on a true path. Most horses have some small defect preventing them using all four limbs in the perfect fashion. The power from this one's hindquarters drove through straight, even limbs, wasting little energy. A true athlete.

There was nothing like him among the 77. I cleared quickly through the bays then, in frustration, watched all the winners. Nothing.

On my fourth coffee and my hundredth curse word, I took a break, and tried to figure out the next move.

There was the faintest chance he'd never raced before joining Bayley. Two things made that unlikely. To bet him with confidence, the man in charge would need to know the extent of his capabilities on the racecourse. Some horses seem champions at home, beating quality stablemates in a gallop, then, for whatever reason, they cannot reproduce the gallops form on course.

The second factor was that when I rode him, even cantering to the start at Taunton, he felt and acted like an experienced racehorse. Okay, he'd won before as Fruitless Spin under Jimmy, but a horse can show greenness in even its fourth or fifth run.

I doodled. Cash signs. Betting slips. How were they getting their money on? Gerry Waldron had said there were no unusual betting patterns on the Warwick or Taunton victories. He'd told me Bayley wasn't a gambler. That should have given me my first big clue that someone else was running this. But how was he making money?

Kilberg had said they'd made some money but not enough. But was he telling the truth or spinning the tale to go with his request for more time?

And where had the horse learned his trade?

Ireland?

All the races I'd watched were on British tracks. I knew Mave avoided Irish racing, claiming there were ten times the number of non triers there than at home. It wouldn't be that high, but the Irish stewards sometimes took a more relaxed view of horses who weren't putting in a hundred percent.

The clock chimed four.

I had plenty contacts in Ireland who might be able to highlight a very promising horse who'd stopped racing there in the past couple of seasons, but asking would mean drawing in more people. That would raise the risk of alerting this guy that I was on his trail.

Too tired to think straight, I laid down my pen and wandered off to bed. My last waking thought was about where Bayley had chosen to run to. Ireland.

THIRTY

I woke feeling hung over through lack of sleep and a gauntlet of bad dreams. It was Monday. I had no rides booked. I'd planned to drive to Stratford on the chance of landing a spare. But I lay dazed and troubled. Frustrated. Stratford could get by without me. I'd use the day to herd my thoughts and form some plans, to pick at my intuition and try to figure out which way it was pointing.

I had coffee and poached two eggs which bled yellow onto the plate. I mopped the yolk with half a dry pitta bread, chewing, chewing, chewing, and wondering how I would eat when I hung up my boots and stopped counting calories.

Twenty minutes later I slalomed on foot among the wet trees, running on auto, aware only of that rhythmical footfall that always helped calm me.

The oxygenated blood fed my brain and it began sorting through the options.

Three dead men. All supposed suicides. Jimmy's wasn't. How likely then that the others were? All three spun on the hub of terminal illness. Of the three, I knew where two bodies were. The next step had to be verifying the reason for suicide.

Showered, shaved and shivering after forcing myself to count out a minute standing underneath freezing jets of spray, I towelled myself dry and checked my watch. I considered calling the sergeant. I wanted the autopsies on Kilberg and Watt to include a check for liver disease and leukaemia respectively. But the sergeant would be too low down the pecking order to organize that. I wondered if McCarthy could swing it with his friend the superintendent.

I phoned him and asked and he said it was a good idea and he'd go and see Sara Chase about it. 'Mac, you've become so amenable, especially when Sara Chase is mentioned.'

'Eddie, you're pushing your luck.'

'I'm kidding.'

'Don't kid. Rumours are easy to start.'

'Mac, I'm kidding you, okay? You know that. Take it easy.'

I hung up wondering at his sensitivity to Ms Chase. Or was it Mrs? Mac would be no more likely to have an affair than the pope. He'd be the type for a late crush on somebody though. I smiled at the thought and wondered what Sara Chase looked like.

I considered calling Mister Sherrick to ask about Jimmy's medical history. But I remembered the care we had to take because of the bugged watch he still wore. Sergeant Middleton's idea, and I hadn't questioned it. Until now.

What was the point of him wearing the watch? It had brought us no benefit. Mave was confident that the bug in it would be transmitting recordings through a maze of hijacked PCs. The cops weren't willing to put a trace on the transmitter in case it alerted Mister Big that they'd discovered the bug.

But our man would have sussed things by now. He was bugging Mister Sherrick, and he'd bugged Jimmy. Surely Watt and Kilberg were being listened to as well? I'd mentioned Mister Sherrick's watch to both of them. So this guy would have heard me, and that made it pointless for Mister Sherrick to continue wearing the watch.

All it would have been transmitting since the bug had been discovered was bland stuff and long silences. Maybe it was time to try and stir up some action.

I typed a note then drove to Mister Sherrick's flat. He opened the door and looked at me then at the watch. He seemed confused and anxious. I put a reassuring hand on his shoulder and gave him the note, saying loudly, 'Mister Sherrick, I'm really sorry, can I use your toilet? Caught short and couldn't quite make it home.'

'Sure, of course. Come in. You know where it is, don't you?'

I went down the hall and opened and closed the toilet door, watching as he read the note. He raised his thumb. I waited a minute then quietly opened the door again, closed it, flushed the toilet, washed my hands and came out as Mister Sherrick was filling the kettle.

I stood with him in the kitchen, small talking for a minute then said, 'Listen, not much point in you wearing that watch anymore.' He slid the watch off and handed it to me as I'd asked him to do in the note. I said, 'Watt and Kilberg were bugged too, although not with watches. He did it with…' I took the lid off the boiling kettle and dropped the watch in. Mister Sherrick smiled.

We made do without tea, leaving the kettle to boil the watch, and we sat by the fire. Mister Sherrick nodded toward the kitchen, 'I bet you didn't clear that with the sergeant?'

I smiled. 'You know me too well. He's got some sidekick now with OCD. It would have taken them six months to approve "Removal of watch, 1, stainless steel, owner Mister James Sherrick senior." Better this way. And quicker. It'll leave our man wondering if we really have found out how he bugged the others.'

'And have you?'

'Nope. Not yet. But I will.'

'I believe you.'

'Good. It must have been pretty miserable having to wear it knowing this guy could hear everything, everywhere. I should have thought of that at the start and not let the cops bully you into it.'

'Well, I'm not sorry to be rid of it, Eddie, although as you get older you find you can adjust to pretty much anything, except, as the man wisely said, a nail in your shoe. So after a day or two I kind of adjusted, I suppose.'

'Well, you're rid of it now.'

'What'll I tell the sergeant?'

'I'll tell him. I'll take it with me. I'll tell him the truth, that I dropped it in the kettle. Accidentally, of course.'

'I guess they got nothing from those pictures they took of it to try and trace where it was bought?'

'Not that I heard of. They might not even have started yet.'

'What about you? Isn't it time to pack this in and get on with your riding career?'

'Not yet. And I don't have a career anymore. Not really. I've got a job I like doing. Careers are for people with a chance of moving upward. I'll be happy to tread water until my muscles or bones or whatever goes first finally give out.'

He nodded in that wise way men his age are entitled to nod, and said, 'You've never been one for treading water, Eddie, never will be. You just need the right horse to come along.'

I thought back to the turmoil Watt's horse had caused in me when I won on him at Taunton. My Mister Hyde leapt from the cupboard that day and kicked Doctor Jekyll aside, just as the old doc was growing comfortable in my skin. And I knew Mister Sherrick was right. The craving returned, and I wondered where the hell that horse had gone and what his name was.

THIRTY-ONE

It was a ten minute drive from Mister Sherrick's to Watt's yard. I could spend half an hour wandering around there on my own. I called McCarthy. 'Mac, what happened with Watt's horses, have they been moved somewhere?'

'Hold on.' He half covered the mouthpiece but I heard him yelling a name. He came back on. 'Eddie, I'm seeing the superintendent in the morning.'

'Good. Will you ask her if they ever got anything from trying to trace where Mister Sherrick's watch came from?'

'The watch you told me was bugged?'

'That's the one. I'm about to call the sergeant and tell him the bug's not working anymore.'

'How do you know?'

'I dropped it in boiling water. By accident.'

'The bug?'

'The watch.'

'By accident?'

'Correct.'

'Hold on.'

I held. He came back. 'Watt's horses have been collected by the RSPCA.'

'What are they going to do with them?'

'Look after them, I hope.'

'What about your guys? The BHA, don't they have arrangements in place for when stuff like this happens?'

141

'No. We have arrangements in place to prevent stuff like this happening, but Watt lied in his application. For eight horses he's supposed to have a minimum of two stable staff and one person responsible in his absence.'

'Who did he name on the application?'

'The responsible person in his absence was Blane Kilberg.'

'Since when?'

'Hold on…since August first last year.'

'Right.'

'Is there anything else?'

'Just let me know what the superintendent says about those autopsies. And the bugged watch.'

'Leave it with me.'

The sun was low when I pulled into Watt's place. I walked round the back into the quadrangle of the main yard. Sixteen empty boxes, half-doors still open on those that had been occupied. When there had been horses in the yard, I had never noticed the eight empty boxes.

Old lights were secured by rusting bolts in the sandstone between each box. I counted nine which worked, leaking weak light through thick casings. They'd be burning power for nothing now. Open boxes. Four windows in the redbrick wall of Watt's house which formed the southern section of the quadrangle. Unprotected windows awaiting vandals. I'd better have a word with the sergeant about getting the property boarded up.

The last of the sun glinted on something high up. A chimney stood at the far end of the building, on the eastern corner. At the top of it was what looked like a CCTV camera with a lens pointing into the yard. I went to the front where I could look almost straight up at the chimney. Another lens covered the drive and approach road. When had that been installed? Where was it recording to?

A square of thick glass was set into the entry door, moulded in four triangular sections and swelling out into a small globe. I went up the step to try and peer through it. I held onto the door handle. It turned. Open. I hesitated, wary. Whoever had come for that horse might have been in the house. Might still be in the house.

But why? What would the point be? The door had been left unlocked because the only two men with keys were dead.

The first thing I checked was Watt's PC. It was still in place. We already had all the data from it. I wandered around hoping to find something I didn't know I was looking for, some clue. What the hell did a clue look like, especially when you'd no idea what the crime was, what puzzle you were trying to figure out.

I went upstairs. I thought back to the night I was parked along the road talking to Gerry Waldron on the phone when I'd seen Blane Kilberg prowling around a bedroom. That had been on the western side of the property. I walked along the hall to the room. No bed. No furniture. No carpet. It smelled damp. In the corner stood a set of stepladders and a pile of rolled up dust sheets. I opened the dust sheets. All that clung to them were paint blotches and small mounds of plaster.

What could Kilberg have wanted in this room? Or had there been something here then that had been taken out? I opened the door of a cupboard: five shelves, all bare. On the floor, sitting on a small rug was a pair of silver dumbbells. I picked them up. Was Kilberg using this room as a gym?

I went back along the hall to the eastern wall, passing three other doors. The door of the room on the corner, the one which would sit below the chimney, was standing open. The brass lock housing from the door frame lay on the bare floorboards. I looked at the gouged wood; three screws stuck out. In the corner, an electric fire had been hauled from the wall. I crouched beside it. Five cables hung from the chimney void into the old fireplace, the stripped wire at their ends still bright. I took a picture with my phone of the hanging cables which had, I assumed, been feeding the CCTV footage into whatever machine had been there.

That told me I needn't spend any more time searching the house. Whoever had taken the horse had taken the evidence with him. And what else had been on there?

In the car I called Sergeant Middleton and told him Watt's property was open to vandals and anyone else who happened along.

I sensed he was about to ask what I'd been doing there and then thought better of it. No point in getting all formal about someone who was on your side. He said he'd see what he could do about securing it.

'Do you think there'll be a problem getting it boarded up?'

'Well, it's not a police matter, really. We don't own it.'

'It's a crime scene, isn't it?'

'In what way?'

'Didn't Kilberg die there?'

'Suicide.'

'Didn't you tell me all suicides are treated as suspicious?'

He sighed. 'I did.'

'Also, Kilberg claimed suicide. We know different.'

'You know different, Mister Malloy, or you think you do. You can't prove it.'

'Sergeant, you've got three dead men since Christmas, all relatively young. Correction one dead man you don't have is Jimmy Sherrick because you've no idea where his body is. Come to think of it, there's every chance your two most recent corpses could have told you where Jimmy is, but it's a bit late to be asking them any questions. Kilberg is-'

'I'm aware of all the arguments, Eddie, and I'm not saying I disagree with you, but at my level you have to deal with red tape, much as I'd like not to. Now, I'll try and get something done to secure the house. I'll speak to Watt's solicitor in the morning.'

'If you knew for sure it was a crime scene, would that help?'

'Yes.'

'Well somebody stole a horse.' I told him about Fruitless Spin, then added the fact that Watt had assaulted me with a wok. I was tempted to throw in the most obvious one, that Watt had been running a major fraud with the ringer scam. But bringing that up might compromise Mac and the BHA. I knew that keeping the scam quiet was top of his agenda with Sara Chase next day.

'Leave it with me. Please.'

'Sergeant, before you go, I had bit of an accident today with Mister Sherrick's watch.'

'The bugged watch?'

'I'm afraid it's now a boiled bugged watch. I dropped it into some very hot water. Clumsy of me.'

'Where is it now?'

'In a drawer in my kitchen drying out.'

'I'll call by and see Mister Sherrick tomorrow.'

'You don't seem too upset.'

'The benefits of using it were questionable.'

'Did your guys do anything to try and track down where it was bought?'

'I would need to check the progress on that.'

'I'd best let you get on then.'

'Eddie…there are other things going on that we need to deal with, you know. I appreciate how frustrating it must be for Mister Sherrick, I really do.'

'Tell him that tomorrow. And come and take the watch into custody. It won't ask for a lawyer, and it'll do its time without complaint. Should make a nice change for you guys.'

THIRTY-TWO

As midnight rolled us into Tuesday, Maven Judge was examining the picture I'd taken at Watt's of the cable ends dangling in the fireplace.

'Quality stuff, Eddie. Not a cheap system, going by the cables alone.'

'Were they connected to a laptop or a PC?'

'Just a hard drive. A big hard drive that would be programmed to record to its capacity then start recording over the oldest files.'

'What if you needed to see the oldest files?'

'Well, we're talking weeks here, maybe even months, before it would delete. He'd be reviewing it before that and saving anything he needed. Email me that pic, will you? I want to take a closer look on my screen.'

I mailed the picture.

'Give me a minute,' Mave said.

'What do you think you've got?' I could see her leaning forward. 'Maven Judge, you're screwing your eyes up. You need glasses, my friend.'

'Eyes like a shithouse rat, me...listen...I can see the supplier's name on the cable. They're the best in the business and, if I'm not mistaken...' She keyed quickly and leaned back, clicking her mouse three times, '...they offer free backup for the first year for all files.'

'You think they have a copy of all the footage from Watt's camera?'

She was clicking rapidly. 'I think, I think, I think...yep, free backup is automatic. Watt would need to have opted out rather than in to reject it.'

'Backed up to where?'

'The company's servers.'

'The site you're looking at now?'

'Keeerect, my friend, and I anticipate your next question. Yes, I probably could get in, though I don't know how long a job it would be. A warrant from your sergeant buddy might be quicker.'

'Only if it's going to take you the rest of the year to crack their system.'

'Let me have a nose around tonight.'

'Thanks. I appreciate it.'

'Sure you do.'

'Mave. *Mave...*'

She stopped typing and turned her plain, gaunt face to the webcam. I'd rarely seen her express emotion. Her brown eyes always had a guarded look, as though she was constantly assessing whatever she was seeing. A handful of times I'd broken through with a wisecrack that had made her expose those crooked teeth in a smile, giving me a ridiculous feeling of accomplishment, almost like riding a winner. 'Listen,' I said, 'I am really grateful to you. I'm not just saying it. You ask nothing in return for the favours you do.'

'Oh, don't go all soppy on me, for God's sake. You're an investment for me. I'm looking after that investment, despite its propensity to dash around on a white charger. You were born in the wrong century, Eddie. You should have been on earth when there were dragons to slay and maidens to rescue.'

'An investment, eh? There was me thinking I was your friend.'

'Never contract friendship with a man that is not better than thyself. And I'm still waiting.'

'Sayeth who?'

'Sayeth me for the second part and sayeth Confucius, the first.'

'You're a big softy, really, Mave. Thou shalt blubber at my grave, I do not doubt.'

'Any blubbering from me at your grave will be no louder than it would for watching a casket of banknotes being lowered into a furnace.'

'Well, at least I'm precious to you all the same.'

'You are. You are. Now go away and let me get on with this.'

'Ping me if you find anything on that CCTV footage.'

'I will take great pleasure in waking you up.' She moved her hand toward the webcam until it took up my whole screen, then fanned her fingers in a goodbye wave and closed the connection.

THIRTY-THREE

On the way to ride at Warwick on Tuesday, I left a message on Peter McCarthy's voice mail. I needed to drag him deeper into this and the lure was his fear of the ringer scam reaching the media. Racing depends on income from betting. If punters lost faith in the BHA, and in Mac's department in particular, the sport was in big trouble.

Punters didn't mind a degree of skulduggery. Many clung to it as a ready-made excuse for their poor judgement. What chance did they have with their money and hard-won knowledge of the formbook if trainers and jockeys were pulling stunts?

But most of those stunts were limited to running a horse over the wrong trip or on ground it didn't like or when it wasn't quite fit. Little tricks to try and get its handicap mark down and its odds up. That was 'fair cheating' in the eyes of the punter. But if news broke that one horse was running in the name of another, and a good horse at that, then the game changed. When somebody writes a horse's name on a betting slip and stops to question if it might not be the horse whose form figures he's based his assessment on, then racing will be on its way out.

Mac must have got the message in more ways than one. Rather than return my call, he came to Warwick. I saw him walk past the paddock as I went out on a leggy chestnut to ride in the handicap chase. He raised a hand, but kept walking, miming the turning of a steering wheel. He wanted to meet me in the car after racing. I nodded and he hurried off toward the weighing room.

Brawny Rogue carried me and sixteen pounds of lead plates to the start. He'd been allotted eleven stones five pounds in this three mile race and had eight opponents. His handicap mark allowed me the luxury of two layers of thermal underwear next to my skin. A canter to the start in mid-January was often driven by wishes of getting there as close to the off time as possible to save circling in the teeth of the wind.

Once racing, as thigh muscles contracted and pumped and arms and shoulders and back flexed and warmed, you could begin to enjoy it. But the pre-race minutes were cold ones, more so for those on the long shots, the hopeless cases. Anticipation of a winner was a fine warmer, and I was on the favourite.

Brawny Rogue was an old hand. Good in some ways - he was a reliable jumper and knew his job - bad in other ways as he'd become an idler. Once he reached the front of the pack, he believed he'd done enough and would prick his ears and down tools. He needed kidding along through the race then an urgent message late on that he'd better get cracking if he was to pass the post in front.

I enjoyed riding Warwick. It was a much trickier jumping test than it looked. The fences were far from frightening to look at. But a row of five of those black birch jumps came pretty close together down the back straight, often catching horses out. Most tracks had a reasonably spaced run between fences, and horses grew used to that, to jumping and settling down to gallop for a while before preparing again for take-off. At courses like Warwick and Sandown, they had to adjust their thinking and timing.

Some horses enjoy measuring their approach to a fence, but many rely on the rider to count them in and ask them to rise on the correct stride. A horse with no confidence in himself must have confidence in his rider or he will end up in the mud, the air whooshing from his huge lungs as his half ton body meets the planet. Welcome to earth.

And in the race, we lost three to those five jumps on the second circuit. Mine found himself having to jump a fallen horse just after landing, and that lit him up, scared him into acceleration to try and escape this melee and reach the safety of the front, of the clear view and open air.

But he was determined to make his move four fences too soon, and thus began the mind games. His instinct was saying let's get out of here. I was trying to send him a telegram down the reins saying take it easy, big fella, no need to panic. All is well. They were only kidding you, messing around. You know the score, steady up, plenty time. But he wasn't quite sure I was telling the truth and he quickened again going into the third last, and I decided to do the opposite of what I usually aim to do, which is to fly the fence and land running. If I did that here, there might be no holding and he'd pass the four horses ahead then chuck it.

He had a tendency to go slightly left approaching each fence, and half a dozen strides out, I hauled him to the right and he hesitated and thought about it and took the extra stride I'd hoped for, and put in a short one, almost hopping the fence rather than flying it. He landed awkwardly and by the time he'd collected his senses, the speed and the fizz had gone from him and I was in control again.

I nursed him over the last two fences, landing three lengths behind two bays battling up the run-in, and I eased him out and onward and gave him a couple of quick slaps with the whip and his ears flicked toward me as if to ask why I couldn't make up my mind whether I wanted him to speed up or slow down and I gave him another across his flanks to settle the argument.

We passed the tussling pair of bays and won by a neck.

As we walked into the winner's enclosure, the applause was warm on this cold Tuesday at a small midlands track. Winning favourites are always popular. I undid the girth and slid the saddle, squeaking off his steaming back, talking as I did so, telling the trainer and owners, a small pub-based syndicate, how well he'd gone and what a reliable and consistent horse he was.

The excitement and celebrations of winning owners was something I never tired of seeing, especially with syndicates. There might be a dozen people sharing the costs and the ups and downs, but each thought of the horse as his or hers. One hatless dark haired girl whose warmth I envied in her white fake fur coat, put her arms round my neck and stood on her tiptoes to kiss me full on the lips…for quite a long time, and I found myself smiling and blushing to kindly jeers as I walked off to weigh in.

Mac was smiling too, watching from inside the weighing room as I approached, still feeling slightly bewildered at an intimate moment with a stranger in such a public place. 'You're crimson,' Mac said. 'I think she heated you up more than the ride did.'

I smiled and waved him away as I sat on the scales. 'Eleven five. Thanks, Eddie,' said the clerk of the scales. 'Thank you, Michael,' I said as I rose, only to feel Mac's hand on my shoulder, steering me into a corner, his six-two bulk in that long dark coat making him look like my bodyguard, or probation officer. I looked up at him. 'Don't you be thinking of kissing me, too.'

He screwed his face up. 'That's gross.'

'Gee, thanks.'

He'd turned me so my back met the corner of the room. He put a hand on each wall, his coat opening so that anyone behind him wouldn't be able to see me. I waited. 'You don't have anything in the last two, do you?' he said.

'Not yet.'

'Will you give them a miss? There's somebody I want you to meet.'

'I might pick up a spare, Mac. Can't it wait until after racing?'

'She's a very busy woman who's broken an appointment to do me a favour. And Nic Buley will be there too.'

Buley was chief exec of the BHA. The fact that he often corrected people about the spelling of his first name told you pretty much all you needed to know about him. 'You lot must be running scared over this, Mac. What's happened?'

'Nothing. We've just decided to step this up a few gears and box it off before it gets out.'

I looked at him. 'Box it off? Mac, you've been spending too much time in Buley's office. Management speak comes from dickheads trying to fool people into believing they know what they're doing. Fucking hell, don't fall for that, please?'

'He's doing his best. He's sharp enough to realize how important this situation is.'

'Probably after you sat on his skinny gym-bunny ribs and rolled around a bit to persuade him.'

Mac, pushed his hat back and raised his eyebrows and smiled. 'Close. I must admit, You're close.'

I smiled. 'Okay. I'll leave after the fourth, but only on condition I hear no more bullshit management speak from you.'

'I'll try. It can be catching when everybody in the office is at it.'

'Catching like the black plague. Shun it, Mac. Resist. You're too old to be a clone, anyway.'

He lowered his arms and straightened and reached in his pocket to give me an envelope with an address scribbled on it. 'It's not far. Down by the river, tucked away in a cul-de-sac. I haven't got a postcode but call me when you leave. I'll talk you in.' He went to turn away. I grabbed his arm. 'Mac! Mac, don't *talk me in*, just give me directions, okay?'

He smiled. 'See you there.'

THIRTY-FOUR

The Old Barn was one of those big conversions some people gloried in. I didn't care for them, with their floor to ceiling plate glass, their atriums and their echoing vastness. It must be like living in an office block or a hotel foyer. Mac led me in to where a 'living flame' fire burned in a hearth that would have dominated my house. But in this cavernous room it looked as though someone had a struck a match and set it against the wall.

Our footsteps click-clacked off the oak as we approached a set of sofas laid out like a Tetris puzzle. Nic Buley and the woman I took to be Sara Chase were laughing together, not looking at us. Behind them through the cinema screen window, mist was rising from the river Avon at the foot of the long garden. A small yacht was moored there. Tiny lights on the boat, on its outside came on as dusk deepened. I took them to be some sort of parking or mooring lights.

We stopped in front of the seated pair. Still they didn't look up. Their shared joke was in the air, and I was already getting angry. Until recently, jockeys were treated by the racing establishment as little more than servants. In front of the stewards we used to be addressed by surname only and told to stand up straight. That had died out in the past few years, or at least I thought it had. I'd yet to be introduced and was already getting the impression they thought I was the butler or the coachman or something.

Mac said, 'This is Eddie Malloy. Eddie, this is Sara Chase, superintendent with Thames Valley police, and you know Nic Buley, don't you?'

'I don't believe we've met formally,' I said. Buley didn't get up. He reached a hand and touched mine, almost brushing it off. The woman's handshake was firmer. 'Hello,' she said, then turned back toward Buley.

'Hello to you,' I said, and she looked at me again, more keenly this time. Mac sensed the tension. 'Eddie was good enough to leave before racing finished to join us.' She nodded, still eying me. Buley stretched a flowing arm, 'Sit down, the pair of you.' It was more order than invitation. He was one of these professionally slim people who ate just enough to fuel their daily gym workouts and their sense of superiority. His dark suit was narrow-cut in case anyone might not have noticed how slim and fit he was. And he glowed. He glowed like he'd stepped from a shower and massage. His reddish hair was thinning, although he'd be mid-thirties at most.

'Do you want me to make tea, or fix you two some cold drinks or something before I sit?' I asked, glaring at them.

Buley didn't get it. He turned to the woman and raised an inquisitive eyebrow, 'Sara?'

She seemed amused. 'I think Mister Malloy was being, eh, satirical.'

Buley looked confused. 'Why? Were you?'

'Yes. I was.'

'Oh,' he straightened, angling his body away from the prim Sara Chase in her checkered cravat and uniform blouse. 'Take a seat,' he said.

'I'll sit when I'm ready.'

Mac deserted me and slunk off to sit on the edge of a pale green sofa.

Buley and Chase watched me now. Buley wasn't yet done with the Alpha Male stuff. 'What's the problem, Edward?'

'You're the problem. And don't call me Edward. It's Eddie, or Mister Malloy. Got that?'

He shifted in his seat and I could see him trying to weigh things up, but he was away from his office domain and the ranks of yes men, and I watched him puff himself up. 'Had a bad day at the races, I take it?'

'You take it wrong. My day was fine until I walked in here to be ignored by you and the superintendent. I'm not some lackey, summoned to speak when I'm spoken to. The indenture system in this country died out years ago. Has nobody told the BHA?'

'Well, I'm sorry you choose to adopt that attitude. I thought we could work together.' He joined his hands in a finger clench to reassure himself.

'Don't dig yourself deeper by patronizing me, Mister Buley. I'm not choosing any attitude. I was born with the inclination to resist being messed around by people who believe they're better than I am.'

'I don't think that at all. I find that most offensive.'

'Tough.'

Buley looked at McCarthy who looked at me. Sara Chase stood up. 'Mister Malloy, I apologize. It was rude of me to seem so distracted when you arrived. Mister Buley and I were sharing a joke at the expense of an old colleague, and I got a bit carried away.'

She was taller than she'd seemed sitting, which sounds daft, but she must have been long-legged and short-spined. Her brown hair was tied back and she had a deep fringe. The tops of her ears stuck out - only the tops - and were inclined slightly forward as though Darwinism had bred a race of professional listeners, and I wondered if she kept her hair behind them to make the most of her hearing power.

Her brown eyes were narrow. Her mouth smiled, but for all her professional effort at repairing the social damage, those eyes couldn't generate any warmth. The windows to the soul, right enough.

I nodded, the only response her 'apology' was worth, and she saw she hadn't won me over so she did what she must always have done, she reached and patted my shoulder, the smile now a dismissive one. And she sat again, but noticeably farther from Buley than when she'd risen.

I looked at Buley. He couldn't hold my stare and turned to Mac. 'Mister McCarthy, would you care to sum up where we are?'

Mac did a tiny eye and head shift, a plea for me to sit down and listen. To my left was a glass-topped round table with five chairs. I took the six strides away from their cozy gathering, took a chair, and spun it to face them. Mac told the story, glancing at times not at his boss, Buley, but at Sara Chase. For what, I wasn't sure;

approval, or encouragement perhaps. But none of what he said was news to me. Buley took over, leaning toward me, elbows on knees. 'We just wanted to give you the heads up first.'

The heads up. The fucking heads up. My most hated bite of management speak, and I had to swallow the curse and keep it down or I'd have strangled some plain English out of him.

He turned to Sara Chase and said, 'The police want us to make sure we have all our ducks in a row.'

Aw, Jeez! I was going to kill this guy. I stared at my shoes, composing myself, then looked at him. 'Three of your ducks are dead.'

'And that's why the police are going to be playing a bigger part from here on.'

'So what do you want from me?'

'We're keen to get maximum leverage from your involvement so far.'

I stared at him, trying to imagine what his poor wife had to put up with. God help his kids. I tried irony. 'Sweat the assets, eh?'

He beamed. 'Exactly!'

Sara Chase sat back, crossing her long legs, and settled linked hands in her lap. 'Who do you think might be behind this, Mister Malloy?'

'I don't know.'

'If I put a gun to your head - not that I would,' she smiled at the others. She'd used that line before. 'What would your best guess be as to the motive, here?'

'Money.'

Buley pitched in. 'We've spoken to all the major bookmakers. The biggest bet on any of Watt's ringers was fifty pounds, and that from an online customer they know well. A habitual loser.'

'What about the exchanges? Were others being laid in those races?'

'Nothing that was above the radar, and these guys have their radar set very low I can tell you.'

More bullshit. I turned back to Ms Chase. 'Have you anything on the origins of the bugged watch?'

'Not yet.'

'But you're looking?'

She watched me. I thought she was trying to decide if it was worth persevering with the sidesteps. 'I don't hold out much hope on that line,' she said.

Some straight talking at last. I nodded. 'What about Jimmy Sherrick's corpse?'

'Nothing.'

I was warming to her. 'Fingerprints in Jimmy's house, or on the chain?'

'No marks.'

'Watt's place? Kilberg's?'

'No indications they were involved in crime.'

'Autopsies?'

'Mister Watt's body will be flown home tomorrow. I'll make sure both autopsies are done by the end of the week. Did Peter tell you the outcome of the tests by Irish police on Mister Watt's corpse?'

No Mister McCarthy for her. No Mac. *Peter.* 'Not yet.' I said.

She looked to him, and Mac said, 'There was enough cyanide in his system to kill ten men.'

'As per his supposed suicide message by email,' I said.

'Why do you say "supposed"?' Sara Chase asked.

'Because I don't think he sent it. And I know Jimmy didn't make the message he was supposed to have left. And Kilberg's was by email too. Jimmy's meant to have ordered cyanide online, which he didn't... couldn't. Whoever's behind this had access to the PCs and phones of Jimmy and Watt and Kilberg. He could fake messages easily. And my bet is that he was there at each death, and he forced them to take the cyanide, then faked the notes. How many suicide notes are by email or voice recording? People just write them down with pen and paper, don't they? Or don't leave one at all.'

All three watched me. Now *I* felt superior. Sara Chase said, 'Bayley Watt killed himself. He took cyanide by his own hand. I'm not saying his mobile phone wasn't hacked, but he did commit suicide, for whatever reason.'

'How can you be certain about that?' I asked.

'Because the Irish Police had to break down the door of his cabin on the ferry. It was locked from the inside.'

THIRTY-FIVE

I drove home, helped by the arctic wind that had been forecast. I could feel it sweeping the car south almost as though it too was heading for Lambourn. It was. When I got out, long gusts swept through the woods, rattling the bare branches and making the limbs of the old trees groan. I had to lean against the car door to close it.

Even inside, behind the locked door, the house was surrounded by the groaning sounds of the forest resisting the wind. This little valley of mine became a whirlpool of air in times like these.

I switched on the lights in the Snug and watched what was left of the dead leaves of last summer come alive again, the sogginess they'd gathered being tumble dried or frozen stiff in the vortex of arctic blasts.

I boiled water for coffee. It had turned out a good day in the end. I'd come from that meeting with the promise of a direct line to Sara Chase. I wondered what it had cost Mac and that fool Buley to get her in on this personally. They'd been desperate for me to keep my mouth shut.

Racing looks a big industry from the outside, but it's a compressed hive of people who know each other, who are looking for a way to the top, or maybe just to stay alive. Gossip can mean more than simply today's main topic, it can mean someone is on the way down, or out and that his or her horses, are up for grabs among trainers, owners and jockeys.

Racing is a huge family that supports its members, celebrates with them and sometimes mourns. But there are many egos, much greed and envy and in-fighting. The one enemy many were ready to rally against was the ruling body, the British Horseracing Authority. It was rare to meet anyone who didn't believe they could do a better job running racing than the BHA did.

And now that I'd spent an hour in Buley's company, I realized a monkey could do a better job. He'd been in the post less than a year having come from some government position associated with the success of the London Olympics. But he was a bullshitter to anyone who wasn't smitten with the King's New Clothes syndrome.

All his Let's Do It! Bollocks had permeated the BHA. His public statements were littered with buzzwords and choked by long sentences which meant nothing. And apart from all that, he had proved to me within a minute of being in his company that he regarded most of his fellow human beings as lesser creatures. I hated that.

If it hadn't have been for Jimmy Sherrick and his father, I'd have walked from that meeting promising nothing. What did I care about Watt or Kilberg, or Buley's reputation?

But I cared about Jimmy and his memory, and his father. So I traded silence for some power; a direct line to Sara Chase. She was a tough woman, but she was practical and ultra-political.

I looked again at the swirling leaves. If wind behaved like water, so did Sara Chase, she flowed with the terrain until she reached a position of strength. And now she was flowing with me. I didn't know why and I didn't much care. Perhaps Buley still had friends in the House who could help advance her career.

I sipped black coffee and went to my PC. Buley couldn't be altogether stupid. He was the type to tell jockeys to do something, not bargain with them. But Mac knew me as well as anyone did, and I smiled as I pictured him pleading with Buley not to try and bully me. It had taken Buley less than five minutes to discover that Mac had been dead right.

I sat at my desk and hit the link to Maven Judge, and she raised a thumb to the webcam and pushed it right up close.

'A big fat thumbs up welcome from me to you, Mister Malloy. I hear you are getting a blast from the North Country.'

'There'll be trees down in the morning.'

'A taste of reality for you soft southerners.'

'I love wild weather, Mave, makes me feel alive.'

'A rare sensation in the valley of the dead, my friend. In fact, someone ought to change that road sign outside Lambourn from The Valley of the Racehorse to the valley of the dead. Any more corpses to report?'

'None. Three's enough. What do you know?'

'I know that many hours of footage from Watt's CCTV cameras awaits your perusal. Doubtless ninety percent of it will be of trees and fields and weather, empty of villains, free of humans of any sort.'

'Have you watched much of it?'

'Five minutes. The most my boredom levels can stand. Seriously, if you intend sitting through this, even on fast forward, you will develop the mental equivalent of pins and needles.'

'Is it all time stamped? I mean obviously time stamped. I don't need to toggle things on and off?'

'Date and time are there on the screen.'

'The first thing I'll check is the night I visited, the night Watt did a runner.'

'You won't, I'm afraid. The system was switched off a week ago today at thirty eight minutes past seven in the evening. There's not a second of footage after that.'

'January eighth.' I counted back the days.

'Eddie, are you okay? Your face has gone that awful contorted way it does when you try to think. I've warned you about overtaxing a very weak organ.'

I smiled at Mave, and she looked away from her screen, directly at her webcam and smiled back warmly. 'Mave, I've got to make a call. Do you want to hold a minute or will I ping you back.'

'I'll hold. I love to hear the rusty cranking of your brain and I can see it is trying to grind something out.'

I phoned Mister Sherrick and asked him if he could recall exactly the day he'd told me the police had contacted him for permission to exhume Jimmy's body. He confirmed what I had thought: January eighth. I told him I'd had a meeting with the police and was trying to help them double-check all their details. I tried to keep the excitement from my voice.

I hung up and Mave turned again to the webcam and raised an eyebrow.

I said, 'Could the CCTV have been switched off remotely, or would Bayley Watt have to have done it?'

'Either.'

'Had it been off at any point before the eighth?'

'No. It was installed and fired up on August eighteenth last year and ran non-stop until a week ago.'

'A stupid question, but just to check, it recorded at night, too?'

'Crisp and clear.'

'I don't suppose you'd like to get the next train down here and help me start digging in Watt's fields for Jimmy Sherrick's body?'

THIRTY-SIX

Next morning the air was still. The winds had moved south, leaving behind downed trees, broken power lines and the sorrowful family of a young girl who had died on the south coast. I switched off the car radio and drove on to Ben Tylutki's to fulfil a promise to ride out.

From Ben's I'd drive the seven miles to Grenville Tarrant's to ride out third lot there. This was the dawn merry-go-round for so many jockeys seeking rides. Helping at morning exercise was an unpaid job. We did it in the hope of getting a call up, a favour returned if a jockey was needed, hopefully in that elusive big Saturday race.

There had been times, long past, when trainers called me, or my agent. Days when I had my pick without having to hurry from yard to yard like some salesman hawking invisible wares. But those days were long gone and, more sadly, had been unappreciated by me, a youth who thought it all came with the talent I had, and that it would last forever.

But there were millions with worse commutes to work. In Lambourn, getting from one trainer to the next is often no more than a matter of walking across the road. Planning laws keep the village looking much as it did in the eighteenth century, when the first trainers moved in. The downs above the village had never been ploughed, as the soil was too poor for agriculture. But the springy turf was easy on the legs of racehorses, and the sloping land rising from the River Lambourn ideal for fitness training.

I remembered my first time on Mandown gallops, looking around wondering where JRR Tolkien had sat with his family and his picnics. What part had this land played in his fiction? And what of the fiction of Bayley Watt and Blane Kilberg? Who or what had driven their lies and their actions, and what was I to do to get Bayley's property checked for the corpse of Jimmy Sherrick?

I could ring Sara Chase, or Mac and ask them to send a team of diggers out there, but how was I to justify it? I couldn't tell them a friend had hacked into the database of a major so-called security company. And even if I persuaded them to dig up an acre, was my hunch right? Had those cameras been switched off so Watt and Kilberg could drag Jimmy's body from a van or a horsebox to bury it again somewhere on his land?

It would have made sense to them to bring a stolen corpse to somewhere they knew they wouldn't be disturbed. Lord knows, there were thousands of acres of countryside and woods around here, but nowhere you could stop with the certainty of privacy, and begin digging. A grave of any depth would take hours to complete, and neither Watt nor Kilberg were hardened to manual work beyond mucking out a box.

As I drove northeast toward Wantage and Grenville Tarrant's place, I pictured Bayley's land and tried to estimate the acreage he'd have secure access to. He didn't need to own it all, but I thought of that snowy day we'd ridden to the Ridgeway, across what seemed a wilderness of white. Bayley would have been intimately familiar with much of that land. Jimmy could be anywhere. I ditched the idea that had been growing that I could walk the area or ride it, quartering it like a gun dog, looking for ground recently disturbed.

But if Watt planned a burial away out in that open country, why switch off the cameras? Their range would be limited to the confines of the house and yard. Was Jimmy's corpse hidden in the house, or the hay barn? Was there a cellar or an abandoned loft on his property? That would have been quickest and least messy; no hard dirty work.

The cold snap had been with us then. Digging through deep frost without a machine would have been close to impossible. They'd have managed it at the grave easily enough, given that the soil would barely have settled since the burial.

If I was right and Watt had stolen Jimmy's corpse, there had to be a strong chance it had been hidden on the property rather than buried. If that was the case, maybe I could find it myself.

The gossip at Grenville's was as it had been on Mandown gallops an hour before; the suicides of Watt and Kilberg. From stable lads and jockeys I'd heard theories about serious illness. Someone knew someone else who'd seen medical records or had spoken to a doctor involved. Cancer was mentioned a few times, and one of Grenville's grooms said she'd heard they both had Aids.

Given that Kilberg's email to the police claimed he'd done it because I'd been harassing him and Watt, nobody asked me about it. There was a chance it hadn't yet filtered into the gossip stream, but it was more likely that fingers were being pointed at me as I rode away.

From Grenville's yard, I drove to Ludlow where I rode a winner. On the way back, I decided to call in at Watt's in the hope it hadn't yet been boarded up.

It had been. Roughly, but effectively with wooden boards and padlocks the size of my fist. I'd need to ask for access or break in.

I could phone my new contact, Sara Chase, but she'd be wary, she'd want to do things by the book, especially given my bolshie attitude yesterday. Maybe I should ring Mac, let him do the explaining and cajoling.

Should I warn Mister Sherrick first? I didn't want to raise his hopes.

Raise his hopes.

Suddenly, it seemed an obscene expression. Raise hopes of finding the decomposing corpse of his son in an empty, shuttered house. That decided it for me. I'd keep it from him.

I'd be passing Mac's house on the journey, but he always seemed uncomfortable at the prospect of visitors. His wife, Jean, was agoraphobic. Maybe Mac felt her domain had to be protected. Anyway, I called him when I got home.

'Mac, can you ask Sara Chase to get a warrant, or whatever she needs to inspect Bayley Watt's property? I think Jimmy Sherrick's body might be hidden in there.'

'You think?'

'An educated hunch.'

'Who's the teacher?'

'A contact with the security company that ran Watt's CCTV system. It was switched off on the day Jimmy's corpse was stolen.'

'That could have been for any number of reasons.'

'Mac, I'm not going to debate it with you. What about all that cooperation I was promised, everything we talked about yesterday?'

'Eddie, how am I supposed to justify asking for a warrant here? On the basis of some hunch you have? What if that gets out to the press?'

'My hunch?'

'The bloody warrant!'

'Calm down, Mac. I was kidding.'

'You've got a macabre sense of humour.'

'That's one of the reasons I like talking to you Mac, I get to hear words like macabre. Look, cool it. I know you're under pressure, and I'm trying to help you here. Give me until tomorrow. I'll have a look around it again in daylight.'

'Eddie, don't be breaking in-'

'Mac! Just trust me, will you? Have I ever let you down?'

'Yes!.'

'Only for your own good.'

'Eddie, listen, just be prepared if anybody finds you snooping around Watt's place. No mentions of ringers or even of any of his horses,'

'I know, Mac, I know! Relax! You're coming close to pissing me right off now. There's an old man sitting alone in the middle of Lambourn who lost his son, remember? That's a hell of a lot more important to me than keeping Bayley Watt's business quiet. Remember that!'

'Okay. Okay. Fair enough.'

'One thing you can do for me, send me a copy of Watt's email to his solicitor.'

'I won't ask why you want it.'

'Good.'

The copy was in my Inbox ten minutes later.

The summary was that Watt had asked that the horses be allowed to complete the current season under Kilberg's care, for which Kilberg was to be paid fifty grand from his estate. He said that he hoped the BHA would look kindly on Kilberg's application for a trainer's licence as all prize money earned by the yard that season was to go to the Injured Jockeys Fund, as was the remainder of the funds from his estate after Kilberg had been paid.

I printed it and carried it to the kitchen where I read it twice more while waiting for the kettle to boil. Whoever had written it wanted Kilberg to be in charge of the horses. Plan A must have been to carry on the ringer scam if Kilberg could get his licence. When I had confronted Kilberg, with our man listening in somehow, he then decided Kilberg had to be taken out too. So long as he got the horse he'd know he could keep going. Lie low for a while, a year maybe, then start over with nobody any the wiser as to who he was.

Mave's early call that this guy was the real deal had proved spot on. Three men were dead. The horse that had got them killed had disappeared. No witnesses left alive. Not the faintest of tracks leading to this Mister Big. Nothing on Bayley's PC. Had he kept another one somewhere? What about Kilberg's belongings, his electronic paper trail?

I called Mac again and asked him to find out what the police had done about searching Kilberg's place, his stuff, for clues. He put up no resistance and said he'd come back to me soon.

THIRTY-SEVEN

I sipped black coffee and played around with Watt's email, the email someone had hacked into his phone and written, probably after Watt was dead. But how had this guy forced him to swallow a handful of cyanide in a locked cabin halfway across the Irish sea? Where was Watt heading for that night if not to meet the man who was bossing this? Was the guy based in Ireland?

Or was Watt running *from* him?

I tried Mave. It was dark outside, so there was half a chance she'd be around. She was.

'You're up early,' I said.

'Couldn't sleep for the noise of the wind sucking and spitting like it was trying to hawk up a gob of phlegm the size of the moon.'

'That's what coastal winds do, Mave. That's their job in winter. The price you pay for living on a cliff.'

'Yea, yea, yea. What do you want?'

I told her about yesterday's meeting and how Watt's place had been boarded up and that I thought Jimmy's body could be inside. I reminded her of her foresight when she'd predicted how smart this guy was and said, 'I'm convinced he hacked Watt's phone and sent that suicide note email, and that he did the same with Kilberg. By the way, I'm trying to get hold of Kilberg's PC for you to have a look at.'

'Oh, really? I can't wait!'

I smiled but she wasn't looking at me. 'Listen, Mave, could he have had some sort of remote control of Watt and Kilberg, and maybe even Jimmy? Could he have had them hypnotized or something, to react to a word or command or a certain sound from their phone?'

'Anything's possible. Some trigger for them to take a cyanide pill, you mean?'

'Yes. Why would Watt go on the run then suddenly change his mind? He was eccentric and moody but he wasn't a quitter. And Kilberg, he thought far too much of himself to just give it up out of the blue. He was a fair bit younger than Watt too. And Watt had just supposedly left him all his horses to train with the promise of fifty grand at the end of the season. No way did he kill himself deliberately.'

'But if your man had them pre-programmed somehow... hypnotism would have been very chancy. I'm no expert, but I'd have thought the effects would last hours at the most, not weeks or months.'

'What about these hypnotherapists who claim success with long term problems, smoking and weight loss and that sort of stuff?'

'That's just persuading people to change habits. But sending some keyword or sound where the subject drops everything and takes a pill that'll kill him, you're in the realms of fiction there, I think. Science fiction. Also, even if he had found a way to trigger that action, how could he be sure they'd be carrying the cyanide pill at the time?'

'True.'

'I wouldn't discount the claim about the serious illnesses, especially if you say you'd seen a few physical changes in Watt. This fella obviously had something on them too. The threat of exposing them, plus a reminder that they might not have had much longer to live anyway, could easily have been enough to push them into taking the pills.'

'You think he had something on them beyond their involvement in the ringer scam?'

'Well, how did he get them into that in the first place? And why? It doesn't look like it was doing them any good, because nobody was betting or laying, according to your contacts. In which case, why was your man doing it? It's a hell of an intricate plot if no money was being made, and the only way to make it was through betting. Could your bookie contact be wrong?'

'I doubt it. That's his job, or part of it, he'll have a string of contacts from Perth to Plumpton plus all that monitoring software they have online now. That would be set to pick up anything of any size, even if he was spreading the bets around different bookies.'

Mave glanced at her webcam, fingers still working that keyboard. 'What about bookies overseas?' she asked. 'Could he have been placing bets in the far east or somewhere like that?'

'I suppose he could. I could ask Gerry to take a look at that.'

'Your bookie man? His tentacles reach that far?'

'Gerry's made an awful lot of friends in his life.'

'A singular talent.'

'It is. I'll call him now.'

'You're on a roll here, Eddie, by the sound of it.'

'I want to find Jimmy. Soon. I want into that house.'

'Well, I'm here if you need anything.'

'Thanks, Mave. What I need is a break. Even finding Jimmy won't get me any closer to this guy.'

'Motive and relationship. The motive's got to be money. If this fella wasn't betting them, somebody else was. And what was his relationship with the dead men? If you can crack that, you're on your way.'

'You've changed your tune, Maven. You're usually trying to talk me out of it.'

'I've decided to stop wasting my time. The sooner you get this done, the better chance I have of getting you to concentrate on helping me.'

'So you're in with me?'

'Yep. I'm going to start my own little mind map tonight and see what I can come up with.'

'You serious?'

'Never more so. With a brain your size, you'll be at this for years. I'm going to let you hook it up to mine for a while.'

'Like giving me a jump start?'

'Well…sort of…a very low power one, toned right down, if you know what I mean. A straight feed from my brain to yours would fuse your box. Blow your mind.'

I smiled. 'I believe it would, Mave. I believe it very probably would.'

THIRTY-EIGHT

I sketched a rough picture of Bayley's house, ran through in my mind what I could recall of the interior, wondering where Jimmy's body might be hidden. Would Bayley have been able to sleep at night knowing the corpse of his stable jockey was under the same roof?

Somewhere in the outbuildings would make more sense. My PC beeped and I clicked the link to take Mave's call. Unusually, she was looking straight at me via her webcam. 'Did you tell me that Jimmy had the same watch as his father, the one that was bugged?'

'I think Bayley told Mister Sherrick that Jimmy had bought it for him for Christmas, but when we discovered it was bugged I just assumed that Watt had been lying and that he'd provided the watch through whoever is running this. Why? What are you thinking?'

'Jimmy was being bugged somehow. If they were using a watch for his dad, there's no reason they wouldn't try that with Jimmy, is there?'

'Why are you saying "they"? You think this is a gang?'

'No, *they* as in whoever's behind this plus Watt and Kilberg.'

'Oh, I thought you'd found something out. Yes, I suppose the bugged watch could have been used with Jimmy, why?'

'Because if there's a radio transmitter in it, it might still be broadcasting a signal.'

I dropped the pen and looked at Mave. 'How would we pick it up?'

'With a scanner. If you think Jimmy's body is at Watt's place, we take a scanner there and run a search.'

'We? As in you and me?'

'Don't you want my help?'

'Mave, I'd pay good money just to get you out of that cliff top eyrie for a day. If you're saying you'll travel down here to help me out, then there's nothing I'd appreciate more.'

'You're a right charmer, aren't you? I'll bet you run riot with women and you're one of these guys who doesn't like boasting about it.'

'Mave, the only woman I want to see at the moment is you.'

'Lord, you're a silver tongued devil, right enough.'

'Listen, you know I'd give pretty much anything for your help in this. Even if it's only with finding Jimmy. In fact, you might be right about the transmitter. Maybe that's why they wanted the body out of the way before the police exhumed it. If the cops traced the transmitter that could have led them to-'

'It wouldn't have led them anywhere, would it? They found the bug in Jimmy's dad's watch but it was untraceable.'

'So why was this guy worried about Jimmy being exhumed?'

'Exactly.'

I drew a watch on the page then tapped the pen against my teeth trying to remember if Jimmy wore a watch. I looked at Mave: 'You got a hunch as to why they wanted Jimmy's body out of the way?'

'Not yet, just a curiosity. It couldn't have been for the transmitter, if there was one buried with him. But something about Jimmy, even dead, has made this guy nervous enough to want to keep him away from the police.'

'Maybe it was Bayley and Kilberg. What if they'd left some sign, some mark or DNA tying them to Jimmy?'

'Maybe, but it's unlikely to have been anything Watt couldn't have explained away through his regular contact with him. You know, if they found a clipping from Watt's fingernail or whatever, Watt would have said, well I saw the guy every day, was legging him up on horses all the time, driving him around. No, it's something else. If I've got a hunch, it's that this guy has blundered somehow with Jimmy.'

'Even a tiny hunch is good enough for me, Mave.'

'As Quasimodo said when he was speed dating.'

I laughed, looking forward to having Mave and her razor wit staying with me for a while. 'So, when are you travelling, and how?'

'I'll get the kit together and book a train ticket. Can you pick me up from Newbury?'

'Sure will. I'll even paint the guest bedroom pink if you want.'

'Nah, the usual dust covered cobwebbed garrett will do for me.'

'Have you got a scanner?'

'I know a man who has.'

'One who doesn't ask many questions?'

'Unlike you, Edward, he doesn't ask any.'

THIRTY-NINE

I woke to what I'd decided was lucky Friday. I had three mounts booked at Newbury, my nearest track, and Mave's train was due at Newbury station half an hour after the last. Everything felt as though it was about to click into place.

Also, I was set to ride the hot favourite for Ben Tylutki in a valuable handicap hurdle. Ben led me out onto the track. Before letting go the reins he said, 'Let him get on with it in his own sweet way. With a bit of luck, you'll see nothing else.'

Ben's regime for his horses was tough. His belief was that if your horse was as fit as it could be, it could beat better horses that were less fit. It was a policy that had served him well and he was steadily attracting more owners.

He got horses hard fit and put up jockeys he trusted. Ben would say his granny could win on many of his horses so all he required was a rider who was straight and could point a horse in the right direction. No complicated tactics: "jump off in front and improve your position".

And that's exactly what I intended doing on Burbank, this bay gelding built more like a greyhound than a racehorse. We flew the first hurdle ahead of sixteen others, then it was simply a matter of relaxing and trusting the trainer's fitness regime. Aboard many horses I'd have judged this pace to be too fast to see out the two miles, and would have been fighting, trying to settle him, slow him down.

As with many of Ben's, he couldn't wait to reach the next jump, so I just perched above his withers and tried to look stylish and enjoy the ride. Ben trained his horses to gallop alone. Most trainers would work horses in pairs. But Ben wanted his to feel at ease out in front, and Burbank blazed away, leading this pack of decent horses.

Approaching the fifth, I spotted a photographer raising his camera. I crouched lower, trying to look part of the horse, man and animal, a single smooth racing machine, and I counted in the stride to his usual take-off point and set my final position for the picture. But Burbank rose too soon and pierced the hurdle below the top bar, locking his legs in the frame, depriving him of the chance to save himself, and he somersaulted and threw me like a half-ton judo expert would onto the turf.

Even in that split second between launch and landing, your instinct kicks your feet from the stirrups and prepares you for impact. Sometimes in a fall from a 'chaser, you're higher up and travelling more slowly and you have a chance to tuck in neatly and aim to land and roll. But being fired off at that low hurdling trajectory, the best you can do is put your hands out to break the fall and hope it doesn't cost you a wrist or forearm fracture.

I was lucky. He sent me along the turf like a fast-skidding bowling ball on my front, and as I came to a halt, I knew the real trouble was on its way. My left ear was to the ground through the padding of my helmet strap, and I could hear eight tons of galloping horseflesh coming. The earth shook. I curled up tight, trying to offer a small target. A horse will do what it can to avoid stepping on a man, or on another horse, but all sixty four hooves would be unable to avoid me. All I could do was hope for the best.

They broke in shell bursts over my head.

Noise.

The gorse in the hurdle crackling, rapping hooves on the frame, the thump of front feet landing on turf, a whip smack, shouts from the jockeys, then metal-shod feet on my helmet, stunning me. The catch on my goggles broke and suddenly everything was brighter. A hoof caught my knee, stepping on it and I yelped and reached instinctively to cover it, raising my head, and something hard and sharp and fast hit me across my eye from forehead to cheekbone in a diagonal. I remembered that detail and then nothing.

I regained consciousness after what I took to be few seconds as I saw the doctor hurrying toward me, and I knew I had to cut through the fuzziness of concussion and prepare some answers to the inevitable questions. Loss of consciousness meant an automatic holiday of at least forty eight hours, and I tried to remember what the usual questions would be, as well as the answers.

I sat up, as the doc reached me. That would impress him. He knelt, looking at my eyes and I tried playing for time. 'It's my knee, doc. Got stood on.' And I lay down again, trying desperately to call home the logical thoughts scattered among my neurons, fleeing at the first kick in the head. Cowards.

He examined my knee. I had to play a tight game. Too many flinches or groans would see me sent to hospital for an X-ray, and I had two mounts to come with no intention of letting anyone else ride them.

He moved away from my knee. 'Nothing broken. How do you feel?'

I thought of answering from the prone position, but that wouldn't look good. I sat up. 'All right, thanks. Have you seen my goggles?'

'Never mind your goggles. Look at me.'

I looked at him. He had a tough job. If there is an opposite of hypochondriacs, jockeys are it. A nightmare for doctors whose job it is to protect us from ourselves.

'What was the name of the horse you were riding?'

'Eh, Burton...Burbank!'

'Which track are we at?'

'Newbury.' I knew that more because I recognized the surroundings than remembered where I was.

'Which trainer were you riding for?'

'Ben. Ben with the hard name. I've never been able to pronounce it. Starts with T.'

He smiled. 'You're a trier, I'll give you that. Listen, Eddie, you took a kick in the head there. That's what broke the clip on your goggles. If you were out, even for a few seconds, you'd be a fool to ride again today.'

'Doc, I never lost consciousness. I was a bit stunned by the noise and everything, but I knew what was happening. I knew my goggles had come off, that's why I asked where they were.'

'Can you walk to the ambulance?'

'Sure.' I tried to spring to my feet but the left knee almost gave way. I walked. He watched, looking for signs of poor balance. Concentration got me to the ambulance and the ambulance got me to the weighing room in time for my next ride.

Maven Judge came off the train lugging a heavy holdall. I leant on the wall watching her scrawny outline against the string of platform lights. She hoisted the bag on her shoulder, the weight dragging open the zip of her leather jacket. She hadn't seen me and I watched her come toward me out of the lights, the bag's weight making her hobble on her right side. I was in the shadows and as she drew level I said, 'Carry your bag, madam?'

She stopped and quickly lowered the holdall. 'The white knight,' she said, then looked closer and saw the cut on my forehead and the long bruise the loose horseshoe had left in my earlier fall. 'Who lost a fight…What happened?'

'Fell off just before a horse decided to pry a shoe loose and fire it at my face.'

'Could have been nasty if one of the pointy ends hit you.'

'It's a scratch.' I took her bag and started walking.

'You're limping.'

'One stood on my knee. In the same race.'

'They had it in for you today, didn't they?'

'They did. Come on. It's whiskey time.'

'Jeez, this is axe-murderer country,' she said as we trundled the final mile downhill to the house, headlights bouncing on the trees, making them look as though they were moving.

'You hardly live in the heart of the metropolis yourself.'

'But at least I can hear the sea and smell the ozone.'

'And I can hear the silence and smell the woods in the rain.'

'Aww, you've gone all romantic on me.'

I smiled as I stopped and pulled on the handbrake.

In the kitchen, I put the bag on the table. She unzipped it and hauled out another bag, thickly padded to protect her laptop, and a wet-sack type bag with a roll top.

'I thought you were staying for a while?'

'I am.'

I nodded toward the bag. 'Is that all your clothes?'

'It's all I've brought. You want to audit them or something?'

'It just doesn't look much. For a woman. Are your shoes being shipped in a crate or something?'

'I travel light. I never buy knickers that don't dry in an hour.'

'Before washing them or after?'

She swung the bag at me and I stepped away laughing. 'Come on. I'll show you your room.'

Half an hour later we were at my desk. Mave was in my usual seat and my laptop had been pushed aside for her supersized silver one and a mug of tea.

It was strange seeing her live, crouched over her keyboard, fingers working it as though they'd been made to do nothing but that. 'What are you doing?' I asked.

'Importing today's results into my programme.'

'When do we get on to the scanner stuff?'

'When I've finished this tea.'

'I didn't see a scanner in that big bag of yours.'

'Would you know what one looked like?'

'Fair question.'

She hit her last keystroke with the panache of a concert pianist and turned and smiled at me. 'But you're right. I'm scannerless at the moment. There's a guy from Vodafone in Newbury getting one for me.'

'When?'

'As soon as you want. He's got it. I told him it would probably be tomorrow before we could pick it up.'

'Can you get it tonight?'

She took out her phone and opened contacts.

FORTY

The shutters on Watt's house looked daunting in the dark, the full moon burnishing the padlocks, exaggerating their thickness.

We started at the front. Mave wore headphones attached to the scanner which was in her jacket pocket. I walked beside her, pointing the flashlight on full flood beam. Every ten steps or so. I'd glance at her and she'd shake her head. We skirted the house and I imagined the architect's original drawings as we followed the line of the walls, around the gable end, down into the main yard, the moonlight now on the cobbles making a group of them look like a tiny range of smooth hills.

We turned at the corner along the base of the U shape, moving slowly and Mave never faltered. We completed a circuit without stopping even once and she took off the headphones. 'Zilch. You mentioned outbuildings. Where are they?'

There were four buildings behind the house, between the yard and the paddock fence. The doors on each faced east, otherwise, there was little uniformity. Different sizes. One with a tin roof, another with half a roof, and yet the security guys had sealed the doors and windows. I knew one had held the hulk of an old red tractor. The largest of them was used as a grain store and secondary barn. The big haybarn was attached to the complex and we'd covered that in the first run.

I changed the angle of the light beam, pointing it right in front of our feet trying to pick out old wire and masonry in the shin-high grass we stalked through. Hoping too for some disturbed ground, a shallow grave, and wondering if the bug would transmit through a few feet of earth.

No luck.

None of the buildings offered a sound.

We stopped and looked at each other. I turned the beam to narrow and aimed across the paddock over the fields, more as a reversion to a childlike compulsion than in any hope of seeing something. I switched the flashlight off. Mave removed the earphones.

'Can we do one more circuit?' I asked.

'We can do as many as you like. I'll keep narrowing the parameters each time. At least that will filter out a lot of the foreign stations and general crap.'

'What are you listening for? If the bug's in a watch then it would have to be a digital watch for it to have a battery, and digitals don't tick, do they?'

'Some of them have a tick programmed in. I'm just seeking a strong signal. The wave will still be transmitted even though there's no sound being recorded.'

'What you're really saying is that it could be a long night?'

'That'll make me feel right at home.' Mave adjusted the headphones and I turned the flashlight beam on and twisted it to wide angle.

Three more circuits brought nothing. We stopped by the haybarn. 'Would it help, if we could get inside?'

'Mave set her jaw and stared at me as though I was stupid. 'What do *you* think?' she asked.

I smiled. 'I think it was a silly question. Wait there.' I went to the car and returned with a set of lockpicks.

'You know how to pick locks?' Mave asked.

'I used to know. It's a delicate skill, and I haven't used it for a long time.' I was working on the lock on the back which secured the window into the kitchen.

'Where did you learn to do that?'

'Correspondence course. Lockpick dot com. You get a certificate and everything.'

She leant around my right side so she could see my face close up. I smiled without looking at her. 'I learned in prison.'

'Oh, I forgot about that. Jailbird.'

After six attempts, we were in.

I switched the lights on in the kitchen. Mave grabbed my arm and whispered. 'What are you doing!'

'Why are you whispering?'

'Because you turned the lights on. Somebody might see us!'

'All the windows are boarded up. The one we came in is at the back. Just fields and trees out there. Take it easy.' It was the first time I'd seen any vulnerability in Mave. Her eyes were wide. 'Come on.' I said, 'we won't be long.'

We covered every room. I showed her where the hard drive had been for the CCTV. All the wires hung as they had when I'd taken a picture of them. As we walked down the hall to the opposite end of the house, I told her about seeing Kilberg that night prowling around this end room.

She scanned every inch. Nothing. 'I think Kilberg was using it as a gym,' I said, opening the cupboard door and taking out the silver dumbbells. 'Bayley was never into physical fitness.' I did a couple of bicep curls with them. 'Come on, Eddie, let's get out. I feel safer in the dark.'

As I laid the dumbbells on the mat in the cupboard, the edge of one caught the corner of the mat and moved it. Below the mat was a hatch, like an old floor safe. It was hinged, but there was no handle or catch, no obvious way of opening it. 'Mave.'

She came over. I pushed the sharp end of a lockpick down the right edge and eased the wooden lid up. The space below was shallow, maybe six inches deep. Resting across beams was a soft neoprene case with a zip. Inside it was a black laptop.

Outside, I relocked the padlock on the window shutter, and carried the laptop under my arm. We headed out of the quadrangle of boxes on our way to the car, when something came back to me. This was the route Watt and I had taken on that ride-out in the snow. When Watt had wanted to stick to the roads and I'd suggested we go through the gate and up onto the Ridgeway. And my horse had spooked crossing a particular piece of ground. Spooked and seemed scared afterward.

I turned to Mave. 'Is that scanner still on?'

She switched it on and pulled the earphones up again as I told her what had happened and led her toward the gate. Then I stopped. That ride out had been less than a week after Jimmy was buried. His body had still been in the graveyard. I steered Mave toward the main buildings.

Crossing the open ground between the outhouses and the yard, Mave stopped and held up a hand. I looked at her. She took two steps back then three forward. I swept the beam across the ground around her. She turned north and went four steps then spun and walked south...and walked...and kept going.

We passed the muck heap on our left and moved toward the paddock. She stopped and turned and went the length of the rear wall of the muck heap, ten strides, then along the side wall, across the open front and back along the third wall where the pile of old droppings and straw was at its lowest. I remembered that Bayley emptied the wheelbarrow from the northern side.

Mave took off the earphones and just looked at me.

I pointed to the muck heap. 'In there?'

She nodded.

FORTY-ONE

It took McCarthy five minutes to get in touch with Sara Chase and she had a team there within an hour. The vans parked on the drive, their headlights blinding. I shielded my eyes and saw four men dressed all in white emerge from the light carrying bags, coming toward us. Two had cameras, the straps around their necks, tripods under arms.

Mave had taken the laptop and her gear and returned to the car, uneasy about possible formalities. The men in white stopped in front of me. One nodded and began setting up his tripod. The others pulled up the hoods on their white jumpsuits and began emptying the bags.

'Mister Malloy?'

I remembered the voice, and turned, baffled at how DS Wilmslow had managed to approach unseen. He looked no more human than he had that day when Sergeant Middleton brought him to interview me after Kilberg died. He was looking at the muck heap and grimacing.

He told me the men in white were scene of crime officers and that they'd have a fair bit of work to do before the muck heap could be searched. A vehicle bringing arc lights was on its way.

'Arc lights and shovels?' I asked.

He looked at the heap of droppings and filthy straw, from its top at chest height to ground level. A shallow tide of urine surrounded it, ebbed to about six inches. But the stains of its high tide mark darkened the concrete two feet from the heap. The

January cold had chilled the smell to little more than a light odour, one I'd never found unpleasant anyway. But Wilmslow seemed disgusted by it. 'They won't use shovels,' he said. 'Might damage the corpse if it is in there, and contaminate evidence.'

One of the SOCO men returned to the vans, their headlights still blazing, engines running, and returned with four telescopic rods. 'Probes,' Wilmslow said.

I turned away. It had been bad enough waiting for them to arrive. The thought of Jimmy hauled from a grave that had been sprinkled with holy water and blessed by a priest, to be reburied in a heap of horse shit in a yard from which he used to ride out with great hope was beyond sickening. My anger at the thought had faded to deep sadness. I told Wilmslow I'd wait in the car.

Mave was lying across the back seat. 'What are you so scared of?' I asked as I closed the driver's side door and settled into the darkness.

'I'm scared of spending months of my life giving statements and attending inquiries and maybe prosecutions. I'm not here. Okay? I've never been here.'

I sighed and pulled out my phone. Mave sat up and grabbed my shoulder. 'Eddie, keep me out of this. I'm serious.'

'Okay. Okay. Cool it.'

'Who are you calling, then? What are you doing?'

I put the phone down and turned to her, my eyes adjusting to the darkness again after what had seemed a long bath in bright light. She looked worried. 'Mave, listen. I know how you feel about authority and government and cops and all that stuff, and if it's anything to do with me, you won't be asked a single question. But buried up there in that pile of horse shit is a friend of mine. He saved my life one time. Give me a break, will you?'

Slowly, she eased back in the seat, taking her hand from my shoulder. 'Jimmy's dead, Eddie,' she said. 'He won't have felt a thing. It won't matter to Jimmy where he's ended up.' She said it quietly, trying to console me. 'It matters to me where he ended up, Mave.'

She nodded and slowly reached and squeezed my shoulder. She lay back down, and I dialled McCarthy's number and told him where the police were at. 'Mac, I need a big favour.'

'I'm listening.'

'If they find Jimmy in there, I want the police to say he was found in the barn, among the haybales, wrapped in clean blankets.'

'Why?'

'Because I don't want his father to find out.'

Mac exhaled in that long sigh which many would have interpreted as frustration and impatience. I pictured him blowing out his cheeks and looking down at his feet and trying to figure out how he could help me. 'Let me speak to Sara Chase.'

'Mac-'

'I know, Eddie. I'll make sure she realizes how important it is to you.'

'Thanks, Mac.'

I put the phone on the seat beside me and slumped back, my head on the soft rest. I could hear Mave's even breathing and thought she'd fallen asleep, but after a minute she spoke quietly into the darkness. 'I think I made a mistake coming here, Eddie. Spending too much time with you will make me soft. I know it. I just know it. If you turn me into an everyday member of the human race, I'll never forgive you.'

I smiled, though she couldn't see me. I watched the moon.

'You hear me, Malloy? I will not forgive. Ever.'

FORTY-TWO

Getting into the black laptop took Mave less time than it took me to make tea and sandwiches. As I put the plates on the desk, she groaned. I looked at her face, which was lit mostly by reflected light from the laptop. Her head was withdrawing in what looked an ultra-slow motion recoil. 'You okay?' I took two steps to get behind her and see the screen, but she quickly snapped the lid closed.

'Child porn. Gross. Gross pictures.'

I moved back and sat across from her. She stared ahead as though the screen was still open, her face frozen in disgust and shock. I reached slowly for her hand. She withdrew it and folded her arms, sticking her hands beneath her armpits.

'Mave...'

She looked at me. 'There is no God,' she said, her face a mix of anger and hurt, tears rising.

Even in the palest of light from the small desk lamp, I could see the colour had gone from her. She stood, holding onto the desk as though fearful of falling. 'Can I go and lie down?' she asked, almost whispering.

I got up and put an arm round her shoulder and led her to her bedroom. She sat on the edge of the bed staring, shocked. I eased her shoes off. 'Lie flat. I'll cover you up.'

She lay near the edge of the double bed. I went to the other side and gathered the covers, rolled them over her. She turned onto her side and curled up. I sat beside her. Still she stared. I rested a hand on her shoulder. 'Put a pillow over my face,' she said.

'Mave-'

'Eddie. Please! I need to be blind.'

I leaned across and picked up a pillow and laid it gently across her head. 'Leave me, now,' she said.

'I'll sit a while.'

'Leave me, Eddie. Please.'

'Okay.'

'Turn off the light.'

'I will.'

I shut the door softly and went back along the hall. I stood looking at the desk, at the closed PC, and walked away from it, to the Snug at the back of the house, to stare through the big window at the darkness and try to take everything in.

Watt and Kilberg and their blackmailer - I had to assume he'd got into Watt's PC - faded now. Mave held my thoughts. She'd been the queen of logic, the chief among cynics. Who understood human behaviour better than she did? What was it she'd said ..."A dispassionate view of humanity for one year will tell you all you need to know." Maybe she knew it from reading about life, maybe from observing people from that remote emotional standpoint. But the reality of this part of humanity had skewered her.

Mave was the most unusual woman I'd ever met. Now she'd gone from invulnerable in my eyes, to helpless. Her protective layers had been stripped away by the images on a PC screen. Stupidly, I wondered what it might do to her love of technology, to her working night spent in front of a screen. Would she ever again be able to open a laptop without seeing what she'd just seen?

What should I do? How could I help her? I put the laptop out of sight in my floor safe. Even handling it made me afraid after seeing Mave's reaction. As a child I'd read Greek mythology, and the Gorgon came to mind.

Standing by Mave's bedroom door, I listened, hoping to hear the even breathing of sleep, but fearing the sound of crying. There was nothing. I pictured the room, trying to remember if there was anything there she could harm herself with, then I chided myself for believing she might.

I went back to sit in silence, and half an hour later, I heard the bed creak. Mave came into the room, the shock gone from her gaunt face, replaced by a furrowed brow and clenched jaw. 'Where's the laptop?'

'I locked it away.'

'Go and get it.'

'Sit down. Give yourself a day or two.'

'I don't need to. I want to examine the metadata in those files. There should be leads to others. It must have been some kind of ring. I want to get the rest of them.'

'The rest of the people involved?'

'Yes.'

I was about to tell her they could be all over the world, but her eyes were telling me she wouldn't be listening. I went and got the laptop.

She put it on the desk and pointed at me. 'Stay back. Don't look at these. I won't be looking at them. I'll search the file data for each.'

'Okay. You want a whiskey?'

'No. Thanks.'

'Coffee?'

'Please.'

I brought a mug of coffee and some chocolate biscuits. 'Thanks. Go away, now, please.'

'Are you going to be all right?'

'I'm going to get these bastards.'

'I'll leave you to it. I'm going to see Jim Sherrick. I need to know before I go if Jimmy might be involved here.'

'None of the pictures I saw had Jimmy Sherrick in them. From your descriptions, I'm pretty sure it was Watt and Kilberg, neither of them at the same time, so I'm assuming one was taking the pictures.'

I watched her, that fierce expression still on her face. 'Mave, as much as I don't want to, I'm going to have to see those pictures. I need to be certain that it's Watt and Kilberg, and I have to check that Jimmy's not in any.'

'Eddie, there are hundreds of pictures. I only saw maybe twenty.'

'I'm prepared for it, Mave. I'll try to look at nothing but the men in it.'

She got up and went into the kitchen. 'Call me when you're done.'

I moved to her chair, more nervous than I'd felt before any Grand National. I raised the lid and tried to force my vision into a narrow channel as I scrolled through pages of coloured photos taken at high resolution.

Watt and Kilberg. Watt and Kilberg.

Page after page.

No Jimmy Sherrick.

I closed the lid, feeling exhausted by concentrating on looking only at the faces of the adults. 'Done,' I called to Mave. She walked through, and stood in the doorway watching me. 'I'm okay,' I said. 'I managed not to look.'

She walked to me and put a hand on my shoulder and smiled sadly. I hugged her and we stood in silence for what seemed a long time.

FORTY-THREE

On the drive to Jim Sherrick's place, I knew I still could not be certain about Jimmy. I'd have bet my life without hesitation that he wasn't a paedophile. The police had found nothing on his laptop. The mirrored laptop that was left at his house had nothing of that sort on it.

So what did the blackmailer have on Jimmy? How had he shut him up over the ringers? But when I thought back to those newspaper cuttings I'd found at Jimmy's house, only two had been of the ringer. Maybe it was after the second one that he realized what was happening and had called me to say "Things aren't right" and that he was packing the job in. A day later he was dead. Maybe he hadn't been blackmailed.

Mister Sherrick was as welcoming as he'd always been. It was a late visit, but I wanted to make sure Jimmy's dad would hear it from me first. And I needed to cement the story the police had agreed to, then tell Mac it had been done. That way, Sara Chase could have no second thoughts.

'Coffee?' Mister Sherrick asked, filling the kettle in the small kitchen.

'Please. How have you been?'

'Fine, thanks. I've got a gig, as you youngsters say.'

'Doing what?'

'Fiddling.'

I smiled. 'As in violins, I take it?'

'I'd never call myself a violinist, but I can carve out a few jigs.'

'A jig gig, then?'

He laughed. 'In the Church hall, playing for the old folks on Friday evenings.'

Old folks. He didn't see himself as an old man. I briefly wondered what age I'd be before regarding myself as an old man.

'Are young folks welcome, too? I'd like to hear you.'

'I'll make special arrangements.'

Five minutes later, in our usual chairs by the fire, Mister Sherrick was trying to take in what I'd just told him. 'In Bayley Watt's hay barn?'

I nodded. 'In a bed of hay cleared out from the middle of a huge stack of bales.'

'Still in his coffin?'

'No, he was wrapped in fleece blankets.'

He stared at his shoes, shaking his head slowly. 'Why would Watt have done that?'

'This should bring us a step closer to the answer.'

'How did the police find him? Someone else must have been involved.'

I told him about Mave's hunch with the transmitter. 'So the bug was in Jimmy's watch, same as mine?'

'We think so.'

We sat a while in silence then he said, 'When can Jimmy be re-buried?'

'I'm going to speak to Peter McCarthy in the morning. I'll ask him.'

He looked up at me. 'There won't have to be another funeral, will there?'

'No, no, I'm sure there won't. Just quietly lay him to rest for good this time.'

His head went down again. I got up and crossed to him, put a hand on his shoulder. 'I'd be proud to come with you if you want me to, to the cemetery. When the time comes.'

'You've been like a son to me, Eddie.' He spoke quietly, still staring at the floor.

'And you've been like a father to me.'

He looked up. 'I've done nothing.'

'You've taught me a lot about courage and dignity and respect.'

'Three things you needed no lessons on, Eddie, least of all from me.'

'I don't know. It's easy to imagine how you would act, I mean me, not you, when certain things happen, but doing it's much harder. Jimmy would have been proud of you.'

He got up and turned to me. His eyes were wet but he wouldn't let the tears fall. He reached to shake hands with me, then put his left hand on my arm and squeezed. I wanted to hug him, but he was not of the hugging generation, and his back stiffened and his head went up and he stood tall in his grief yet again.

Mave was in the kitchen when I got home, drinking whiskey, 'I helped myself. Hope you don't mind.'

'Of course not. How are you feeling?'

'Like shit. But I'll be better tomorrow.'

I nodded, wanting to ask what she'd found, but wary of raising it, and she sensed my hesitation and spoke. 'The pictures were originals. There's no sign of them having been emailed anywhere or put online. The last time they were opened, by someone other than me was July last year. When did you see Kilberg in that room?'

'The night Bayley died. A week ago, Friday.'

'Whatever he was there for, it wasn't to look at those pictures.'

'Maybe he was just checking the laptop was still there?'

'Could be.'

His marriage to the sixteen-year-old now made sense. Disgusting sense, but now I could see the logic in it from his side. And in hers, for running back to Romania. 'So we need to get Kilberg's PC and see what's on that,' I said. 'If they weren't viewing the pictures on Watt's, they must have had access elsewhere.'

'You going to tell the police?'

'We have to, don't we?'

'Sooner the better.'

I called Mac.

FORTY-FOUR

On the way to Fakenham for three rides, I tried four times before I raised Mac on the phone. I'd forgotten to tell him the night before that Jimmy's dad had accepted the story about the hay barn. Mac said he was with Sara Chase at that moment and he'd probably have some news for me by the time racing had finished.

'What kind of news?'

'Well, we're not sure yet. Another autopsy is being carried out on Jimmy. He wasn't wearing a watch.'

I stared through the windscreen, passing a line of bare beech trees, trying to make sense of what Mac had just told me. 'Where was the bug?'

'We don't know yet.'

'Mac, come on. What was he carrying? He was buried in a suit and tie, wasn't he? Was he still dressed?'

'He was dressed.'

'In a suit and tie?'

'Suit, shirt, tie, socks, shoes, underwear. No watch. No pens. Nothing mechanical or electrical.'

'It must be in his clothes somewhere! Maybe it was a standalone bug, a tiny battery-driven thing.' I heard Sara Chase say something to him.

'Eddie, look, we expect to have an answer soon. You're at Fakenham today, aren't you?'

'On my way now.'

'Call me after the last. Goodbye.'

'Mac!'

He'd gone.

I pulled over and scrolled through for Mave's number then went back on hands-free as it rang.'

'Mave, listen, you're not going to believe this, I just spoke to McCarthy and-'

'Eddie! Eddie! Listen! Don't talk on your mobile about this. Find a payphone. Ring your home number.'

'Okay. Sorry. I might be a while. Not many payphones in this part of the world.'

'I can wait. And don't ring anyone else. And tell McCarthy not to talk about this on mobile either. He should know better.'

'Right.'

Twenty minutes later I was in an old hooded payphone in the lobby of a country hotel pumping coins into the slot. I told Mave what Mac had said. She hardly needed a moment's thinking time. 'It's in his body. The bug must have been implanted, probably in his neck, or under his collarbone, close to the vocal cords.'

I pictured it, thought of the voice recordings patched together, and of the conversation in the car that night when Jimmy had said he wanted to meet because things weren't right with Bayley. 'You're a genius, Maven Judge.'

'I'm an idiot, actually. The ringer scam was based on moving the chip implanted in a horse's neck. It hardly takes a huge leap of the imagination to transfer the theory to putting a chipped mic in a human neck. I should have guessed this weeks ago.'

'So that's how he was picking up what Bayley said, and Kilberg?'

'That would be my bet.'

'But if they knew they were carrying recording chips, why would they have blabbed so much?'

'Maybe they didn't know.'

'Mave, come on, even I would notice if somebody cut a hole in my neck and shoved something in there.'

'But what if you were told it was for something else?'

'Like what?'

'Like treating cancer.'

FORTY-FIVE

Driving home in the freezing dark was usually easier when you'd had a winner. But on none of my rides round the tight undulating Fakenham track had my mind been on the job. Not even when I'd got that old gelding Excalibur up on the line to win the handicap 'chase. Excalibur had been the horse I'd ridden at Ascot the day before Jimmy died, and here I was awaiting Mac's call to find out if Maven Judge was right about the bug buried in his corpse.

When Mac finally phoned, I pulled over. I didn't want to mishear anything.

'Eddie, the autopsy was completed about an hour ago. They found the bug.'

'Where?'

'Close to where you suggested. It was fixed on the inside of a titanium collarbone.'

Titanium. I remembered Jimmy had busted his right collarbone so often it had been replaced a few years ago. Mave had been spot on and I was frustrated that she could get no credit here, even though that was her choice.

'Sara Chase is well impressed with you.' Mac said.

'Well, if it wasn't on Jimmy, it had to be in him. That was the only logic left. When will the other two be done?'

'Bayley Watt tomorrow, then Blane Kilberg, maybe tomorrow. Depends how long the first one takes.'

I leaned back in the seat and sighed. 'Jeez, Mac, what is going on here? Who is this guy? He can't be doing all this himself. Who performed the surgery on Jimmy? There must be a record somewhere?'

'There are records for the op to replace the collarbone, but there's nothing after that.'

'Well speak to the surgeon who did the replacement. That's got to be specialist work. Find out how many are in that field. Maybe one of them was bribed or blackmailed or something.'

'It might take a specialist to do the replacement, but it's not exactly brain surgery, Eddie, fixing a tiny piece of plastic and metal to what is effectively a metal bar.'

'True.'

'Let's see what comes up in the other two autopsies.'

'You want a bet now you'll find the same bug somewhere around the voicebox area?'

'No thanks.'

'Mac, what is this guy up to? Judging by Watt's laptop, it's blackmail with Watt and Kilberg, and somehow Jimmy got roped in by them. But blackmail for what? Where's the money angle, the betting angle?'

'We've come up empty on that. No betting outside the average, no laying of others in those races. We asked all the major bookmakers today to double check. Zilch.'

'What about bookies in the far east? You know, online only?'

'We're working on that, with more than half the reports in. Nothing.'

'What about Ms Chase or Miss or whatever, has she any ideas?'

'She's working through her contacts.'

'That means no, Mac, doesn't it? I wish you wouldn't give me all this bullshit defensive crap. You need to get away from that prick Buley you work for. What's wrong with just saying no sometimes? *No, we don't know.* We're none the wiser. We're fucking human like everyone else.'

'I'm going to let you go, Eddie. You're getting tired and emotional.'

I drew a deep audible breath and stretched my arms straight, gripping the steering wheel. 'I'm sorry, Mac.'

'Forget it. Let's talk tomorrow.'

'Call me after Watt's autopsy, will you? And remember to get them to check that leukaemia claim.'

'I will. Take it easy on the way home.'

'Mac…remember Jimmy's dad in all this, will you? And please ask Ms Chase to do the same. The guys who dug Jimmy out of that muck heap are going to want to be telling the tale.'

'If one of them disobeys an order from Sara Chase, he won't know what's hit him. Trust me.'

'I'll drop by Mister Sherrick's place on the way home and tell him about the bug. If you keep me up to date, I'll keep him up to date. Saves any chance of Sergeant Middleton or that weirdo Wilmslow ballsing it up with him.'

'Okay. But try and stay this side of the paranoia border, will you?'

'I crossed it a long time ago, Mac. It's helped keep me alive.'

'If that's what you call living. Speak to you tomorrow.'

He hung up.

If that's what you call living.

Huh.

FORTY-SIX

Mave sat at my desk in the dark, light from the PC screen on her face and her long hair. This was the first time I'd seen her without her hair tied back. 'What news?' she asked, and just nodded when I told her she'd been right about the bug. 'I should have sussed it at the start, when you asked me to analyze that recording. I can't believe I missed it.'

'Well, you got it way ahead of her majesty's police force. Want a coffee?'

'Please.'

I talked as I walked to the sink. 'I've just been to see Jimmy's dad, to ask him if he can set up a meeting for me with Jimmy's ex-girlfriend.'

'Why?'

'It's something I should have thought of at the start. If he was likely to tell anyone what was going on, it would be her.'

'Well he didn't, did he?'

'How do you know?' I asked.

'Because she hasn't turned up with a bellyful of cyanide.'

'She might have done, for all we know. He split up with her a while ago. She wasn't in racing. She could have moved to Wales or Scotland or somewhere.'

'So how's Jimmy's dad supposed to find her?'

'I don't know.'

I carried the drinks to the desk and pulled up a chair. 'Put the lamp on at least, will you?'

Mave scowled. Without looking away from the screen her fingers moved, seeking the switch on the small desk lamp. It clicked on and she narrowed her eyes. I watched her, thinking of last night, wanting to ask if she was okay. But I sensed she wouldn't talk about it. She had dealt with everything while curled up in bed, a pillow over her face. Life had to resume now.

I opened the drawer and got my doodle pad and pen and started with my usual crossed lines, hatching, filling in the corners. Mave glanced across. 'High tech, eh?'

'It suits me. My mind doesn't work like yours.'

'Two words too many on the end of that sentence.'

'Very funny. It helps me to write things down and try and relate them.'

She clicked twice with the mouse and opened a mind map on screen. 'Try this, you'll find it much easier.'

'I have tried it and I don't. Pen and paper works for me.'

'Fine. Get scribbling.'

'Key question, or at least key question number one, why steal Jimmy's body? What was this guy afraid the police would discover? He hears through Mister Sherrick's bugged watch our conversation about the police exhuming. He gets on to Watt and probably Kilberg, and the body's gone that night. What did he think the police would find?'

'At that time, nobody knew about the bugs, did they? Maybe that's what he was trying to hide.'

'But why? You said the recordings would run through a maze of different networks in hijacked PCs.'

'That was an assumption. That's what I would have done.'

'And you were right, or at least going by the bug in Mister Sherrick's watch. So finding the bug in Jimmy was no certainty. They were planning to exhume because they accepted what I told them about Jimmy's suicide message being faked and about him being a technophobe. But what would the chances have been back then of finding a bug implanted in his collarbone, and even if they did, this guy knew they couldn't use it to trace him.'

'But think of the information he was getting through Jimmy and Watt and Kilberg and then, after Jimmy's death, through his dad after Watt conveniently delivers this Christmas gift from a dead son. That would have been of high value,' Mave said.

'But that source was never going to last, was it? Between the grave robbing and the house burning he'd surely have realized that the police would guess he was listening in somehow.'

'Ahh, but they didn't, did they? You did. Otherwise the bug would probably still be in the watch.'

'Nah, I know the sergeant is no Sherlock Holmes, but somebody on the case would have worked it out.'

Mave stopped typing and turned to me. 'Eddie, how many cases do you think the cops are working on? It's the same with them as with anyone else in a job, out of sight out of mind. Once your man the sergeant walks out of Mister Sherrick's flat, he's thinking of the next call or of heading home for his tea or his holiday in Benidorm or something. You figured it out because it's a hundred percent for you. It's on your mind constantly.'

I nodded and drank some coffee.

'And also, because you're pretty smart…sometimes.'

'Cheers.' I raised the mug. 'So why am I not smart enough to figure out why the body was stolen?'

'It has to be the bug. If the police do another autopsy and find the bug, they know it's murder.'

I was far from sure. 'So this guy's a tech genius, right? You warned me about that at the start. He's somehow got that bug into Jimmy's collarbone. He's hacked his email and planted an order for cyanide. Watt, who's much more tech savvy has actually ordered the cyanide and somehow got Jimmy to take it. Kilberg said Watt was with Jimmy that night, the night he died.'

'But Kilberg spun you some tale about Jimmy wanting to be sure, not wanting his father to find him and all that guff. Watt's put the cyanide in his drink or something, then strung him up. Very probably with Kilberg there to help him. After you start nosing around, they decide they'd better go in and clean up a bit in case they've left any traces.'

'But they haven't cleaned up enough for whoever's their boss and he sends them back to burn the place down. Drink your coffee, will you? It's a waste of hot water.'

Mave smiled and picked up the mug. 'You going to nag me for the next however long I'm here?'

'Yes.' I picked up my pen again. 'Turn your screen off. Bear with me for ten minutes while I think aloud. Butt in anytime.'

She closed the PC down. The faint buzz from it and the sound of the cooling fan stopped, and for a few moments we sat in perfect silence. I doodled and speculated. 'Okay, let's assume it was the bug he was trying to protect. He's pretty sure he can't be tracked through this network maze, but what if there's a maker's mark on the bug? These things must be pretty specialized.'

'What his main challenge would have been was battery power. It takes some strength to drive that signal out. Even the one in the watch would have struggled, I'd have thought. I'd bet it was one of those chunky jobs with a fat case?'

'It was pretty big. Hung loose on Mister Sherrick, that's for sure.'

'Where is it now?'

'The watch? I dumped it in a boiling kettle at his flat.'

'You told me that, but didn't you take it with you after that?'

'I gave it to the sergeant. Told him it had been in an accident.'

'Can you get it back?'

'Probably.'

'And can you get me the bug they took out of Jimmy?'

'I'll ask.'

She pointed me to the phone. 'Ask now.'

I sent Mac a text asking him to phone me on the landline. He called within two minutes and he was still in cooperative mood. 'Can I ask why you want the bugs?'

'I know a man who knows a man.'

'And how long will this man want them for?'

I glanced at Mave and just guessed, 'Forty eight hours.'

'And he's a discreet man?'

'Very.'

'I'll call you back.'

Mave said, 'We need to nail the communications, here. Will you buy a couple of pay as you go phones for you and me, and advise Mister McCarthy to buy one too?'

'I'll go and get them now.'

'Shops'll be closed, Eddie.'

'All night supermarket.'

She shook her head in what I took to be disapproval, and I said, 'Welcome to civilization.'

FORTY-SEVEN

Next morning, I met Mac in a quiet off road area in Lambourn Woodlands. He handed me what I took to be an evidence bag. It looked empty. I opened it and saw tiny items with very thin labels attached.

'Any word on Watt's autopsy?' I asked

'They're doing it now.'

'Checking for bugs?'

'That's the brief.'

'If they find one, I might need to see it too.'

'Eddie…'

I waited, but he'd decided against saying whatever it was. 'Mac, out with it.'

'This is evidence, critical evidence. Sara Chase took an awful lot of persuading that this was a good idea. If anything happens to them, the case, whatever comes of it in the end, could be worthless. If Sara hadn't been so impressed with your prediction about that bug and if I hadn't known you for so long-'

'Mac, don't worry. Tell Ms Chase this might knock weeks of foot-slogging and thousands in costs off the investigation. My guy would cost a fortune to hire to work on this. He's doing me a favour, and these sorts of things are like jewels to him. They'll be safe. I promise.'

'I take it he doesn't need to know the circumstances surrounding them? We can't have any prosecution prejudiced in that way either.'

'Stop worrying. Without this guy, I very much doubt you'll have anyone to prosecute.'

He sighed and laid back on the headrest. 'I must be going soft in the head.'

'You have mellowed a bit, lately, I'll say that. Maybe you'd better see your GP for a check-up.'

'You're a funny man, Eddie Malloy.'

'Others say that to me too, but I never hear anybody laughing.'

Mave held the bugs under the desk lamp. 'They're different,' I said.

'Completely. The one from the watch looks straightforward. This one from Jimmy looks to me like it's got an RFID chip bolted on, and its own battery source. I don't suppose you have a loupe lying around?'

'As in?'

'The little magnifying eyepieces jewellers use.'

'Afraid not.'

'Did you get those pay as you go phones?'

'I did. But I doubt you'll see much through them.'

'Ha ha. Power one up. I want to speak to my Vodafone man.'

Twenty minutes later we were ready to leave to meet Mave's contact. 'Eddie, no offence, but you're only taxi driving here, This guy won't see anyone else but me. He wants you to drop me off five minutes' walk from the meeting place.'

'How well do you know him?' I gave her the warning Mac had given me about the evidence.'

'The guy's solid, Eddie. I've used him before and I've helped him out with a few home projects. But he's a nervous man with a family to feed and a good job to protect.'

'Fine. Just checking he's not the type to have been got at by whoever's running this scam, given that all of you seem to be in the same business.'

'His nerves wouldn't stand it. Most of what he does he could charge fortunes for, but he gets his kicks from geeks seeing how good he is. When he works something out and explains it to you he beams like a kid at Christmas.'

I dropped Mave off not far from Newbury Racecourse. 'How long do you think?' I asked.

'Don't know. I'll call you, but don't hang around here.'

'Home, James.' Mave said, when she got into the car an hour later looking pleased with herself.

'What's the news?'

'The bug in the watch was just a bug in a watch. Straightforward. The bug fixed to Jimmy Sherrick's collarbone had its own battery, a GPS unit, a transmitter and a receiver.'

'In something the size of a postage stamp?'

'My guy was drooling. He said he'd love to meet whoever put it together.'

'Me too. Any clues on that? I mean do these geeks have their own sort of hallmark?'

'Nothing. Not a thing.'

'What's the point of the GPS? Why would he want to know where Jimmy was all the time?'

'Plenty reasons, maybe. Especially his position in a race, how fast he was going, how he rode it.'

'He couldn't know his position unless all the other jocks were fitted with GPS as well.'

'Who's to say they weren't?'

I rubbed my face with both hands then thought of Bayley Watt's habit of doing that when he was tired. I looked at Mave. 'What about the receiver? Does that mean he could tell the bug what to do, maybe control the volume for recording, or switch it off?'

'It was nothing to do with the recording side. It was programmed to activate another chip.'

'What, like something Jimmy came into contact with, like another bug?'

'No. It was very close range, probably another implant.'

'Inside Jimmy?'

'Yes.'

'Like what?'

'He couldn't tell, but he reckons once the chip had done its job it would have been set to migrate to another part of the body, through the bloodstream.'

'Done its job? You make it sound like some kind of rocket launcher.'

'Effectively, that's exactly what it was.'

Mave was beaming, excited, it was unlike her.

I said, 'You look as if you've caught some of your friend's enthusiasm for all things tiny and technical.'

'I think I know what the signal was launching, as you put it.'

'What?'

'A cyanide capsule.'

FORTY-EIGHT

By the time I got home from Exeter races the following evening, the same electronics that had been implanted in Watt had been found in Kilberg: a transmitter and receiver. Tests were being done on the stomach walls of both corpses to try to find out if the cyanide release had begun there. The police had agreed to leave the transmitters with me, and Mave had spent the day trying to break through the web of feeds that had taken the recordings back to whoever was behind this.

I dropped my kitbag beside the desk and looked down on Mave's chestnut hair and coffee-stained blue mug.

Dusk had long fallen and, as ever, only the PC screen lit the area around the desk. I clicked the lamp on. 'Let there be light,' I said.

'Let there be enlightenment,' Mave replied.

'Is there?'

'No. Just confirmation that this guy must have spent a long time planning this, a hell of a long time. I thought there'd be a couple of thousand hijacked PCs passing this stuff along, but the way he's structured it, we might be talking tens of thousands.' She stopped typing and pushed the wheeled chair away from the desk so that I had to move aside quickly. She stood and smiled at me and put an arm around my shoulders, walking me toward the kitchen. 'Anyway, darling, how was your day?'

I laughed and pushed her away. 'Get off, you crazy woman!' I was pleased to see her back to herself.

'You know, I'm really concerned for you given the lack of women around here,' she said.

'Winter keeps them away. They can't stand the cold down here in the valley.'

She settled at the kitchen table while I filled the kettle. 'What about the groupies at the races?' she asked.

'What groupies?'

'Come on. Plenty women are attracted to men who do dangerous things.'

'Yea, like motorcyclists who dress in black leather and are covered in tattoos. What chance have we in pink silks and bruises?'

'You need to open your eyes, Eddie. You're a good looking fella. Now that cut's beginning to scar over, you have that dark and deadly look about you.'

'Stark and deathly, more like. You want some coffee?'

'Please.'

I sat opposite Mave and slid a yellow mug toward her. She drank, then pushed hair from her eyes and tucked it behind her ear. 'Any winners at Exeter?'

'I rode a third, then nearly got carted in the handicap hurdle. Unplaced in the Bumper.'

'A fairly typical day, then?'

'Pretty much. What about you? Where to next?'

'I'll wait until you get your doodle pad out and we'll do another brainstorm.'

'At least I had Bayley Watt right. I knew he was capable of running, but no way would he commit suicide. Nor Kilberg. He was too far up himself to do his body any damage.'

'Except he's let somebody else do it damage. He's had three devices put under his skin. The transmitter, the receiver and the cyanide capsule.'

'But all they thought they were getting was a cancer cure, or at least the chance of a cancer cure. Carrot and the stick. That's why there'd be no need to blackmail Jimmy. They'd have offered him the cure. He had nothing to lose.'

'Correct,' said Mave.

'I think we've started the brainstorm. Do I need my pad and pen?'

'If you must.'

I got them and returned to the table to doodle and think.

'Write these down,' Mave said. 'Cyanide. Blackmail. Implants. Bugs. Computer genius. Paedophile…what else?'

'Ringer. Horses. Racing. Betting. Trainer. Vet. Jockey. Hair loss. Muscle loss. Cancer-'

'Hair loss?'

'I told you after that ride out with Watt, I spent half an hour googling. He used to have very hairy wrists, to a point where he couldn't wear a watch. The hair was almost gone. And his body looked soft, as though muscle was turning to fat. Kilberg was looking the same, though he was much smaller than Watt.'

Mave had begun nodding before I'd finished. 'Ever heard of Alan Turing?'

'The Bletchley Park guy, a code breaker or something, wasn't he? Didn't they recently pardon him for a conviction?'

'They pardoned him for being gay. He was a computer scientist, and cryptanalyst, the first really big name in the field to get public recognition. In the early fifties, homosexuality was a criminal offence and he was found guilty of indecency. The court gave him the option of probation if he would agree to hormone treatment to kill his libido. There was talk of doing it using implants, but he ended up with a course of hormone injections of oestrogen which left him impotent and with a condition called gynaecomastia: development of breast tissue. Turing was found dead two years later and the verdict was suicide by…what?'

'Cyanide?'

'You got it.'

'Jeez!'

'What else?' said Mave.

'What do you mean?'

'Think of the hormone treatment, and what happened to Watt's hair and his muscle.'

'Hormone implants.' I said.

Mave watched me. 'That's the cure the blackmailer implanted. They thought they were getting cancer treatment, he was feeding them oestrogen. Impotence. That's why none of those photos had been opened since July.'

'Genius.'

'He's bordering on it.' Mave said.

'Not him. You.'

'Idiot is what I am. I should have pulled all this together much sooner. Much, much sooner.'

'Don't be daft. If I couldn't and the cops couldn't…' I tailed off as I watched her face, and I smiled. 'I'm not comparing apples with apples, am I?'

'This time, unfortunately, I suppose you are.'

'And it puts my mind at rest with Jimmy, too. I saw no signs of softness in him. It must have been just the bug and the cyanide.'

'Must have.'

I stood. 'Celebratory drink?'

'Go on, then.'

I poured whiskeys while Mave kept talking. 'We're on a roll, Edward, let's keep going.'

'I'm listening.'

'This guy implants oestrogen. What does that tell us?'

'He has a conscience.'

'Correct. And maybe some history of being abused.'

'From the computer work he's done, what age range would you guess at?'

Mave made a whistling noise and swilled the whiskey round her glass. 'Tough one. Most people with that kind of talent and that kind of appetite for work would be young. Teenage to mid-twenties. But there are quite a few second and even third generation guys, people with the foresight back in the early nineties to realize what the internet would bring.'

'What about that knowledge of Alan Turing, would that point to someone older?'

'Turing was a shot in the dark for me. He might have triggered this somehow, but it would be a sloppy assumption right now.'

'Could it be a woman?'

'If there were someone that capable, I'd probably know her.'

'I always thought it was a rare talent at your level, but I didn't want to seem sexist.'

'I'd accuse you of many things, Eddie, but sexism wouldn't be one.'

I picked up my pen again. 'Right. Motive?'

'Some degree of justice, or revenge, but the ringer scam brings us back to money. You said that all the betting intelligence, from here, the far east, wherever, says nothing unusual. What do they class as unusual?'

'I'll ask.' I reached for my mobile.

'The other one,' Mave warned.

'I know. I'm just getting Gerry's number.'

I spent five minutes talking to Gerry Waldron. Mave didn't have the patience to wait. She returned to her keyboard. When I said goodbye to Gerry, Mave stopped typing and turned to me. 'Well?'

'Gerry says there are patterns for different race types. A big Saturday handicap on TV, they'll take plenty. There are always tips going around and three or four runners in these big races might be heavily supported, but the bookies check what all the tipping lines are giving out. If a constant stream of money was coming for a first-timer or a horse with little form, and it hadn't been tipped by a pro, they'd be very suspicious.'

'But the ringers were in these small midweek races, weren't they?'

'They were. And they calculate from data they have on past races how much they expect to be bet on each horse based on its price. If they suddenly start taking hundred quid bets on one when the normal stake is a fiver, they realize something's up. The biggest bet they logged on any of the ringers was twenty five quid.'

'What about the betting shops? Supposing he had hundreds of agents around the country placing bets of twenty quid a time to stay under the radar?'

I shook my head. 'Nothing like that. Nearly all the tills in shops are computerized now so everything's being logged online. Anyway, this guy looks a lone operator, doesn't he? Maybe he has a surgeon doing implants for him and somebody turning out these bugs, but he's not organizing betting on a grand scale. Somebody would have talked by now.'

Mave got up. 'Let me open my mind map and we'll get all your doodling on the one system.'

I followed her to the desk and her PC. On her screen was a picture resembling a subway map superimposed on itself a hundred times. 'What's that?'

'It's a simulation of the first section of the network he used to carry the recordings from the bugs.'

'When you say first part, what fraction?'

'Of the whole network? Maybe a tenth of a percent.'

'And there's no way the owners of these PCs could know this traffic was moving through them?'

'Nope. He'll have inserted a tiny bug in a mailing list and every email sent would spread the infection to the contacts list of the others.'

'What about security software, anti-virus?'

'No good against this fella. He'd have passed the stage of breaking that years ago.'

'So the last PC on the line is his?'

'I doubt it. Might be, but I doubt it. He only needs access to the data on it and that would be dead easy.'

I looked at the diagram and tried to imagine it multiplied by a thousand. I reached for my phone and hit redial. 'Gerry, what triggers the alerts in your tracking software, stakes or payout?'

'Stakes. Too late by the time it comes to payout. We want to block the bets before the race or change the price.'

'But suppose it was lots of small individual stakes being placed from different accounts. Is there a lower level where they'd be watching for those types of bets, where they'd maybe start aggregating the individual stakes?'

'Good question. Can you hold a minute?'

'Sure.'

Mave was watching me intently.

Gerry came back on, 'A fiver.'

'That low? You're kidding?'

'We don't like taking chances.'

'Thanks, Gerry.'

'Anytime, my friend.'

I nodded toward the diagram. 'Off the top of your head, how many PCs do you think he's controlling?'

'Twenty five thousand.'

'Could he also have used them to open an account for each PC owner with a bookmaker?'

'Easily.'

'Without them knowing?'

'He'd just channel all the communications from the bookmaker to a folder in the cloud somewhere that he could access.'

'How about twenty five thousand bets at two quid each?'

Mave smiled.

FORTY-NINE

'Gerry, sorry to bother you for the third time in half an hour.'

'No trouble, Eddie.'

'Would you mind checking those races I listed for online bets under a fiver, especially from recently opened accounts?'

'Sure. It will take a bit longer.'

It took almost an hour and Gerry apologized for the delay. 'I could have got back to you sooner, but the shower of shit that's now hit the fan is covering the whole industry. We reckon those horses have cost the major bookmakers, not just us, close to three million off the back of thousands of bets, all at four pounds stakes.'

By the time I got off the phone, Gerry had asked me to come and speak to the Association of British Bookmakers at a special meeting in his chairman's house in Surrey the following evening.

Mave high-fived me. 'I told you I'd supercharge your brain, didn't I!'

'You did, Mave. You're a genius.'

'Three million!'

'Now they're shitting themselves in case the news gets out. Their shareholders are going to be picking the heads that will roll furthest. Gerry wants me to meet the big chiefs tomorrow night.'

'What for?'

'To see how a lid can be kept on it, I suppose.'

'So the BHA are running scared and now the bookmakers are with them.'

'By the sound of things the bookies will be sprinting past them very shortly. At least the BHA don't have shareholders to worry about.'

After another call to Gerry Waldron, we figured that the betting accounts had been opened alongside new accounts with a specialist online payment transfer company called PayPunter. The bets had been made and winnings withdrawn to thousands of PayPunter accounts to which only this guy had access. Gerry was going to try and find out where the funds from PayPunter had been transferred to.

'The money will have gone to a handful of accounts which you'll find are now closed,' Mave said. 'So we know the motive, we know the victims, we know how he did it all but we're not one step nearer finding out who he is or where he is.'

'The links are Watt and Kilberg and Jimmy. One of them, or all of them knew this guy.'

The phone rang, the landline. It was Mac. 'Eddie, the autopsies on Watt and Kilberg show no cancer. No disease. Watt's heart was slightly enlarged, otherwise he was fit and well although noticeably overweight.'

I looked at Mave and mouthed "No cancer." 'Thanks, Mac. What about the stomach wall for signs of cyanide residue?'

'None found. The docs say that's unusual. They'd have been dead by the time it had been fully dispersed, so some could have been expected to remain in the stomach. What are your thoughts on it?'

'Just a hunch. It's tied in with something else. Can you ask them to check for oestrogen in all three corpses?'

'That's a female hormone.'

'It is. Trust me on this one, Mac. I'll come and see you tomorrow and take you through how we see it.'

'We?'

'My friend, the genius.' I smiled at Mave and she made a brave attempt at fluttering her eyelashes.

'The one who helped with the bugs?'

'The same.'

'I'll come back to you.'

We moved to the Snug and I threw some logs on the stove while Mave poured whiskey over ice. I opened the curtains and we tried to look through the reflection of the room out into the darkness.

There was something I'd forgotten, and I couldn't bring it to mind. I stared at the fire and listened to the crackling logs. 'Where are you tomorrow?' Mave asked.

'Fontwell.'

'For how many?'

'Two.'

'You do the weights okay?'

I held my whiskey glass up to the fire and filtered the view of the flames through the golden liquid. 'Eleven two and eleven five. No sweat.'

'Literally. Are you meeting McCarthy there?'

'Probably.'

'You going to tell him about the betting coup?'

'Nope. I promised Gerry I'd say nothing until I meet his guys.'

'And you've promised McCarthy you'll say nothing to anyone about the ringer. Should be fun tomorrow night! What's the point of going there and wriggling your way through questions?'

'Because Gerry asked me as a favour. And I think I could raise a fighting fund to help us catch this guy.'

'How much?'

'How much do we need? Is there anything money can buy that would help untangle that mess of a diagram on your screen?'

'Pointless, Eddie, even if they could. It won't terminate at his PC, I'll guarantee you that. What about trying to trace the horse, this Fruitless Spin or Fissure Splint or whatever the hell it's called?'

'Good idea. They'll have plenty experts to call on who might recognize the horse.'

Mac rang back to say the oestrogen test would need to wait until tomorrow. We arranged to meet after racing.

FIFTY

Driving to Fontwell, I began obsessing about where this horse had gone, this Fruitless Spin or whatever it was called. Removing the horse from Watt's place could only mean that this guy intended to find another trainer to put it with, a small trainer who could manage alone.

Nobody with full time staff could do what Bayley had done. A horse being boxed up and sent racing would be known to everybody in the yard. Regular name changes and the bleaching of body parts would soon be public knowledge outside of a one-man operation like Bayley Watt's. Even he was supposed to have two stable staff registered with the BHA. One of those was Kilberg. I'd need to ask Mac who the other was. Probably someone fictitious.

My brain slowly churned through the small yards I knew of, the permit trainers. Tonight I'd make a proper list, and it would be pretty short. That cheered me.

But at the races, I couldn't rest. Even when I wasn't riding, I headed for the paddock to look at the runners, searching for the well-made bay gelding of around sixteen hands, with the athletic walk.

My booked mounts finished second and third. I picked up a spare in the last, but realized after two flights of hurdles that I'd better start trying to think of something positive to say to the losing owners.

Mac was waiting in his car, in the dusk. I'd showered and my hair was still wet and the wind chilled my head as I hurried through the car park..

'You smell like a coconut,' Mac said.

'Shower gel. It is a bit sweet. Open a window.'

'I'll get used to it. What's new?'

I told him about the theory of the oestrogen implants, then watched expectantly. Mac had always liked to build suspense when he knew something and he stared poker-faced for five seconds. 'Watt and Kilberg had extremely high levels of oestrogen, way above normal. None was found in Jimmy Sherrick.'

I felt myself almost slump with relief getting the confirmation that Jimmy hadn't been involved in paedophilia. 'Levels way above normal,' I said. 'I thought levels would be zero. It's a female hormone, isn't it?'

'That's what I thought. The experts tell me every man has oestrogen, just as every woman has testosterone. How do you think he was topping up the hormone feed in Watt and Kilberg?'

'I don't know. I hadn't got that far.'

'The medics say the indications are that it's completely natural in Watt and Kilberg. The oestrogen they found needed no synthesizing by the body.'

I looked at him.

'They found another implant in both Watt and Kilberg, one that wasn't present in Jimmy Sherrick. It was in the back of the neck, at the base of the skull under the hairline. They believe it was sending some kind of radio frequency signal to the brain.'

'To encourage the production of oestrogen?'

'That's the way they're thinking. More tests are planned for tomorrow.'

'Mac, this guy is a genius.'

'You tell me your friend's a genius too. We'd best pray he's a higher grade of genius than whoever's done this.'

'Let's hope we get the chance to find out.' I turned side on to look at him. It was almost dark outside. 'You seem reasonably composed, Mac. Is there something else you're not telling me?'

He shook his head. 'You know all I know. I'm just relieved this hasn't broken yet. I didn't think we had a snowball's chance of keeping it quiet. Every day that passes without it breaking makes it more likely we can keep it under wraps.'

'Well, he's got the horse back. He wouldn't have risked taking it from Watt's if he didn't plan to try again.'

He turned to me. 'That's right, stoke my anxiety.'

'It's reality, Mac. But what we have on our side is that he can only pull this off using a very small yard, probably another permit trainer. There can't be many?'

'Off the top of my head, I don't know.'

'Well why don't you find out and have your inspectors pay them all a little informal visit this week to let them see you're on the ball?'

'I might just do that.'

I told him I was heading off for a meeting with the bookmakers.

'Why?'

'We traced the betting angle. He was keeping stakes below their trigger limit of a fiver and placing thousands through hijacked PCs.'

Mac covered his face with his hands. 'Mac, listen, the bookies will be as keen as you are to keep this ringer angle under wraps.'

He turned to me. 'You can't tell them about the ringer!'

'They've laid the same horse at least three times! Maybe more, to the tune of three million in losses. Okay, the horse will be under different names on their records, but these guys are not stupid.'

'Three million? It sounds like stupid is a reasonable term for them.'

'And what does that make the BHA?'

'Okay. Slag us off, as usual.'

'Mac, what is the point in denying information to the bookies? They've got a thousand times the cash that the BHA has to throw at this and solve it. They'll find this horse long before any of the rest of us will.'

He simmered, then cooled. 'Can you get them to promise to keep it quiet?'

'Yes.'

He leant back on the headrest and sighed. 'Please God, why didn't I take early retirement last year?'

FIFTY-ONE

From Fontwell, I drove thirty miles north to Shalford in Surrey for my meeting with the Association of British Bookmakers. The CEO of Betstore, one of the biggest chains, had offered to host it in his Georgian house. The butler led me through and announced me as he opened the door into a room the length of a bowling alley. The three floor to ceiling windows were big enough to be roadside poster sites.

Eight men and one woman took up a third of the table, chairs askew, drinks at hand and an atmosphere so relaxed it was bordering on jolly. I'd expected to be wading through tears and bitten fingernails.

My friend Gerry Waldron got up and came to welcome me. A handshake and a hug from this big grey-haired man with the kind eyes and genuine look. I felt I'd known him all my life. With an arm across my shoulder, he introduced me, pulled out a beautifully upholstered chair and poured a whiskey and ice for me.

By the time I was ready to leave, two hours later, I had promised them silence on my part about their losses and they'd reciprocated on the news of the ringer. They had committed resources and cash to help find the horse and whoever had engineered the betting coups.

'What about you, Eddie,' asked the Betstore chairman, 'what's your fee?'

'I hadn't thought about it.'

'I feel more comfortable dealing with a man who knows what he's worth.'

I looked at the faces, watching, waiting for an answer. I said, 'The five companies here take how much betting turnover, percentage wise?'

The chairman glanced at the others and said, 'About eighty percent of UK turnover.'

'Okay. If I catch this guy, all five of you give a hundred grand each to cancer research.'

The expectant smiles of these professionals watching this amateur, faded quickly, though the chairman held steady, determined to appear unfazed. 'I'm in,' he said.

The rest quickly followed.

Mave was pleased to hear that Mac had confirmed the oestrogen theory, but she was concerned about the commitment to the bookies. 'How are you going to keep these guys at bay?' Mave asked, 'At a hundred grand a time, they'll want hourly reports on progress.'

'They'll disappear back to their offices now. Details won't matter to them. They've appointed a project manager. I tell him what I want and he gets it done. No questions asked.'

'They sound a dream to deal with compared to the BHA.'

'Pragmatism versus paranoia. No contest.'

She turned back to the PC, and clicked to bring up two windows on screen and said, 'Once you've made fresh coffee, I'm going to lay your doodle pad square on the desk and get you to link the latest theories of Maven Judge.'

I headed for the kitchen, walking and talking. 'Mentioning yourself in the third person, Mave, rarely a good sign.'

'You're right, but, well it's not…'

I filled the kettle, waiting for her to finish, but she didn't. I called to her, 'It's not really you, was what you were going to say, wasn't it? It was your alter-ego. What do they call it these days? Your avatar.'

She said nothing. I carried the coffee to her desk. 'What's your real name?' I asked.

'If I told you, I'd have to kill you.'

'Come on, Mave. We're living together, remember?'

She smiled and drank, looking at me over the blue rim. 'Someday I'll tell you.'

'I know nothing about you except that your brain's as big as the moon and you're half crazy.'

'Never a truer word, Edward, as you will one day find out.'

'Come on, I've laid open my heart and soul.'

'Not for me. You've laid those open for the world, because that's the kind of person you are. We're all different.'

'Some more different than others.'

'Agreed.'

She returned to the haven of her keyboard and screen. I said, 'I'll tell you what, if I crack this before you, and before the cops, you tell me your life history.'

She smiled, keeping her eyes on the scrolling text. 'And if I crack it first, what do you tell me?'

'I tell you I'll never ask again.'

'And you come in with me as a partner in the system?'

'So long as it means I don't break any rules.'

'You might have to slightly fracture some very small ones.'

'We'll see.'

'Okay. This project manager guy the bookies set up, have you got his number?'

I took out my phone. 'In here.'

'Call him and ask for the IP addresses of fifty of the customers whose PCs were hijacked. There's a minuscule chance our man has been complacent enough to leave a route open from the first PC he infected.'

'I thought you said there were thousands of PCs?'

'There are. If I get the details of fifty, I can write some code that will probably identify all of them.'

I dialled the number of the project manager, Ishrat Uppal, realizing I didn't know if it was a man or a woman.

It was a woman, and she proved very, very helpful.

FIFTY-TWO

I came through the kitchen next morning and heard the keyboard clicking. Mave had reverted to her old nocturnal habits.

I took her some coffee. She grunted and kept working. I knew better now than to say any more, and went for a shower. Mave was still in the zone when I left home before daybreak. I had two trainers to ride out for, then three rides at Chepstow.

Driving west to Chepstow, Mister Sherrick called to tell me he'd tracked down Jimmy's ex-girlfriend, Amanda. I pulled over and he gave me her details. 'She said she'll be happy to talk to you.'

'Good. How've you been?' I asked.

'I'm fine, Eddie. Don't worry about me.'

'How's the fiddle gig going?'

He laughed. 'They're dancing in the aisles.'

'That's nice to hear. Listen, I've made some headway lately, are you around this evening?'

'I'll be here. You're welcome anytime.'

'I'll try and see Amanda on the way home, then call in.'

'I'll look forward to it.'

When I arrived at Chepstow, I phoned Amanda. She said she'd meet me at a hotel in Swindon that evening and I was to call her when I was half an hour away.

My final mount was a winner, and I took extra satisfaction from knowing I'd had a lot to do with that. He was an old handicapper who hadn't won for two seasons. He'd lost the habit and, worse, had got comfortable with that.

From the first fence I was gently pushing him, rhythmically, talking to him: 'Come on, you're a decent horse. You're not finished winning yet. Let's show them you can still do it.' And I kept this up, along with the constant urging forward into his bridle, and with five to jump, he began to believe me and he took hold of the bit, and I kept pumping away steadily and his confidence grew on the strength, perhaps, of old memories, and by the time we jumped the second last in third position, he knew and I knew we were going to catch the two in front, that he'd once again be leader of the pack.

I was beginning to get a reputation for regenerating these veteran horses who'd spent seasons going through the motions, like the slow kid in class who's gradually shuffled away into obscurity.

I was still in high spirits when I met Amanda Radicci, and her warm smile and big friendly eyes soon told me how she worked on men. Jimmy's outlook, his lost in the past view regarding technology, summed up his general approach. He preferred simplicity and took things at face value. If Amanda had looked at him with this burning concentration, as if he were all that mattered, Jimmy would have been captivated. His forty plus years must have felt half that. He'd have seen his life open up again.

She settled in the corner of the lounge and asked for mineral water. I judged her to be about thirty. Her eyes and hair were dark, her skin so smooth from expert makeup application that she looked as though she'd been airbrushed. Except for her footwear, she was dressed almost primly: high necked sweater and knee-length skirt under a long coat. Her legs were crossed, and spike-heeled leather boots pointed at me as I returned with the drinks. I wondered how far up under that hem the boot-tops stretched.

I explained I was a friend of Jimmy's and that his Dad was concerned about the way the police had handled things. I was only trying to help him out.

The sultry determined look she'd greeted me with had been gradually toned down when she saw I wasn't responding to it, and she said, 'So long as none of this is official. Not that I've anything to hide. I never met Jimmy's dad, but he always seemed a nice man from what Jimmy told me, and he sounded sweet on the phone.'

I asked her if Jimmy spoke much about his job and the people he worked with. She said that all he ever wanted to talk about was how great everything would be when his divorce was through and they could move abroad and make a new start in the sun. It was that, she said, that gradually wore her down and made her decide to leave. 'I was twelve years younger than Jimmy, but ended up feeling like his mother half the time. It was like being with a kid on a car journey who keeps asking "Are we there yet?"'

That got to me. That resurgence of hope she'd given him that had backfired on the poor sod. I wished she hadn't told me about it. I felt as though she'd whispered some bedroom secret that had wounded Jimmy's dignity.

'Didn't you fancy moving abroad?' I asked.

'I would have if there'd been a proper chance. But Jimmy was a dreamer. He didn't have the money. His divorce was going to be expensive. He kept saying something was being put together, but he wouldn't tell me the details.'

'You think he was making it up?'

'I think he believed it, he kept telling me it was all hush hush. That didn't help things either. Then he went to Ireland for some tests, said it was a medical Bayley Watt wanted him to have as he was getting a bit older. I wanted to go with him, but he wouldn't have it. That didn't help things, if you know what I mean.'

I wondered if that was for the implant, or something to do with Jimmy's cancer. 'How long was he away?'

She turned to me, her big eyes much colder now. 'Listen, this is beginning to sound like some kind of interrogation. Could I get in trouble over this?'

'No, no, not at all. How would you be in trouble? I'm just trying to help Jimmy's dad get to the bottom of things. Jimmy left the house to him and an insurance policy, and the insurance company are arguing about Jimmy's mental health, his suicide. You know how they are with things like that.'

'His mental health seemed fine. He wasn't depressed, the opposite, if you ask me. He was always happy unless we'd had a fallout. Then he'd brood for a day or two, which is hardly abnormal, is it? Tell Jimmy's dad if he needs a signed statement from me or something, I'll do that.'

'I will. Thanks. So did Jimmy go through with the medical?'

'As far as I know, though we still weren't really talking when he came back.'

'And it was Ireland he went to?'

She nodded. 'He bought a scratchcard on the flight to Dublin. I found it in his pocket…when I was doing a washing.'

She watched me and I tried to look as though I believed she hadn't been going through Jimmy's stuff. She said, 'The scratchcard was typical. He was always looking for the "lump sum", as he called it - made me feel like a bloody debt that was waiting to be paid off.'

I looked at her. 'I knew Jimmy for years,' I said, and I told her about the time he saved my life. 'He was a good man. Whatever he was doing it would have been for you.'

'I know it would. I know. He just got too serious, too soon. I kind of tried to get him to ease off, but he was blind and deaf to anything I said unless it was "I love you" or "come to bed". We hadn't been together forty-eight hours and he was making plans, even talking about having kids. It was too much for me, and I couldn't get him to understand that. I'm not some cold hearted bitch who picked him up then dumped him. I simply couldn't cope. I'm sorry.'

I nodded.

'Do you believe me?'

'Yes. I believe you.'

'Does Jimmy's dad think he killed himself because of me?'

'No. He doesn't.'

'Jimmy was sick, you know. I don't think he told anyone else. After we broke up he sent me a letter saying that the medical we'd had the fallout over, had shown he had cancer, that he hadn't wanted to tell me in case it scared me away. He said there was some treatment he was getting, something nobody had ever tried before, and it would either cure him or kill him. He said the illness must have been playing on him and that's why he'd been so obsessional with me, that he was sorry and if the treatment worked would I take him back.'

'Did you-'

'I wrote back to him. I said, yes. I'd give it another chance.'

She was getting tearful, trying to keep her voice low. She looked around to see if anyone was watching us. She took a napkin from the table and dabbed at the corners of her eyes, then clutched it, her red fingernails digging into it as she said, 'You know what I'm most ashamed of? It wasn't the walking out, or the Dear John letter, it was…it was saying I'd give it another chance if he got better, because the first thought I had when I posted that letter was I hope he dies from the cancer and I don't have to keep my promise.'

'Your heart was in the right place when you wrote it, Amanda. We all mess up. All of us.'

She wept, and that palette of makeup she wore left her looking like a clown. She excused herself. I waited, wondering if poor Jimmy had taken bribes to keep quiet about the ringers. Bribes and a supposed cancer cure implanted in Ireland.

He'd have travelled home full of new hope, waiting for the capsule inside him to start its healing work. A capsule containing cyanide. A bug recording his conversations. That call to me just before Christmas was listened to and twenty four hours later the cyanide capsule was triggered, then Watt and Kilberg hoisted Jimmy on that chain for me to find. Poor bastard.

FIFTY-THREE

When I reached the car, I called McCarthy and asked him to get his guys searching in Ireland for what this ringer might be.

'Why Ireland?'

'A few reasons. I'll tell you next time I see you.'

'I thought the bookies were looking for it?'

'They will be.'

'They're keeping quiet about this?'

'Even quieter than you.'

Next stop was Mister Sherrick's flat. I noticed that when he clicked the kettle switch, it boiled quickly and I guessed he'd been expecting me sooner. I carried the tray from the kitchen to the fireside. Mister Sherrick said, 'I met Ben Tylutki when I was at the shops buying those biscuits. He said you gave that Chepstow winner as fine a ride as he's seen.'

'Ah, he's a good friend of mine, Ben.'

'Eddie, we get enough brickbats in life. Don't be shy about taking the compliments.'

'I just hate tempting fate, Jim.'

I told him about the meeting with Amanda, softening the hard edges as best I could. 'What is she like, pretty?'

'Very. Dark, big eyes, nice skin. She's looked after herself.'

'She sounded a nice girl on the phone.'

'She seems all right, though I'm not sure Jimmy would have put up with her for too long, even if she hadn't walked out.'

'Demanding type?'

'I'd say so.'

We sat and talked for an hour, though I had to be careful about what I said. I'd have trusted Mister Sherrick with my life, but didn't want to put him in a dangerous position.

Back home, I opened the door to silence. No keyboard clicks, no cursing. Mave was not at the desk. I found her asleep in the big chair by the fire, chin on chest, loose hair changing colour in the reflection of the fire flames.. It was the first time I'd seen her completely still and calm, and I was struck by her slightness. Her shallow chest drew small quick breaths like a mouse. Her hands were clasped in her lap. I lifted the woollen throw from the sofa and laid it carefully across her.

I made coffee, and sat at the desk with my pad and pen, feeling that I was somehow in Mave's space. As ever, I drew until I had drawn conclusions; piecing possibilities together and trying to break them down. If I couldn't find a flaw, they stayed on the list to discuss with Mave.

Jimmy had gone to Ireland for his so called medical which had to be when the stuff was implanted. I could easily get a list of the dates he'd been away.

If our man was based in Ireland, it was a fair assumption that the horse had come from there, although it might make the animal's identity harder to discover.

So what time had Bayley Watt spent in Ireland? Or maybe Kilberg had been the man to travel? I sensed rather than heard Mave behind me, and I turned to see her shoeless and forlorn, still half asleep.

'Can I help you, madam?' I asked.

'I'm looking for my common sense.'

'Oh. When did you last see it?'

'At home, in Wales. Seems like months ago.'

'Well, that's probably where you'll find it, refreshed and waiting.'

'Get off my chair.'

I got up and Mave sidled over and sat, her fingers reaching for the keyboard like a comfort blanket.

Over coffee she ran the programme she'd built. All it was to me was a one-minute blur on the PC screen. It ended with a twelve digit number. Mave said, 'That's the IP address of the end PC in the link this guy was using.'

'What's IP? Does that tell us who and where this person is, the one who owns the PC?'

'Internet Protocol. It tells us where the PC is down to the city level. With more work, I could break through and into the PC itself, but it would be easier and quicker to get your police friends to get the service provider to give us access.'

'Then what?'

'There's a chance, if your man has been complacent, that I can find out what PC was used to pick up the data from this one.'

I called Mac and got the usual "leave it with me."

I turned to Mave. 'So, how many PCs were in his network?'

'Close to thirty-three-thousand.'

'Jeez.'

'Smart fella.'

'Nice work, Mave.'

'It was, actually.'

We smiled and I thought of what Mister Sherrick had said, and how much easier it was for Mave to accept compliments.

I sat back and picked up my pad. 'Here's my version of coding. Try this.'

'Let me go to the toilet first. A gallon of coffee's bursting my bladder.'

'I'll make some more, to help refill it.'

FIFTY-FOUR

Mave was back at her desk, fresher, coffee mug looking large in her narrow fingers. She rested her chin on the rim and with the cast of the low light, it looked as though her small thin face could easily drop in and sink.

I said, 'That last PC in the hijacked network theoretically puts us within one step of our man, doesn't it? What are the chances? Try and look at it objectively, and tell me the odds.'

'If he's stayed careful, a million to one. If he's dropped into complacency, much, much shorter. Remember I said to you when you told me the horse names that he'd taken a chance by using an anagram? Fruitless Spin, Fissure Splint…what was the other horse?'

'Spiritless Fun.'

'Very clever people sometimes can't resist dropping in a tiny clue to let other clever people know how smart they are. They're not bothered about impressing the masses. But when they think they'll never be caught, they sometimes like to tease. If he believes a network of more than thirty thousand PCs is enough to protect him from anyone, then he could be in for a surprise.'

'Is there any way he could suss you're trying to track him through that network?'

'He could have coded something in to alert him, but he'd have needed some knowledge of the way I code to second guess me.'

'I thought software code was software code?'

'Coding can be as individual as a painting, or a song. I could look at code and tell you who wrote the programme if I'm halfway familiar with his work.'

'So if he's had an anagram moment, he might be just a step away?'

'Could be. Let's see how quickly the cops get official access to that last PC in the line.'

I stood up and stretched and yawned. 'I'll call Mac first thing and press him for a result tomorrow.' I saw myself in the mirror. 'God, I look even more tired than I feel.'

'You've no stamina, Malloy.'

I massaged my face with my hands, rubbed my eyes. When my fingers were at my chin I stopped and stared at my reflection and thought of Bayley Watt. I turned to Mave. 'If you see me doing that face rubbing thing again, smack me on the head with something hard. I don't want any reminders of Bayley Watt lodged in my psyche.'

'It'll be a pleasure.'

'I'll bet.'

'You were going to show me your version of coding, which I take to be some more doodling.'

I told her about my meeting with Amanda.

'So,' Mave said, 'it seems to confirm Jimmy was the only one of the three with cancer. Watt and Kilberg have been straightforward "take the oestrogen and run the ringer scam or you're in deep shit."'

'That seems a fair summary.'

'So the man we assumed had a conscience in trying to disable two paedophiles, can't find any of that conscience when it comes to the only innocent guy of the three. He tells him he's implanting a cancer cure, and he puts in cyanide.'

'Well, when we assumed the cancer treatment, we thought Watt and Kilberg had cancer too. It turned out they didn't. So maybe that wasn't what he told Jimmy.'

'But what else would have persuaded him to agree to an implant? And remember, Kilberg spun you the cancer tale for all three. He didn't produce that from nothing, did he?'

'True. I suppose the best you can say is that our man knew Jimmy was going to die anyway.'

'He knew that all right. If the cancer didn't kill him, the cyanide would.'

'Move your chair, a second, will you? Let me find Jimmy's letter.' I opened the desk drawer and took out the letter and read it to Mave:

Dear Eddie,

I'd been meaning to talk to you for a while. If you're reading this, then I probably never got round to it. Don't think too badly of me. I was just trying to come with a late run. I doubt I'd ever have got up, and the stewards would have taken it away from me anyway.

Life is short. Health is precious. Spend no time trying to make your mark, because we will all be forgotten.

'Don't think too badly of me,' Mave said. 'That says to me he knew about the scam. Plus the fact he said that the stewards would have taken it away anyway. Doesn't that confirm he knew what he was doing was wrong?'

I nodded, a weary sadness coming over me. 'You're probably right.' I got up and stretched and yawned. 'Maybe we'll crack it tomorrow,' I said.

'It depends what kind of stand the ISP takes when the police ask for the ID of the person who owns the PC.'

'You think they'll drag it out for a while?'

'Could do.'

'How long would it take you to find it…if you had to?'

She shrugged. 'Don't know until I try. I might have a go tonight.'

'Mind if I leave you to it? I'm whacked.'

'See how tired you get when you use your brain?'

'You're right. I'm not used to it.'

Mave watched me. 'I haven't said this to you for a while, Eddie, but are you sure you want to carry on? If he has left some code in there to warn him if somebody's getting close to that last PC, he's going to know you're breathing down his neck. I think the only reason he hasn't threatened you so far is that his ego wouldn't allow him to believe you could get anywhere near him. He might have changed his mind by daybreak.'

'I'll be careful.'

'You don't know the meaning of the word.'

I smiled. 'Goodnight, Mave.'

'Sweet dreams, Edward.'

FIFTY-FIVE

Returning winnerless from Exeter, I was driving on dark country roads when Mac finally returned the calls I'd made earlier. 'You're a hard fella to get hold of, Mac. I've been trying since this morning.'

'Sorry, Eddie. No point in me talking to you unless I had answers to your questions. Well, answers that you won't find particularly helpful, but answers nonetheless.'

'Go on.'

'The Internet Service Provider wants a court order before releasing the information.'

'How long will that take?'

'We're trying to push it through today, before the weekend.'

'How hard can it be, Mac? I read about these celebrities getting them on a Saturday to prevent publication in Sunday papers.'

'Celebs can afford top barristers.'

'So if it's not tonight, we give this guy an extra forty eight hours to cover his tracks.'

'What guy?'

'The perp! Mister Big! Whatever you want to call him. The guy who killed at least three men.'

He sighed, long and loud. 'Eddie, look, I've been trying to avoid asking you the tougher questions on the basis that if I don't know something, I'm not compromised at this end. But I think it's time we met for one of our informal chats.'

'You name the place and time, Mac. I'll be there.'

'Where are you tomorrow?'

'Wincanton.'

'I'll see you there. Can you meet me in the car park before racing?'

'Will do.'

'See you then.'

I stabbed the button to end the call and cursed aloud. I'd known Mac a long time. We'd helped each other out over the years, but why was I always left feeling like the patsy? What were they doing camped out at Newbury police station with their so-called incident team? I had a feeling there was one man and a dog on this and they were getting us to do all the running around. If it hadn't been for Jimmy and his dad I'd have told them where to shove it.

'You're a troubled man,' Mave said when I walked in and slung my kitbag down so it slid along the floor toward the kitchen. 'Your face is like fizz.'

I told her what had happened with Mac and about the delay with court order, but every second word was a curse and she ended up laughing. 'It's at times like this a man realizes that the lexicon of swear words is so frustratingly sparse and inadequate,' Mave said.

'Knowing you, you'll invent some new ones.'

'I could do that. Easily. It's making them fashionable, that's the problem. Marketing.'

I sat on the desk, calmer now. 'Any news?'

'Plenty news.'

'Go on.'

'Our man got complacent.'

'He linked to that last PC in the network?'

'Looks like it.'

'Did you get into his?'

'Nope. That's what makes me pretty sure this is the man. It's been more than seven years since I hit a system I couldn't find my way into. I've never come across protection this strong.'

'So are we any further forward?'

'Well, I couldn't get into his PC but after about three hours I broke through from the ISP side and found out where the PC is located.'

'You've got his address?'

'Well, kind of.'

'Mave, come on!'

'It's a company. Based in Dublin. They're called Nequitec.'

'What's their business?'

'There are clues in the name. We could play some nice word games here, but somehow I don't think you're in the mood.'

'Mave!'

'They sell implants to Weatherbys.'

'Implants? Passport chips?'

'For implanting. In the necks of racehorses. Or in Watt's case, for replanting in the necks of several racehorses.'

I slumped in the chair. 'Fuck me!' I laughed.

'I'll pass on that, if you don't mind.'

I opened my arms. 'How easy was that? Why didn't I think to start there instead of end there? I'm thick.'

'It's as easy to be thick in hindsight as it is to be smart.'

I slid the chair across, close to Mave and took her pale face gently in my hands and smiled stupidly at her. She said quietly, 'What are you planning to do with my head?'

'I wish someone had invented a word beyond genius.'

'Super genius?'

'You're the eighth wonder of the world, Maven Judge, and I'd like to kiss you.'

'Hoping the frog will turn into a princess?'

'You're not a frog. You're wonderful.'

'The two are not inseparable.'

I leaned toward her, still holding her cheeks. She put a finger to her lips, blocking me, then said, 'I don't want to be kissed as a reward.'

'It's not a reward!'

'And I don't want a sympathy kiss.'

I let go her face and sat back, feeling embarrassed and ashamed. 'I'm sorry,' I said.

'Don't be. Beauty and the Beast can only work when the girl is the beauty.'

I looked at her and wanted to say that long ago I'd seen through the plain features: the small eyes, the big nose, the thin lips and crooked teeth and untended hair, the tomboy who'd never become a woman because she didn't believe she deserved to. But how do you put that into the spoken word?

'You're a beauty to me.' I said.

'Because you're grateful, and because I've helped you. And because you're a very sweet man.'

'Do the reasons matter? I care for you a lot…an awful lot.'

She smiled, 'Then I'll settle for that.'

I offered my hand, and she shook it.

'What next, do you think?' I asked.

'Your move.'

I found myself doing that face-massage again and stopped halfway through.

I looked at Mave. 'What would you do?'

'I'd write down that address, drive to Newbury police station, hand it to your Superintendent woman and get on with my life.'

'They'll balls it up.'

'How? They move in, take the PC, analyze the data and charge the owner of the PC or the MD of the company or whoever.'

'Do we know who the MD is?'

'CEO and founder and majority shareholder is a man called Miles Shanahan. I haven't had time yet to find out much about him.'

'What if the cops can't find somebody smart enough to get into the PC?'

'They won't even try. They'll just ask for the passwords. Mister Shanahan can hardly say no.'

I considered it, then stood up. 'Whiskey?'

'Celebratory?' Mave asked.

'Contemplatory.'

Mave smiled. 'That's the first five syllable word I've heard you use.'

I smiled. 'I wasn't even sure it was a word.'

She jumped up and put an arm round my shoulder, walking me toward the drinks cabinet. 'But you took a punt, my friend, and you were right!' She slapped me on the back.

'Sit down, you daft bugger and I'll pour.'

We held chunky glasses that kept the heat on the outside, protecting the ice inside. 'Pros and cons about stepping out now?' Mave said.

'Go on.'

'This guy's a top-notcher, you accept that?'

'He's top notch at tech stuff and maybe even surgery. But he could be seventy years old for all we know.'

'True, but he could be twenty seven with an arsenal in the cupboard in his office. He killed three men.'

'Remotely. If he had an arsenal, he could have shot them, if he had the balls for it.'

'His balls might be the size of his brain, but why use them when you're way smarter than the cops? If you hadn't taken an interest, police records would have three suicides marked. Cases closed.'

I drank and looked out into the darkness. 'What about-' My ringing phone interrupted me. It was McCarthy. 'Mac, call me on the landline.'

'Sorry, I forgot.'

He called back right away. 'We couldn't get the court order. Sorry. It'll have to be Monday'

'Okay. Thanks. I'll see you at Wincanton tomorrow.'

'You okay?'

'Fine. Why?'

'No pyrotechnics.'

'I've fizzled out, Mac. Good night.'

'Eddie. There's more. The specialists are pretty confident that transmitter at the base of the skull on Watt and Kilberg was sending messages to the brain to activate oestrogen production. They tested Watt's and Kilberg's samples against Jimmy Sherrick's, who would have shown normal, and those two were higher in multiples of thousands.'

'Thanks, Mac. See you tomorrow.'

I told Mave about the oestrogen stimulation. She put down her drink and hurried to the PC. 'There's no way this hasn't been patented. No way!' She sat down, fingers flying across her keyboard.

FIFTY-SIX

I sat in my car at Wincanton racecourse, listening to the heavy rain on the roof, and watching the entrance for Mac arriving. In my pocket was a single piece of paper with all the details printed out for the police. Mave had talked me into it.

Patents were registered in Germany in the name of Miles Shanahan's company, Nequitec. The patents were for implants that could be remotely activated in order to produce a number of different effects on the human body, among them the artificial stimulation of oestrogen to be used in place of chemical castration implants.

The patent approval was eighteen months old. There was a separate patent filed for chemical castration of animals using the same process. A patent application for the use of remote activation of cyanide capsules in humans had been turned down on the basis that "it will probably be found to violate paragraph two of the German Patent Law — which does not allow inventions that transgress public order or good morals".

Mac rolled in through the rain, my wipers showing his progress toward my car like a time lapse. As he pulled in, I jumped out and ran the twenty yards to his car. I jerked the door handle and almost wrenched my knuckles from their sockets. It was locked. Mac hit a button and opened it. My dripping hair was plastered on my skull as I pulled the door closed.

'Sorry. I forgot I'd locked it.'

'Why do you keep your car locked when you're in it? Fucking hell!'

'Here.' He passed me a clean handkerchief and I dried myself as best I could. 'You can't be too careful these days, Eddie. You read about these carjacking incidents and handbags being snatched at traffic lights.'

'You haven't got a fucking handbag!'

I could see he was trying to contain a laugh. 'Calm down. Or maybe I ought to just give you the bad news while you're already annoyed.'

'What bad news?'

'The police are taking over now, full time.'

'Says who?'

'Says the chief constable. Sara had to brief him last night after the final results of all three autopsies. If you and whoever's helping you don't bow out now, and something happens to either of you, it's a PR disaster for the police.'

'So they're closing in on this guy?'

'Not yet. But the chief constable is confident they can find him without any outside help.'

'And how confident are you?'

'Sara believes it's the best thing to do, and I've no reason to doubt her.'

'Bad move, Mac.'

'Why?'

'How long have you known her?'

'About five years. What difference does that make?'

'How long have you known me?'

'Fifteen, sixteen years.'

'And you trust her judgement over mine?'

'Eddie, it's not personal, for God's sake. It's professional.'

'I'm a professional!'

'You're a professional jockey! She's a senior police officer.'

'How many times have I helped you out of scrapes before the police did?'

'We're not keeping score here, come on!'

'You're not, are you? That's the problem.'

He laid his big head back on the rest, rolling it gently and sighing.

'Sigh away. What exactly have the police done in this case to give you confidence in them? Where would you all have been if I hadn't been feeding you stuff?'

'And Sara appreciates that, believe me. But we need to take the emotion out of it, take a step back. Let them get on with what they do best.'

'What they do best! Are you kidding me?'

'Well what would you do in her position?'

'I wouldn't sack the only guy who's been coming up with leads, would you?'

'It's not my decision, Eddie.'

'That's a fucking cop-out, Mac! Diplomatic bullshit picked up from that chancer, Buley.'

'Okay! Okay! No, I wouldn't sack you, as you put it.'

'Well why not fight my corner?'

'It's a very delicate situation. You're not stuck in the middle of it. You can only see it from one perspective.'

'Mac, do you ever stop and think it might be you who's wrong? When you're trying to see things from all these different perspectives, don't you ever just simply want to do what you feel is the right thing?'

He sighed again. 'Maybe we should talk later.'

'Later being when Sara Chase and her chief constable come up empty? No thanks, Mac. Make the choice now. Am I in or out?'

He did the head rolling and sighing again, then he turned to me. 'I'm sorry. You're out.'

My tantrum lasted until I reached the changing room, until I went into the toilet and flushed the details on Miles Shanahan down the toilet and said aloud, 'Chase that, Sara!'

Three hours later, I nursed a novice 'chaser through two miles of Somerset mud, happy to bide my time, to get him safely over each fence and steadily reel in the leader and pass him yards from the post.

Another winner. It stoked my confidence and my resolve to get on a flight late this evening and head for Dublin to nail the man who killed Jimmy Sherrick.

FIFTY-SEVEN

Mave watched me pack a carry-on bag for the flight, calling out as I dropped each item in. 'Underwear, toothbrush, shaving cream, bullet proof vest, last will and testament…'

'Very funny.'

'Eddie, why are you packing a bag at all? Why are you going there? It's utterly pointless.'

'I don't want the police ballsing it up.'

'You don't want the police getting the glory when we've done all the work. Isn't that what you mean?'

'That too.' I zipped the bag closed.

'What, you want your name in all the papers? You'll have no peace for the rest of your life. All sorts of wackos will be trying to get you to do things. Go and stand out in your summer house and listen to your beloved silence, and say goodbye to it while you're out there. You're going to have the media down here and every weirdo who feels the police should have done better for them and think you should be their white knight. For fuck's sake, see sense!'

'I'm not bothered about any glory. I want to do right by Jimmy and his father.'

'Well, do right by handing over this guy's details. How can the police balls that up? Here's his name and address. Here's the patents he filed. Get his PC and you'll find all the evidence you need on bugged conversations and betting fraud.'

I smiled at her as I lifted the bag off the bed. 'I didn't know you cared.'

241

'Eddie, seriously. You burst in here half an hour ago raving about how McCarthy doesn't trust you. Answer me this, do you trust me?'

I'd never seen her so animated. 'Of course I trust you.'

'You trust my judgement?'

I knew what was coming but had to say yes.

'Then unpack the bag, call McCarthy and give him those details. It'll all be over by this time tomorrow, and you and me can be have Sunday lunch in the pub up the road without watching whiskey pissing out of bullet holes in your belly.'

In the end, I compromised. I arranged a meeting with Mac and Sara Chase that evening and offered to trade the paper I held with Shanahan's details for the right to be there when they went for him.

'No heroics,' said Superintendent Chase. 'We go in first. You stay outside in a safe vehicle. When we've got him and secured the area, you can come in.'

'No deal.'

'Why?'

'I want to see his face when you arrest him for the murder of Jimmy Sherrick.'

She clenched her square jaw in frustration. 'We'll secure the area and you can come in for the reading of his rights, which will be done by our Irish colleagues.'

I settled for that and they began making arrangements with the Garda in Dublin.

'Go home,' Mac said. 'We'll call you when everything's set up.'

I looked at him, then at the Superintendent. I got up. 'Don't stiff me on this, Mac. I'll never forgive you.'

Sara Chase stood up right in front of me. 'Nobody will stiff you or anyone else on this, Mister Malloy. You have my word,' she reached to shake hands. 'I'll send a car for you when the time comes, but we'll need some patience to put things in place with our counterparts in the Garda Siochana. Red tape doesn't get any thinner when you cross the Irish sea, I'm afraid.'

I'd been hoping for a dawn raid on Shanahan's big house in Ballsbridge, but it looked like I'd be having that Sunday lunch with Mave instead.

They set it for midnight, Monday. That meant I could make my rides at Uttoxeter, and if all went to plan, I'd be back for Ludlow on Tuesday.

At seven p.m. a police car picked me up from home and took me to Heathrow. I'd expected Mac to be there, but it was Sara Chase who greeted me and we both checked onto a flight as standard passengers. As we strapped on seatbelts and watched the usual chaos of boarding, I said, 'I expected a private airfield and a police helicopter with armed SWAT teams or whatever you have.'

She smiled. 'We're on tight budgets, Mister Malloy. And I'll be there for liaison only. Our Garda friends will lay on whatever firepower they think necessary.'

'Do they know Shanahan?'

'They know of him.'

'Has he got any kind of record?'

'Let's just say they never expected him to slip up.'

'Well connected?'

'Very.'

'Well enough to be tipped off about tonight by someone in the Garda?'

I expected an angry rebuke, but she was calm. 'What would be the point of him running? The best he'll try is to blame someone else. I'd be pretty sure this PC that's been controlling everything won't be found in his office at Nequitec.'

She was wrong. That's exactly where it was found. And that, along with the look on Shanahan's face when they charged him told me that whoever killed Jimmy Sherrick was probably still on the loose.

FIFTY-EIGHT

With Shanahan in custody in Dublin in the very early hours, I had plenty time to fly back, go home and get ready for Uttoxeter. I'd sent a text to Mave saying an arrest had been made. She was waiting for the details, mug of tea in hand.

'Shanahan's suspected of making his money years ago in attacks on business PCs, those DDOS things that you used to read about.'

'Distributed Denial of Service. Where they bombard a company's servers with so much traffic, the site seizes up.'

'That's the fella.'

'He was under suspicion in the early days of online betting for doing that to bookmakers, but the police couldn't find enough evidence to take him to court.'

'It's a tricky subject for non-specialists.'

'Anyway, he's always been into racing. He buys a small company producing ID implants for leisure horses, like chipping them for theft prevention and stuff, and he uses his racing contacts to win the big contract supplying implants for thoroughbreds in the UK and Ireland. And he's close to signing up the racing authorities in the USA.'

'Not any more, he's not.'

'Seems that way. But I don't think he's our man.'

Mave knew me well enough now to just watch my face and wait. I said, 'Shanahan might be an accomplished liar, but he seemed genuinely shell shocked when they read him the charge. The PC you traced was in his office, on his desk. He happily gave the passwords for it and they're going through it today. When things cooled down and I had a chance to think, the first thing that came to mind was that, tough as it has been to trace this guy, in the end it was too easy.'

Mave sipped tea then nodded. 'I kind of know what you mean.'

'If Shanahan did this, using a PC in his own office, in his own company, which is worth pots of money anyway…well, there's complacency and there's being a complete idiot. You've always said how smart this guy is. You've called him a genius. Is this what a genius does? Even a complacent one?'

'Normally, no.'

'Mave, if you'd seen his face…There are actors and con men, but, if he is guilty here, those few seconds of facial expressions deserve an Oscar.'

She sat at her desk. 'When do they expect to have the data analysis from the PC?'

'I don't know. I can check with Mac. He texted earlier and said he'd see me at Uttoxeter before racing. But I'm happy to bet now that they'll find the recording of Jimmy's message, copies of the emails sent as suicide messages by Watt and Kilberg, lists of the betting accounts opened, the whole nine yards.'

Mave pushed her hair behind her ears. 'What you're saying, Mister Malloy, is that I've been led up the garden path to the very door our man has wanted me to paint a big red cross on.'

'I'm not blaming you! Don't be daft. I just thought back to how Jimmy's death was made to look so signed sealed and delivered. Especially for the police. They're no different from the rest of us. They love an easy job. This looks like another classic case.'

She nodded. 'I did say I'd be astounded if that last PC in the link was his.'

'You did. And you were right.'

She smiled that crooked smile. 'You are such a sweet man. Your diplomacy is not wasted, Edward, even on a cynic like me.'

I laughed. 'You're only a pretend cynic, Mave. You're as soft as the rest of us deep inside.'

'Soft centre, hard shell. Is that what you're saying?'

'Your shell's getting steadily thinner.'

'I'm beginning to feel like a tortoise.'

My phone rang. It was Mac. I asked him to call back on the landline. He did. 'Eddie, you were there when they arrested this guy, why are we still having covert conversations?'

'My naturally cautious nature, Mac. I'd sooner wait until he's convicted before dropping my guard.'

'Ha! Since when was the word caution ever associated with Eddie Malloy?'

'I keep telling you, older and wiser. That's me.'

'Listen. I can't make Uttoxeter. Can we meet at Hilton Park Services?'

'When?'

'Eleven?'

'Okay.'

Mave waited until I'd hung up then started tapping her keyboard. 'What are you up to?' I asked.

'I want to see if another access point's been used for Shanahan's PC.'

'His PC's in a Garda station in Dublin.'

'But the server's still where it was, for now. Once the cops get a specialist in, the server will be removed too, or locked down. Might as well make hay.'

'You're not planning to go home, then?'

'I've grown accustomed to your face.'

She smiled at my baffled look and said, 'A song title. Paraphrased. One of my dad's favourites.'

'That's the first time you've mentioned another soul you are linked to in any way.'

'Despite everything you've assumed about me since we met, I do indeed have a father and mother. Or had.'

'Are they…aren't they still alive?'

She smiled sadly. 'No, they aren't, I'm afraid.'

'I'm sorry.'

'I am too.'

I sat by the desk and looked at her. She didn't seem upset, still working her keyboard. 'Do you want to talk about it?'

'Not now, thanks. Go and meet McCarthy. You'll be late.'

'Will you be all right?'

'I've been all right for a long time, but thanks for asking. Now bugger off.' I went to the bedroom to pick up my kitbag.

Mave had that knitted-brow look I'd come to know well. I said, 'You've been here over a week. That qualifies you for a goodbye peck on the cheek, but it means you need to have my pipe and slippers ready when I get back.'

'I'll pass. Thanks.'

'See you later.'

'Mmm'

My backup phone rang. I didn't recognize the number, but it had to be somebody involved with this caper. 'Mister Malloy?'

'Who's speaking, please?'

'It's Ishrat Uppal, project manager for, well, that project.'

'Oh, hello. I'm sorry, I didn't have your number in my contacts.'

'That's okay. Can you talk just now?'

'Sure.'

'Our team in Ireland has found your horse.'

'Literally? The horse, or the identification of the horse?'

'The identification. It ran previously at the beginning of last season, before an injury caused it to miss the rest of the season.'

'What's its name?'

'Colossus.'

I knew of it. The horse had won two top novice races in Ireland. It had never raced in the UK under its own name. I could recall the trainer but not the owner. 'Do you know anything about what happened to it after it was taken out of training?'

'It went to its owner's farm.'

'Who's the owner?'

'Enda Magultry was the owner.'

I'd never heard of him. 'Don't tell me...he sold it to a man called Miles Shanahan?'

'Close. He left it to Mister Shanahan in his will.'

'He's dead?'

'Er, yes.'

'When?'

'July eighteen, last year.'

'Suicide?'

'He ate an apple that had been injected with cyanide.'

Mave had stopped tapping and was watching me. I smiled at her and said to Ishrat, 'Your team in Ireland are very efficient.'

'You don't seem so bad yourself, Mister Malloy, if you don't mind me saying.'

'Thanks. Do you think they could find out everything they can about the history of Enda Magultry?'

'I'll get them started on it right away.'

'Good. Thank you. I'll put your name in my contacts now.'

'You have my number?'

'Is this one the best to get you on?' I asked.

'Day or night. And I mean that. If you need to call me at three in the morning, don't hesitate.'

'You'll go far.'

'I try.'

'Speak to you soon.'

'Goodbye.'

I told Mave.

'An apple injected with cyanide? Guess how Alan Turing died?'

'An apple injected with cyanide?'

'That's what was assumed. They found a half-eaten apple by his bed and cyanide in his system. They never tested the apple for cyanide.'

'You're kidding?'

'Dark forces and all that cold war stuff. Turing was thought by many in the establishment to be an international accident waiting to happen.'

'You think MI5 killed him?'

'I don't think anything. Many do believe that, though. And what about Shanahan now? If that horse is in his ownership, it looks like game over.'

'It does.'

'Which hammers a big hole in your instinct. And mine.'

'Let's see what Mac has to say. Want me to call you after the meeting?'

'It can wait.'

'See you tonight.'

'Keep your guard up, Eddie.'

'You too. Lock the door behind me.'

She did.

FIFTY-NINE

Mac was in the big service station cafe. Beside him was an empty plate, the thin sauce from baked beans showing a smear of drying yolk and tracks from mopping bread. Mac was drinking a huge mug of tea - trucker size.

I slid in across from him. 'Good breakfast?'

'Brunch, really. Well, I'll count it as lunch too.'

'Why not? Take the weight off the calorie conscience?'

'It's all right for you whippets. Try having a dodgy metabolism. It's not easy.'

'So they tell me. Anyway, what can I do for you? I need to be at Uttoxeter in an hour.'

'You can help me out on the best way forward with this. We'd still like to keep it under wraps. We've got the right man,' he said, 'I don't doubt that. The horse isn't going to run again. I just would rather know where it is.'

'Ask the owner.'

'We don't even know *what* the bloody horse is!'

I told him about Magultry and his will.

'How did you find this out?'

'Through the paid contacts of the bookies.'

'Shanahan's dead in the water,' he gulped tea.

'Too dead for my liking, Mac. It's like somebody sent us a jigsaw puzzle with the parts all numbered on the back.'

'Well you've changed your tune. Forty eight hours ago you were saying it was only because of this genius of yours, whoever he is,

249

that we were anywhere near catching Shanahan. Now you think it was so simple he's the wrong man?'

I explained it as I'd done to Mave, but Mac's glowering look didn't change. 'Eddie, you're a one off. Nothing's ever straightforward in your world. If Shanahan was being set up, why not just place the clues in the suicide messages, or leave something on Watt's PC, or Kilberg's. Instead, we've had to pick our way through a maze of over thirty thousand hijacked computers. Why not five thousand computers, or five hundred if it was meant to be easy?'

'*You've* picked your way through? You mean *we*, I think. Anyway, I take your point. It was very tough early, very.'

'See, you forget the difficult things that happened a while ago and just concentrate on the breakthrough moments.'

'Fair point. Okay. Let me think a bit more about it.'

'I'll get Sara to ask her Irish colleagues about the horse. They tell me Shanahan handed over his PC passwords willingly. No reason why he shouldn't tell us where the horse is.'

'Okay. I must get off to Uttoxeter and you'd better get going for your meeting in Birmingham with the Gambling Commission.'

He stared at me. 'How did you know about that?'

I smiled and tapped my nose. 'Elementary my dear McCarthy.' I got up. Mac reached and clasped my arm. 'Seriously, Eddie. Who told you? This is private and was only arranged late last night. That's why I had to call off the Uttoxeter trip.'

'Mac, cool it. It was a guess. You couldn't make Uttoxeter. We live ten minutes from each other yet you wanted to meet me fifteen minutes from Birmingham. I ask myself, who's big enough in Birmingham to make Mac cancel a meeting? That's where the Gambling Commission have their HQ. There's been a lot in the news about integrity in sport. Two and two made four for once, now I wish I hadn't bothered. You're bruising my delicate skin. Let go.'

He did, but he didn't let go the mistrustful look he had.

I smiled. 'Mac, it's known as the power of deduction. Not something you'd be familiar with, hence your suspicion.'

He walked with me to the car park, warning me to keep quiet about the ringer business, even though it looked done and dusted. He said, 'I'm astounded it hasn't been picked up by anyone else, and I want to stay astounded.'

'May you be in a constant state of astoundment. Call me if you find out where the horse is. Ring my backup phone.'

He grunted and got in his car.

SIXTY

The nice little midlands track of Uttoxeter yielded me a winner and a third. On the way home I called in to see Jim Sherrick and told him about Shanahan. Mister Sherrick sank back in his chair by the fire. 'All for money then, in the end, Eddie.'

'It looks that way.' I hadn't mentioned the paedophilia. Even though everything pointed to Jimmy's innocence on that front, I didn't want Mister Sherrick to even have it in his mind.

'What will he get? What sentence, I mean?'

'Shanahan? Who knows. Life, I'd have thought.'

He stared into the fire flames for a while then looked at me. 'This'll sound a bit silly, but if they find all the stuff he recorded with those bugs, on Jimmy and on me, could I ask for them to be destroyed?'

'It's not silly. Perfectly understandable. I'll ask the question when the time comes.'

'You know what makes me happy over all this?'

I waited. Happy was a strange word to use.

'That you've come through it without any damage, Eddie. I've been worrying about you since it all kicked off.'

'I'm fine. I took no risks. And I had plenty help from a good friend of mine.'

He smiled softly. 'You're some man for passing the credit to somebody else.'

'I haven't done that much, honestly.'

He shook his head, still smiling. 'You'll be glad to be finished with it.'

'I'll hang in until I actually see a conviction.'

'That shouldn't take long, from what you tell me.'

I resisted saying what I felt, and I stood up. 'No. You're right. It shouldn't.'

'When it's done, I'll take you out for a bit of a knees up.'

'I'll look forward to it. Bring your fiddle.'

He rose and put a hand on my shoulder. 'Oh, I've packed that in. I'm learning the bagpipes now.'

'Hmm.'

'I'm kidding.'

'I'm glad.'

'Safe home, Eddie.'

SIXTY-ONE

That night, we drank, Mave and I. Whiskey.

Her work was done.

She'd underestimated the Garda. The server for Shanahan's PC was taken down within half an hour of her starting work on it. 'There's nothing more I can do, Eddie. Time to go home.'

'I'll miss you.'

'Aww!' she mocked.

'I mean it. I'm not coming on to you, or anything. I'd miss you if you were a man too.'

'I almost was, I think.'

'Why are you so hung up about your looks?'

'Because I'm a woman. Please don't give me any skin deep or in the eye of the beholder stuff, will you?'

'I won't. I know almost nothing about you except that you're a lot like me only ten times smarter. And I enjoy your company more than anyone else I've ever met.'

'Well…me too.'

'Come and see this. Bring your drink. Put a coat on.'

She decided against the coat, but followed me out to the garden and into the summer house. Sitting opposite her on the wraparound bench, I told her about it, how it was supposed to be my place of contemplation, of relaxation.

She shook her head slowly, glass at her lips. 'You've told me all this before. You're drunk.'

'But you've never been in here! It's different hearing about it when you're sitting here.'

'Freezing my arse off.'

'Well, I just wanted you to know what my dreams were. Daft as they seem now.'

The light from the house window lit one side of her, halving her thin face. 'We all kid ourselves, Eddie. The right brain makes excuses for what the left brain decides to do. Or is it the other way round?' She held up her glass and stared at the whiskey, one ice cube glinting in the light. 'I'm drunk too, I think.'

'What about you, Mave? What do you want to do?'

She shrugged. 'Finish my project. Keep my head inside the box.'

'I thought you geniuses, or is it genii? Anyway, don't you think outside the box?'

'I think outside it, but live inside it. Otherwise I see things I don't want to see.'

'What kind of things?'

'Life.'

She wouldn't look at me.

'What happened?'

Now she looked at me. 'I happened.'

'Who are you?'

'I'm the daughter of the son of a preacher man.'

'Songs again.'

She nodded, and drank. 'Big part of my life, songs. How I got my name.'

'You're not going to make me guess through about fifty years of chart hits, are you?'

'Jolene.'

'As in, what do you call her, the one with the big knockers...'

'Dolly Parton.'

'That's her,' I said.

'You know the song, what it's about?'

'A wife begging some hussy not to take her man.'

'Some beautiful hussy. Her stunningness described in every detail. My dad was a big country fan. Completely ignoring the fact that when I was born I looked like a slightly overweight prune stone, he decided to call me Jolene.'

'It's a nice name.'

'Not for a girl with a face like mine. You heard of Janis Ian, the singer songwriter?'

'Mmm, vaguely. I couldn't tell you any of her songs.'

'Check the lyrics in a song she wrote called At Seventeen. I was the girl in that song. Dad just got us mixed up.'

'I'm sure you were always Jolene to him.'

'I always was. Love is blind, right enough.'

'When did he die?'

'When I was fifteen. Electrocuted on stage when helping some shit country band set up their gear in some fucking Yorkshire backwater club. Fuckwits.'

'How old was he?'

'Thirty-nine. Just six years older than I am now, which I cannot get my head around.'

'I'm the same age as you! When's your birthday?'

She drank. 'Yesterday.'

I put my drink down and stood. 'Yesterday? Tell me you're kidding!'

'I'm kidding.'

'Are you?'

'No.'

'It was your birthday yesterday, and you didn't tell me!'

She glanced up at me. 'What was I supposed to say, good morning, Eddie, it's my birthday?'

'You could have, well, hinted or something.'

She was smiling at my aggravation. 'Oh, like. Guess what day it is today? Or, you'll never believe who was born on this day thirty three years ago. All this apart, of course, from the fact that you were in Dublin.'

'Aw shit! I feel awful now! You stuck here alone on your birthday.'

'Well, I'd have been stuck alone on my birthday in my own shack in Wales. It makes no difference. Sit down and stop fussing like an old hen.'

I smiled and sat. 'Next year, I'll take you out.'

'What, with a Kalashnikov or something while I'm not looking?'

'Very funny, Maven.'

She watched me finish my drink. 'Thanks,' she said.

'What for?'

'For calling me Maven. I thought you'd take the piss and start calling me Jolene all the time.'

'I will. Once I get used to it.'

'You dare!'

'I'm kidding. And I'm cold. Let's go in and fill these up.' My phone beeped. I checked my watch: 11.30. It was a text from Ishrat to say she had information if I wanted it now. I told Mave who it was and I called her, listening as I looked out on that yellow rectangle of light on the dark lawn: 'Magultry was seventy three years old, a retired priest who was left a farm and almost four million Euro by a parishioner. He abandoned the priesthood at sixty three after accusations of child abuse dating back to the sixties. Lawyers for the Church managed to get a conviction against him quashed and he was quietly pensioned off to Roscommon. He returned to Dublin five years later when he got this inheritance. There were public campaigns against him, seeking retrials, but the campaigns fizzled out.

'He settled to a reasonably quiet life. The only time he was seen out was when one of his two horses were running. We found no direct personal links between him and Miles Shanahan, but he owned shares in Nequitec to the value of quarter of a million Euro.'

'When were the shares bought?'

'July first, twenty-seven days before he died.'

'Anything else?'

'That's all for now. Want them to keep digging?'

'Please. Those public campaigns against him, can you find out who was driving them?'

'I'm sure we can.'

'Good. Thanks, Ishrat.'

'My pleasure. Sorry to trouble you so late.'

'No trouble.'

'I hope to have more information for you tomorrow, at a more sociable time.'

'Don't worry about that. Call me anytime. If I'm not around, leave a voicemail.'

'I will. Goodnight, Mister Malloy.'

'Call me Eddie. You make me feel old.'

'Goodnight.'

I turned to Mave. 'You hear that?'

'I did.'

'Still heading home tomorrow?'

'Can I sleep on it?'

'Please do. I've got a very strong feeling the fat lady is still waiting in the wings.'

SIXTY-TWO

Unusually, Mave was still in her room when I left to ride out for Ben Tylutki. When I returned, she was sitting in the Snug, fully dressed, jacket too, watching the birds peck at the feeders I'd hung in the trees.

Her laptop wasn't on the desk. Her bag was packed and strapped. She turned as I crossed the room and sat beside her. 'Homeward bound?'

She smiled. 'Who's talking in song titles now?'

'Why don't you stay, just a little bit longer?'

She laughed, her eyes sparkling. 'You'll run out of songs before I run out of resolution.'

'I know, I'm struggling already.'

'It's been good, Eddie, but I'm beginning to feel a bit useless now, and I don't like that. The geeky stuff's done, or at least, if it's not, I can do as much at home as I can here.'

'I don't think Shanahan is the man, Mave. The big geek is still out there.'

'I suspect you're right. But the cops have closed down my only route to finding him. It's down to you now. You should chuck it, too, but you won't.'

'Too close.'

'It's nothing to do with being close, Eddie. It's your utter refusal to pull up once the race has started. You cannot stand to see something unfinished.'

'I try. I've been kind of coaching myself as I get older to think more before getting involved.'

'Good. That's the key. If you don't commit to starting, you don't need to finish.'

'Prevention being better than cure?'

'Exactly.'

I watched her, She held my gaze, but pursed her lips. I said, 'I'm not taking any more bookings after tomorrow. I'm going to Dublin after racing on Saturday. Why don't you come with me?'

'I'm nocturnal, remember? I don't care for the light, especially limelight.'

'You should be there with me, Mave. This project team the bookies have got working are going to cut through what's left of this case in days, I'm sure of it. Nobody's done more to get us this far than you. I want you to be there when we finally nail this guy.'

She turned in her seat to face me straight on. 'This is the guy we talked about a couple of days back who could be twenty-seven, with an armoury in the attic?'

'Or seventy. With just a big PC and a big IQ.'

'Eddie, even if I wanted to, it would be stupid. We can't be seen in public together if you're serious about helping me with my project. I don't want the authorities to even know I'm alive, especially the racing people or the bookies. I can't afford to. I feel like my life's invested in this, and I'm doing an Eddie Malloy...I ain't giving up.'

I nodded, and watched her face until it was calm and she was looking at me. 'I'll miss you,' I said.

She stood up. 'No you won't. You're a solitary soul, like me. We're happiest with our dreams, and nobody around to dent them.'

'Hey, wait a minute!' I stood and faced her. 'I'll have you know that I saw every one of your dreams since you've been here. They floated under your door and into my room and I lay there and watched them and didn't put a single dent in any of them. Never even touched them.'

She laughed again and pushed me back down onto the couch. 'Take me to the station, will you?'

'Why don't you wait until tonight and I'll drive you home? I'd feel awful just dumping you at the station.'

'Don't be daft. I like riding on the train. Always did, since I was a kid. Come on,' she picked up her bag.

'Give me that.'

She handed it over.

I bought her a first class ticket. I'd bill it to the bookies. 'Ping me tonight,' I said as the train approached.

'I will.'

'Take care of yourself.'

'I've been taking care of myself for years, Eddie.'

'I know you have. But you look like a stiff breeze would down you.'

'I bend in the wind. Stiff knees might down me, if I live long enough.'

'You'll be a zillionaire by then. You can change knees once a month.'

'And you'll be a millionaire once the system gets rolling full time.'

'I wouldn't have a clue what to do with it.'

The train pulled in. I kissed her. She kissed me. We waved to each other…that final gesture we make as though some invisible physical link remains stretched between two palms, broken only by the loss of eye contact.

I walked slowly to the car, trying to figure out if a heavy heart was meant as a counterweight to the sudden void in my gut. Every parting is a tiny death.

SIXTY-THREE

Forty eight hours from February, I thought, as I pulled out of the Plumpton car park. Dusk was stretching noticeably now on these late afternoon drives home. I'd returned voicemails before setting off, rejecting, as nicely as I could, three offers of rides early next week. One message was from Mac. When I called, he asked me to meet him on the way home in a pub near Lambourn.

Mac was waiting. He sat by the fire, hat on the table, half pint of Guinness to hand, one of the few in there not looking at his phone screen. I walked through the low buzz of conversation and sat across from Mac. 'Bet you didn't expect it to be this busy,' I said.

'It's usually one man and a dog,' he said, looking around.

'Usually? When were you last in here?'

'About three years ago.'

'Say no more.'

Five minutes later, we were in Mac's BMW in the corner of the dark car park. 'What's happening?' I asked.

'Shanahan denies ever meeting Enda Magultry or ever setting eyes on the horse Magultry left him. And he says those patents aren't his.'

'The patents for the implants?'

'He says he stole the ideas for them from some kid who came to see him a couple of years ago.'

'Nice man. What was the kid's name?'

'He can't remember.'

I laughed. 'When did he come up with this tale?'

'Just after noon today. He said he'd been ashamed of doing it, that's why he hadn't mentioned it earlier.'

'How did the police react?'

'The same way as you did. They plan to make formal charges of murder against him in the next twenty four hours. His PC had all the evidence they need, even without the patents. What they don't have is knowledge of where the horse is, or where the money is. There's an offshore bank account in his name, but Shanahan says he can't authorize access to it for the police because he didn't open it.'

'How long will it take them to get into it via the diplomatic route?'

'Years?'

I turned toward him, but could see little detail in his face in the darkness. But I knew from his voice he was worried. I said, 'You sound like you wish there was something to these protests of Shanahan's?'

'I could just do with a bit longer before everything's made public. I want that horse found.'

'Of course...once they announce charges, you'll have to reveal the scam.'

'But at least we'll have been seen to do our jobs. Much different from the news getting out before anyone had been caught.'

'The "we" being the BHA?'

'Oh, Eddie...I've got enough on my plate without a debate about who did what. Give me a break!'

'Did I say anything?'

'You were going to.'

I smiled. 'Maybe I can buy you some time here, Mac. Can you get me a description of this kid who's supposed to have had the ideas for the implants?'

'Why?'

'Do you want help or not?'

'I need something to justify the request to Sara.'

'If you think that one will take some justifying, try this. Ask her to ask the Garda to exhume the corpse of Enda Magultry and check it for implants. Tell her I think Miles Shanahan might be telling the truth.'

SIXTY-FOUR

The house was strangely silent without Mave. She'd never made much noise, but I'd always known she was around. I sat on the couch where we'd talked this morning, trying to figure out why the gap her absence left felt like a brick was missing from the wall, and a cold wind was blowing through the hole.

She had fitted here.

I'd thought the house was perfect. All had seemed whole until Mave arrived. Something was missing now she'd gone.

I looked at the desk…the empty chair, still trying to work out how I felt. I wasn't pining the way lovers do. This was a new feeling for me. I lay back, cradling my head in linked hands, thinking.

Mave fitted.

Nothing in my life had ever fitted. Nothing.

She had slotted into it, into a space I hadn't known was there, and…fitted. So precise a fit that not an atom of space was left.

I went to my PC and pinged her. She answered in a mock robotic voice, 'Normal service has been resumed.'

'So I see. Including a webcam which points anywhere but your face,'

'You've seen enough of that to last a lifetime.'

'This house misses you. I miss you.'

'Peas in a pod, Eddie, you and me.'

'Long distance pod, now though.'

'None the worse, for it, believe me.'

'How was your trip?'

'Uneventful.'

'Your shack okay?'

'It hadn't blown over the cliff. What remains of my heart lifted when I saw its creaky outline and crooked chimney against the western sky, and heard the sound of the waves in Hell's Mouth.'

'Why do sailors scare the shit out of themselves by naming coves Hell's Mouth? What about Heaven's Haven, or something?'

'That's for townies with no sense of drama. Any more news from your bookie woman?'

'Not yet.' I told her about the meeting with Mac.

'He stole the patents from a kid?'

'The ideas, he says.'

'Sounds plausible.'

'It does. Let's assume somebody set Shanahan up. Could he have opened an offshore bank account in Shanahan's name without him knowing.'

'Easily.'

'Okay, how's this? Shanahan's kid is real. When the kid finds out Shanahan has stiffed him over the patents, he starts working out how he can get revenge. Magultry has this child abuse charge hanging over him. If the kid finds some proof, like images on his PC, and blackmails him into taking the same implants as Watt and Kilberg, he's then got control of Magultry.'

'Makes sense so far.'

'Right. He gets the horse from Magultry and moves it to Watt. He tells Magultry to buy the shares in Nequitec and leave the horse in his will to Shanahan, then he activates the cyanide implant, eats half the apple, injects the remainder with cyanide, and leaves it beside Magultry's body, a la Alan Turing.'

'If the cops exhume Magultry, get them to check the teeth marks. If the apple survived, that is.'

'Good point. How does the rest sound?'

'Well when you add it to the fact that the kid, if there is one, also stands to win millions and, if he is a kid, and if he eventually gets caught, he'll know that by then Shanahan will have confessed to stealing his patents. Suppose he's twenty-two, and he gets fifteen years in jail, it's hardly the end of the world to come back out at thirty-seven with millions in the bank from his patents.'

'If he got fifteen, with good behaviour, he could be out by the time he's thirty.'

'He could. Now all you have to do is prove it.'

SIXTY-FIVE

It was almost eight o'clock before Ishrat rang. 'Sorry, Mister Malloy, I shouldn't have tempted fate last night by promising to call you at a more sociable hour. Are you okay to talk just now?'

'Sure, what have you got?'

'Those campaigns against Father Magultry, or ex-father Magultry, if you prefer, were organised by a teenager called Finbarr Quaidd.'

'Teenager? What age, do you know?'

'He was sixteen when he started and was still campaigning after his seventeenth birthday.'

'Precocious for a public campaigner. Was he accusing Magultry of molesting him?'

'His father. He was campaigning on behalf of his father, Kegan Quaidd. He claimed Magultry's abuse of his father when he was at a seminary as a young man in the nineteen sixties, ruined his life.'

'So when did young Quaidd give up?'

'About four years ago. His last public statement was that he'd dedicate himself to protecting children from paedophiles. Two years ago he set up a company called The Raglan Unit on Raglan Road in Dublin.'

'What is it, like a drop-in centre for kids or something?'

'It offers counselling and support for people of any age who've suffered sexual abuse. Open twenty-four-seven all year.'

'How is it funded?'

'Quaidd's company, The Raglan Unit Limited, sells implants to third world countries. He holds the patents on several hi-tech inventions.'

'Any idea what these implants do?'

'His main revenue comes from ones which protect livestock in Africa from disease. There are trials going on with them in humans. So far the trials have been a hundred percent successful in protecting against malaria and typhoid.'

'A go-ahead young man. I'm surprised I haven't heard of him. He sounds a classic youth hero for the media to feed on.'

'He keeps a very low profile. Puts his father up for interviews and as spokesman for the company while he concentrates on the tech side, although he spends each Sunday at the unit helping out, talking to people.'

'Have you any pictures of him?'

'None recent. Only from his campaigning days.'

'Can you email them to me?'

'Sure. I've got your details. I'll do it as soon as we finish this call.'

'Ishrat, you've been brilliant.'

'I'm just a coordinator, Mister Malloy. The team in Ireland deserves the credit.'

'You're a brilliant project manager. I give you the vaguest of requests and you come back with the most comprehensive results I could have wished for.'

'Ha! All in a day's work.'

'Listen, will you ask the team to find out all they can on Miles Shanahan, who owns a company-'

'Nequitec. We're already on that. I thought you would want something on him. Should be ready tomorrow.'

'You're way ahead of me. I need as much factual stuff as possible. I know there've been plenty rumours about Shanahan. Your guys might be able to get evidence to back those up. I'm guessing they've got contacts who wouldn't speak openly to the police?'

'We'll get what you need. Is there anything else for now?'

'Just those pictures, please.'

'I'll send them within two minutes.'

She did as promised and I sat staring at a ginger-haired, stern-faced boy, half a head taller than the adults around him. He carried the same banner as a dozen of his supporters. It was properly printed; none of your rough paint and bad spelling: "Arrest Sinful Priests".

And I knew then that five years or so after that press picture was taken, this kid had sent a signal across the Irish Sea on a late December evening activating a cyanide capsule that killed Jimmy Sherrick.

SIXTY-SIX

On Sunday morning, February 2nd, Rory Moran, driving a blue Toyota, picked me up at Dublin Airport. Ishrat had arranged it. Moran was the head of the Irish team the bookies had commissioned. On the drive into the city, he told me of his history in the Garda and in what he called the Irish security industry.

He told me too about Miles Shanahan, a man he'd known for many years. Yes, Shanahan had commissioned DDOS attacks on major UK bookmakers fifteen years ago. No, he hadn't murdered two prostitutes in north Dublin in 1997. Shanahan would never risk anything like that. He had plans to be a politician. But he'd had the girls murdered, and their weighted corpses dropped into the sea.

The girls had tried to blackmail him when he'd announced his intention to run for office. He was questioned by the Garda but never arrested. A year later, Shanahan's wife was killed in a fall when they were on an Alpine holiday. Shanahan said they'd been walking in the mountains when Alice had strayed onto a cornice which collapsed. There were no witnesses other than her husband, and he withdrew from politics then, citing 'a grief that would never leave him'.

Moran told me the burden of grief was lightened considerably by an insurance payout of half a million Euro. Moran used it to help fund the purchase of the company now known as Nequitec.

He dropped me on Raglan Road, about a hundred yards from The Raglan Unit. 'Want me to wait?'

'If I'm not out in five minutes, you can go, and come back in an hour if that's okay?'

'Grand. See you then.'

I walked the tree-lined road and stopped outside the three storey redbrick with arched doorway. I counted a dozen steps, my hand on shiny black railings. The door was closed against the winter. A sign said: 'Don't ring, come in!' I turned the brass handle and walked into a warm hall, with what looked like old school benches on either side. Coats hung on long wall racks. A tartan bin held umbrellas, and a long mat led to a desk as old as the benches. A man and two women were talking. I could smell fresh coffee as I approached them, but could make out little of the conversation, the accented words too fast for me.

A dark haired woman with a welcoming smile said, 'Come in. Take off your coat, and warm yourself here by the stove. Will you have some tea or coffee?'

'Coffee would be nice, thanks.'

'Are you a milk and sugar man?'

'Black would be fine, thanks.'

'Sit down, now, and I'll bring it over.'

I sat. A straight staircase went up, and to its right, one went down. I was conscious that Moran was waiting along the road. The woman brought the coffee. 'Well, January's behind us. We're on our way to summer,' she said.

'Yes. Thanks.'

'No trouble. I'm Dolores. Shout if you want anything.'

'I was hoping to speak to Finbarr.'

'He's downstairs. I'll give him a shout. Should I say who's waiting?'

'Just a friend…from England.'

She nodded, still smiling, and went downstairs. A minute later she was back, the smile as wide as when she'd left me. 'Finbarr will be with you shortly.'

'Thank you.' I'd no doubt there'd be a basement exit, but I could hardly go racing down there. If he left, Rory Moran would probably spot him.

I heard footsteps on the stairs, and turned to see first a clump of curly red hair shining under the lights, then blue eyes, then the long narrow face of Finbarr Quaidd. Watching his feet as he climbed, he seemed doleful, then he looked at me and smiled and held out his hand as he approached. I stood, He was at least six-three. The smile was genuine as he looked down on me. 'Eddie. Nice to meet you.'

We sat in his office. The walls held pictures and posters of what I took to be African villagers and their cattle. Letters and postcards and children's crayon drawings were pinned and taped around the place. Some of the pictures featured a very happy looking Finbarr with squads of black, smiling children.

'You're a popular young man,' I said.

'With some.'

I nodded.

We watched each other.

He spoke. 'I wasn't quite sure you'd get here. I thought I'd done just about the perfect job.'

'I have some very clever friends.'

'You do. You do indeed. But not clever enough to bring you this far. Give yourself some credit.'

'I also have a dead friend.'

'I know. I'm sorry.'

'Did you kill Jimmy, or was it Bayley Watt?'

'I did. I told Watt and Kilberg Jimmy had killed himself and that they should go and stage the hanging to convince the police not to ask too many questions.'

'You killed Jimmy for money.'

'I suppose, yes. I had to make a decision on it, and make it quickly, after he spoke to you on the phone about meeting him.'

'And how did you balance out that decision, against all your good deeds?' I gestured toward the walls.

'Jimmy had weeks to live. He was determined not to tell his dad, or anyone close to him about the cancer, though he broke that in an effort to get Amanda back. But he'd have died a horrible death on his own.'

'Cyanide poisoning doesn't seem a particularly peaceful passing, either.'

'It's a hell of a lot quicker than pancreatic cancer. Jimmy's had been diagnosed too late. It had spread to his liver. It's likely it would have reached his bones and maybe lungs.'

'What was he planning to tell me that night?'

'About the ringer, I think.'

'I thought he was in on it?'

Quaidd shook his head and his thick bright curls swung. 'No. I didn't think he'd agree. Watt believed he would. I told him to leave it and see how Jimmy reacted after Stifles in Spur won.'

'Fruitless Spin on his second run?'

He nodded. 'The one where we'd find out if Jimmy had sussed it or not.'

'You don't know much about jockeys if you believed he wouldn't.'

'I thought he would, but that he'd kid himself for a while. He'd told Bayley about the cancer, to give him a chance to start planning who his next jockey would be. Then he blew his top after Stifles in Spur.'

'And that's when you offered him a potential cure?'

'That's right. Through Bayley Watt.'

'So why did Jimmy change his mind and decide to talk to me?'

'I don't know. He kept asking Watt when the symptoms, the pain from the cancer should start easing.'

Tears rising in my eyes surprised me and I raised a hand to my forehead.

'I'm sorry. I wish I could have found another way. I'm working on a cancer cure through implants. It's a long way off, but the money I raised from those bets will be a big help in getting us there. Well, would have been a big help, I suppose I should say. I'm sorry, Eddie.'

I felt like the kid in the room, with Quaidd the adult. He was moving through the stages of explanation as though it were some technical project.

He scooped a Kleenex from a box on his desk and offered it. I took it and dried my face and looked at him. 'This all seems just matter of fact, to you.'

He smiled slowly, shaking his head. 'I've done all the pain and the heart-searching and questioning. Been through it with my dad since I was old enough to cry only because I saw him crying. That was what my life was, and that's all it would have been if I hadn't decided to change things.'

'How did you find out about Watt? Had he been involved in the abuse of your father as well as Magultry?'

'No. When Magultry bought those two horses, that's when I started thinking that there must be paedophiles in racing, same as in any other walk of life. I hacked the database of the DVLA in the

273

UK. Almost everyone who's been on the sex offenders' register in the UK changes their name. The only national agency they formally need to notify is the DVLA. I ran a query on current trainers, jockeys and vets. All I got was Watt and Kilberg.'

'Kilberg was American.'

'Kilberg was born in London. He never lived abroad. He was a vet who ran a small animal practice in Yorkshire, where he set up something called Happy Saturdays for kids to supposedly learn about raising pets. It was a cover for child abuse. He served three years and changed his name from Kevin Rudging, then started moving around the country.'

'Watt?'

'Real name Quentin Rudyard Collins. Been abusing since his teens. Ran a kid's animal farm in Cornwall, in one of the busy holiday areas. He left the local children alone and preyed on the holidaymakers. He got away with it for nearly ten years. He served six of an eight years sentence. Changed his name, moved to Scotland for five years and worked on the oil rigs to get the cash together to buy a couple of horses and get himself a permit to train.'

'You had that info plus images from their PCs?'

'Correct.'

I watched him. He was calm, confident looking.

'What happened with Shanahan?'

'I was looking for funding to develop the implants. I'd read about Shanahan and his fancy talk about plans for the community when he was getting into politics. Then I saw he'd bought this company, so I went to see him and offered him a share of profits if he'd help me develop the ideas.'

'And he stole them?'

'He did.'

'Did you threaten him when you found out?'

'No. I called him to ask what was happening. He'd been ignoring all my emails since our meeting. He told me on the phone to check the patent register and to count myself lucky he'd taught me a relatively cheap lesson so early in my life.'

'And what did you say to that?'

'I told him it was a lesson I would remember for a long time,' he smiled.

'Shanahan's told the police about you.'

'I knew he would. At least I get the patents back. They can fund The Raglan Unit while I'm in prison.'

'What about the three million in betting money?'

'It was six. Six million.'

I recalled my meeting with the top guys and realized they'd put me away. If word of the scam had leaked, it would sound only half as bad.

'Where is it?'

'Safe. It'll be there when I come out.'

'How much is in the account you opened for Shanahan?'

'Half a million. Just in case the police did manage to get into it somehow.'

'Where's the horse, Colossus?'

'He's in a livery yard near the Curragh where the owner's waiting for another letter from Mister Shanahan on where his inheritance is to be sent for training.'

'Another letter?'

'The police should find a letter emailed from Shanahan along with a bank transfer from Nequitec for five thousand Euro. Advance payment for livery fees.'

I shook my head slowly. 'You did a very, very neat job.'

'Not neat enough. I knew you were on it. I knew you had top grade help. I still didn't think you'd crack it. What let me down?'

'Those word game apps on your phone.'

He stared at me. 'My phone is unhackable. How did you know about those?'

'A guess. I knew you liked word games. My genius of a partner sussed that.' I pulled the press photo from my pocket and laid it on the desk. He looked at himself carrying that banner. I said, 'Fruitless Spin. Spiritless Fun. Fissure Splint...Sinful Priests.'

He smiled, partly in surrender, partly, I think, in admiration.

I stood and picked up a cardboard coaster from his desk. It was green with gold letters: *The Raglan Unit*. 'Can I offer you another, Finbarr?'

'Go on.' He watched, unblinking. I tore off the top section, leaving Raglan Unit, and laid it down. 'Alan Turing.'

His smiled widened and he nodded slowly.

'Good luck,' I said.

'Where are you going?'

'Home.'

SIXTY-SEVEN

A winter Sunday dusk. One of my favourite times to sit in the Snug by the fire with my special lead crystal glass, a gift from Martell, who used to sponsor the Grand National. Half full of whiskey and ice, it was luxuriously heavy.

I sipped and watched the last of the light fade over the garden, the sun house. I'd pinged Mave, but she'd reverted quickly to old habits and was still asleep in her Welsh eyrie. I'd called Mac and told him to forget about the request to exhume Enda Magultry, that my suspicion Shanahan was an innocent man had been wrong.

I told him where Colossus was. He didn't ask how I knew, and just said he'd arrange to have the horse picked up.

An innocent man.

Shanahan was not that. I had not lied. He hadn't killed Jimmy, or any of the others in this. But he was a worse man by far than the young red-headed executioner.

Finbarr Quaidd had made no special plea. He'd denied nothing. He had accepted that if somebody turned out to be smarter than he'd been in dispensing his own form of justice, then he was willing to put his hands up.

Jimmy had been sacrificed for the success of Quaidd's project. With a few months, at best, to live, Jimmy would have given his life anyway if Quaidd had explained the end game.

I think.

Who knows?

Young Quaidd might live another sixty years. How many could he kill in that time, if he chose to carry on pursuing paedophiles? Would more Jimmy Sherricks die too for the cause? Did paedophiles deserve summary execution? Would Quaidd give every one of them the chance to save themselves with the implant?

Did Watt and Kilberg and Magultry deserve death?

Mave's terrible anguish when she saw those images came back to me. If I'd seen those images, would I have wanted to kill those in that paedophile ring?

Yes.

I stared into the fire flames. Then my selfishness kicked in as it had done after Jimmy's death, when I thought I could get the rides back at Watt's. Maybe I could free myself of responsibility here by shifting it to the shoulders of Mister Sherrick? Here's the story Jim, now, do you want me to hand Finbarr Quaidd in?

Cop out. Passing a burden to an old man who'd buried his son and would have to do so again. I shook my head, ashamed at my own weakness.

The burning logs crackled. I glanced up and through the double doors to the desk, half-expecting to see Mave there. Then I rose and turned to put down my glass on the mantelpiece above the fire. My reflection looked at me from the mirror and we watched each other a while. 'You're a gloomy bastard,' we said. 'Cheers.' We drank to each other and I went to ping Mave again.

No answer.

I pulled out my phone like a sixgun, as Bayley Watt would have said, and called my bookies' man, Gerry Waldron.

'How was Dublin?'

'I saw little of it, Gerry, but it was good to meet Rory Moran who did such fine work in helping me nail Shanahan, and find the horse.'

'I didn't know you'd found the horse.'

'Peter McCarthy's arranging to have it picked up and put away somewhere it can't do you guys any more harm.'

'So Shanahan's the man?'

'All the evidence points that way, and there's plenty of it.'

'I hear he has our money in an offshore account.'

'So they tell me. Let's hope he hasn't spent it.'

'Your man at Betstore wants you to work for the Association of British Bookmakers as Integrity Director. I told him he'd be wasting his time, but I promised to mention it.'

'Where does he want the integrity directed to? And where do I find it in the first place?'

Gerry laughed. 'I knew your answer would be something along those lines.'

'I'm a jockey, Gerry. The brains behind all this was someone who hates the limelight.'

'The thing is, Eddie, it takes a lot more than brains, this kind of thing. That's what you've got.'

'So does a pig. And a mule.'

He laughed again, a soft genuine sound that I liked. 'Maybe when you retire, eh?'

'Who knows?'

'Anyway. I'll pass on the news. They'll probably wait for Shanahan's conviction before paying that charity money.'

'That's okay.'

'Cancer, wasn't it?'

'Yes. See if there's a special one for pancreatic cancer, Gerry, will you?'

'Of course I will.'

'Thanks, my friend.'

'Look after yourself.'

'You too. Oh, Gerry…Your young project manager, Ishrat. She's an absolute star and deserves to go far.'

'I'll tell her boss.'

No going back now. Once you start something you've been putting off, momentum can kick in. Rather than holstering my phone, I dialled Mister Sherrick's number and told him the police were confident they had the man they'd been after.

'It's been a long road, Eddie.'

'For you especially.'

'It feels more like six years ago than six weeks.'

'It does. I'll come and see you soon, if you don't mind. We don't need to talk about all this. I used to enjoy those long chats we had by your fire.'

'Me too. You're welcome here anytime.'

'When's your next fiddle gig?'

He laughed. 'Friday.'

'Can I come to that?'

'You'll be the youngest there by forty years.'

'I'll bet there'll be plenty feet can tap quicker than mine.'

'You'll have no peace from the women. How's your dancing?'

'My dancing's more likely to injure me than riding.'

'The old dears will steer you right.'

'Pull me up, more like.'

'Ha! We'll see. Seven o'clock start.'

'I'll be there!'

Halfway through refilling my glass, Mave pinged me, and I felt a little burst of excited anticipation, whiskey swishing as I hurried to the desk. She was staring right at me, wide-eyed. 'You're a persistent sod in waking a woman up!'

'So I've been told.'

'I'll bet. What do you want this time?'

I laughed. 'Some friendly banter.'

'My banter tank is in for a refill. You emptied it last week. How did it go in Dublin?'

'It went well in the end.'

'In the end? Did you find the kid?'

'I did. He wasn't what I thought.'

'As in?'

'Well, put it this way, I spoke to him for half an hour and came away pretty sure that Shanahan was the man after all.'

'The man for what?'

'For locking up.'

'You're being evasive.'

'I am.'

'Why?'

'I don't want to lie to you.'

She smiled slowly, shaking her head, still looking at me. 'You are a man-child. If we ever lived together, I would marvel for a while at the novelty of your character, then I'd kill you out of frustration.'

'How long is "a while"?'

'A month. Max. Probably half that.'

'Forewarned is forearmed. Book me in for a week in summer.'

'Can you swim?'

'Like a dolphin.'

'Can you climb a cliff?'

'A small one. Well, a sand dune, really.'

'In a raging storm in Hell's Mouth, could you keep your head when all around you are losing theirs?'

'I very much doubt it.'

'Will you help me with this bloody project?'

'Yes.'

'Then name your dates for the hotel Cliff Shack.'

'First week in July.'

'Any special dietary requirements?'

'Chewing the fat.'

She looked at me for what seemed a long time. I tried to keep smiling, keep my wit sharp, but the impetus had gone. Mave said, 'You're quipping your way round your problem, Mister.'

'You know me too well.'

'Tell me about this kid Quaidd.'

I told her.

'Why were you so certain it was him?'

'Because of you. When you spotted the ringer names were anagrams, it opened my mind up. I saw Sinful Priests on the banner the kid had and realised it had been his starting point for Fruitless Spin and the others. And Raglan Unit hit me right between the eyes with Alan Turing.'

'That was clever, Eddie.'

'I had a fine teacher.'

'You did, and now she's going to teach you something else. Are you listening?'

I nodded.

'Ever heard of the greater good?'

'I have.'

'What you've done is for the greater good. Forget you've been involved in any of this, and just imagine somebody gave you a piece of paper on each of them. One on Quaidd and one on Shanahan, laying out what you already know. You're asked to choose which should stay free for the greater good. Who would you choose?'

'Finbarr Quaidd.'

'So would I. So would ninety nine percent of law abiding people.'

I nodded. 'Okay.'

'Right. Now some homework.'

I looked at her.

'That little elasticated head lamp I saw on your coat rail, does it work?'

'Like a light house.'

'Put the drink down. Put the headlamp on and change into your running gear. What's your favourite run?'

'Through the wood behind the house.'

'Get going then, and leave all that crap that's in your mind out among the trees.'

'Yes, Miss.'

'There'll be questions on it when you get back.'

'A check for mind crap?'

'Correct. I'll be waiting here. Off you go.'

I got changed and went out.

And I raced through the wood in the dark, each step pounding my doubts into the forest floor, creating a rhythm, reviving a song, and echoing my inborn urge…keep on running.

Dear Reader,

Thanks for buying Dead Ringer. The next Eddie Malloy mystery –
Aim High – is already underway. For the release date, you can
follow on twitter @pitmacbooks, or sign up for notification at
pitmacbooks.com

Best wishes
Joe McNally
January, 2014

Printed in Great Britain
by Amazon.co.uk, Ltd.,
Marston Gate.